I0586624

Also by D.M. Chappell

The Truth About

Fairy Tales

(Matchmaking Agency)

By D.M. CHAPPELL

For my wonderful husband and sounding board, Eric.

Copyright © 2018 by D.M. Chappell

Cover Illustration: The Book Design House

Interior Illustration: Dahn Tran Art

Library of Congress Control Number: 2018902862

ISBN 978-0-9981183-7-6

All rights reserved. No part of this publication may be reproduced, stored in a retrieval system or transmitted, in any form or by any means, without prior written permission of the author, nor be otherwise circulated in any form of binding or cover other than that in which it is published and without a similar condition being imposed on the purchaser.

This book is a work of fiction. Names, characters, places, and incidents are the products of the author's imagination or are used factiously. Any resemblance to actual events, locales, or persons, living or dead, is entirely coincidental.

Printed in the U.S.A.

ACKNOWLEDGEMENTS

Thank you to Jenny, Jason, Leanne, Shelly, Belinda, Gabriella, and Scarlett for their help with this book. Without your help, it would never have become what it is.

The Truth
About Fairy
Tales

(Matchmaking Agency)

HELP?

And they lived happily ever after...

Those are six words all little girls around the world know. Most of us held onto the idea that all would be right in the world if we could just find the right man: our knight in shining armor.

When we grew up we realized those words were a lie. Okay, so maybe that's a bit harsh. They might not have been so much a straight-out lie as they stretched the truth. In real life finding Prince Charming is hard and finding happily ever after... Well, that is rare. Really rare.

I was no exception. Don't get me wrong, I was prepared to kiss a few frogs along the way to find my Prince Charming, but I was okay with that. At least until I ended up with nothing to show for it except warts, or more precisely, divorce papers.

We at TAFT know from experience the pitfalls women face. We also know that few men nowadays are raised to be chivalrous, much less charming—unless of course they are trying to get you in bed.

The truth of the matter is, it only takes the dangle of a pretty girl in front of said Prince Charming to distract him enough to go down a path that does not lead to your tower for rescue.

This is why myself and my partners, Sara and Julia, created TAFT Matchmaking Agency. To help all women find potential mates—who are truly ready to settle down.

Our proprietary software, data collection, and selection methods allow us to match each of our clients with the right person for them.

How do we do this you ask? Well, without giving away our secret I can tell you we show them what each match is really made of, flaws and all.

TAFT has a success rate of 90% and a Platinum A+ rating with the Better Business Bureau.

We hope you choose to join our agency, and we look forward to working with you to help find your FOREVER Prince Charming.

- Calla Lily Bloom, Co-Owner of TAFT

Chapter One

The young lady across from me was cast from the same mold as the majority of our clientele: under thirty, at least a seven, with a net worth easily over one million. The money, of course, was all thanks to her family fortune, not her own hard work. Which was true for the majority of our clients, who were all female. Most were either sent here by their mothers, or they came because of a recommendation given to them by someone at one of the many local clubhouses in the area. Belmont, Georgia, was famous for its golf, wealth, and trophy wives, in that order.

While TAFT was known for having the best of the best sign with our service, and I was thrilled we were successful, I sometimes wished we had more "average" clientele.

Being an average looking woman myself, I knew it was hard enough to find, much less keep a man, without having to compete with the types of beauties that normally decorated TAFT's doorstep. A perfect example was the young perky blonde who'd whisked away my husband of ten plus years.

Not that our marriage had been perfect. How could it be? We'd gotten married right out of high school and hadn't ever really had a chance to explore the world, or other people for that matter. Marrying your high school sweetheart sounded like a dream come true, but dreams and reality were two different things entirely.

It was because of TAFT's personal reasons for operating a matchmaking agency that our rates were not published, nor set in stone. We tried to accommodate anyone who walked into our agency: supermodel or girl next door. We wanted *everyone* to get the opportunity to find true love. It wasn't our fault we had more of one type than another in our town and that type had thick wallets.

Don't get me wrong, we'd *never* intentionally swindled people out of money. We charged according to their net worth. Fair? Maybe not, but we viewed the fee as a way to balance the playing field. Not that average looking women couldn't be rich, you just didn't see many of those in Belmont.

"Our brochure should give you a general idea of what TAFT has to offer you, and how it works. As soon as you sign up for our matchmaking service we can begin to make your profile," I said, sliding the bi-fold, color brochure across the table.

April Weaver carefully slid the brochure towards her, fingers extended as to not mess up her fresh, crimson-red manicure. On any other person, the color would have screamed foul because of its brightness. But on April, whose skin was tanned within an inch of its life, no other color would have even stood out enough to be seen.

"The Truth About Fairy Tales. What a cute name. How in the world did you come up with it?" she asked.

"Well… My business partners and I—"

"My friend said you will give us all of the dirt you have on the men we are interested in?" April cut in, not waiting for me to answer her first question.

I sighed inwardly. These young women had no sense of patience. It was too bad, because of all the questions prospective clients asked me, how we got our name was the one I'd always enjoyed answering. I felt intense pride in the creativity we'd displayed in our company name.

When Sara, Julia, and I had finally become successful enough to turn our hobby of matchmaking into a business, we knew the first to-do item was coming up with a company name. We each brainstormed where we had first learned about men, love, and marriage. Surprisingly enough, our answers were all the same: Fairy Tales.

"Yes. Your information is accurate. TAFT profiles list both the positive details of the male candidates in our selection pool and the items they'd like to 'sweep under the rug' until after the wedding bells have rung," I replied. "We refer to this information as 'negative references' on our profile form."

"Do I have to list *my* negative references?" Her skin tried its best to pucker between her brows, but the Botox won the battle and only a hint of a line showed.

"While we would like you to be as honest as possible under the 'personal areas of weakness,' we do not require the same list our 'selection pool' candidates give us."

"Where do you get the negative references?" she asked.

"I'm sorry, April. That's proprietary information. If we shared that, anyone could do what we do," I said, letting out a light-hearted laugh while pasting my best false smile on my face.

The statement was a partial lie. Anyone could call the reference numbers the men listed: his mother, any female siblings, his last three ex-girlfriends, and the last four women he had dated and get the scoop on the guy's biggest flaws and failures. However, they wouldn't have the detailed algorithm we had created to best make use of the information gathered. The juicy details that data gave us was TAFT's alone.

When we'd first created the algorithm, my mother had asked me, "Why in the world would a man want to be a part of an agency who asks for disclosure of his dirty laundry?"

The answer was simple: men want women, no matter the cost.

"Do I need to pay for services up front, or when a match is made?" April asked.

"We require a retainer fee to begin services. This covers the data compilation and background checks. Then an automatic payment, in the amount agreed to in your contract, will be deducted each month from your bank account. That amount allows you to access up to three matches per month."

"Background check? Do you do those on both the clients and the selection pool?"

"Yes, April. We find it's in the best interest of all parties that we perform a full background check, for everyone's safety."

I stood, walked over to my filing cabinet, and pulled out a form. I returned to my seat and slid the paper forward.

"The information listed at the top is what we need from you. The bottom explains the process and what types of results we get back. You can find and complete this form online."

April leaned forward and looked at it but made no move to add it to the pile of other documents I'd given her.

The truth was, we hadn't done background checks when we'd first begun. It wasn't until after a couple of unlucky ladies were scammed out of money by their matches that we'd started. We had thought our reference checks were sufficient, but simply put, we were scammed by the scammers. They learned of our reference check and make sure everyone we talked to was in on the plan. They all gave us the dirt, just not the truthful dirt.

It only took us those two epic failures to add the important piece of background checks to our procedures. As they say, "Fool me once, shame on you; fool me twice…" Any client found to have a past arrest record, a history of questionable financial transactions, or abuse charges of any kind were denied entry.

My phone, which was sitting beside me, let out a soft *DING*—giving me an excuse to get out of the meeting if I needed to. Realizing April was more interested in getting dirt than finding true love, I decided there was no need to waste my time with details she didn't really care about.

"I'm sorry, April. That is all the time I have for today. Do you have any other questions before I walk you out?" I asked, standing. "As I said, you can always read the pamphlet, look at our website, or call and speak with our receptionist to get more information."

"I think I have everything I need. I'll have Daddy write you a check and drop it off as soon as he's done with golf," she said.

She stood and followed me out of my office door and to the lobby, which consisted of several chairs for waiting clients, a coffee cart, a coffee table, and a receptionist desk.

"It smells lovely in here. Just like a coffee shop," April said, breathing in deeply.

"Thank you. We like it," I replied.

I didn't feel like sharing my little secret with April. The aroma actually came from the beautiful Greta Armani painting that was situated on the wall above the coffee cart. One of my old friends had turned me on to her work. Greta, a Cuban artist, used instant coffee to create paintings of rural landscapes and other scenes. Her paintings were even more unique because she made sure that the aroma of the coffee wasn't lost. It lingered in the air for years.

The colors in her painting complemented the colors of the room, which consisted of browns and tans. I'd been told her technique was to mix different quantities of coffee powder in water, in order to achieve various shades of brown.

After the door shut behind April I grabbed a small bundle of rubber bands off of Eva's—our receptionist— desk, plopped down unceremoniously on the closest waiting room chair, and launched the bands one-by-one at the wall—opposite my favorite painting of course.

"That good, huh?" Eva asked with a laugh.

"You could say that. Another gossip girl with daddy's money to burn. I guess I shouldn't complain, they're our bread and butter."

"Yes, they are," Eva agreed with a frown, as she stood and started towards the copy room. "At least you only have a half-dozen more of those to speak with today."

"Just kill me now!" I said as I sighed, stood up, and

headed back towards my office as I waited for my next appointment.

Chapter Two

The next day didn't start on a great note. I'd been so exhausted at the end of the previous day that I'd been too tired to sleep. You would've thought exhaustion equaled sleeping like the dead, but no such luck for me. This morning, I'd done my best to apply my makeup to hide the shadows under my eyes.

Climbing in my car, I'd left the house in search of the one and only thing that might help redeem the morning... CAFFEINE! My hopes had been dashed at the sight of the line at the drive-through. There was no way I had time for that. Sighing, I continued on to the office.

Eva was on the phone when I walked in, so I only gave a quick wave before passing her and moving into my office.

Sitting down in my chair, I opened the bottom drawer of my desk and slid my new purple Marc Jacobs clutch into it.

I'd gotten into this habit after Sara had her purse stolen off the hook behind her door. Although it was found in the trash dumpster outside, with all the cash and credit cards missing, we'd never figured out who it was that had taken it. To be safe, we'd all decided a new hiding place was necessary for our purses going forward. In addition, we'd added these cute little buttons that were actually tracking chips. Now, if one of our purses walked away, we could track it.

Swiveling back around, I saw the red light on my phone was blinking. I groaned inwardly. Nothing like starting off a no-sleep, no-caffeine day with a bunch of voicemails to listen to and calls to return. I reached forward and grabbed a pen and paper to jot down numbers. The first paper I turned over, in hopes that it was blank and could be of use, ended up being last month's TAFT newsletter, which I'd printed out to read at my leisure. I picked it up and flipped to the dog-eared page: Julia's advice column. I hadn't had a chance to read it before it went out to our clients. Deciding to deal with the voicemails later, I leaned back and began to read:

HOW MANY CARATS ARE YOU WORTH?

The biggest fights couples have in the beginning are about one of two things: sex, or money. Today I'll speak on the latter, MONEY!

My advice on this one is simple… Make sure you know how many carats you are worth before jumping into the dating pool. Why should you do this? Because I promise you, you'll never get a ten-carat ring if you pick a four-carat guy.

Sounds crass? Maybe. But the truth is, if you want any chance at all of having success in your marriage, you'll need to be smart and only choose the man, or woman, that can provide you with the lifestyle you think you deserve.

I know your next question is, "What about love?" I promise you love will soon fade away if your Tesla turns into a Gremlin and your glass Jimmy Choo's turn into Crocs.

So, please, take my advice. Learn from someone who has been there, done that—not just once, but four times—marry the person that meets your carat criteria. It will save you many nights of fights, tears, and tubes of mascara.

This public service announcement is provided to you by TAFT

I couldn't help but chuckle at Julia's article. If anyone knew the do's and don'ts before marriage, it was her. I really believed Julia's biggest issue with longevity in a relationship was due to the fact that she was in love with the idea of being in love. She didn't really want anything that came with it.

Sara, on the other hand, was only in it for the chase. She just had to have the man she was after until she actually caught him. By then, she was bored and ready to move on to the next conquest.

Among the three of us, we didn't have the best track record or stance on relationships. It was only because of our parents, and my Grandma Olive that we knew marriage and love really could exist. Not that my parents hadn't had their fair share of fights. I remembered a doozy or two during my childhood. But somehow, they'd always come back to one another. I was fairly certain it was a generational thing that had pushed the divorce rate up. Women no longer felt the need to allow a man to open a door for them, and men no longer felt the need to do so. Back in the day, Grandma would've taken Dad by the ear if he hadn't opened the door for her or my mother.

The crackle of the intercom burst into my reminiscing.

"Callie, there's a Detective Brown here to see you," Eva said.

"Did he say what he wanted?"

"No, ma'am. Do you want me to ask him?"

"It's fine. I'll be out in a moment."

This day just keeps getting better and better! I stood and started towards the door, taking a quick peek in the mirror on the wall to make sure I was properly coiffed, or at least as put together as I could get given the start to my day.

My emerald-green eyes stared back at me, showing me that my rich, auburn-red hair had managed to remain frizz-free—smoothed back in an artful French twist, and my makeup still looked fresh. Seeing everything was in order, I went to the lobby in search of my unexpected guest.

***

As I rounded the corner into the lobby, I gave Detective Brown a once-over. He was tall, lightly tanned, with brown hair. His shirt was stretched just enough over his chest to tell he was fit, in a lean way.

I guessed he was somewhere in his early forties. Out of habit, I checked to see if he wore a wedding ring on his finger—or had the shadow of one recently removed. It was bare. While he would have been my cup of tea, had I been in the market for a man, I was not. So, I moved on from my appraisal to find out why he was here.

"Good morning, Detective Brown. How can I assist you?" I asked, my hand outstretched.

He took my hand in his and with a firm grip, gave it a single shake before letting go.

"Good morning. Please call me Jack. I need to ask you questions about some of your clients," he replied in a deep, smooth radio announcer voice.

I felt a little shiver of attraction run down my body. I quickly collected myself.

"I'm sorry, Jack. All client information is confidential without a release. If you would like to speak with the clients and get them to give you one, then I can answer any questions you might have."

"I'm afraid I can't do that," he replied.

"I promise it's very easy. I can even provide you with a—"

"I don't think you're understanding me. A form won't help."

I couldn't help but shuffle from foot to foot as I tried to understand what he was attempting to say. "You're right. I don't understand."

"I can't get a release because your client is dead."

"Dead?" I knew there was more I wanted to add, but my brain had just gone too numb to ask a logical question. Ironically, all I could think about was my statement from the day before when I'd said, *Just kill me now.*"

Jack reached forward and gently grabbed hold of my elbow. "Maybe we should go into your office where you can have a seat?"

"What…" I said, my legs feeling as if they'd turned to jelly.

Saying nothing further, he turned me and walked us into the office just ahead, leading me to one of the plush chairs. I took a seat and a deep breath.

"I apologize, you've caught me off guard. Let's start over. You said 'clients,' plural. Is there more than one dead person?" I asked, looking up at the detective who was still standing beside me.

He moved over to the chair across from me and sat down.

"At this point, no. We have only one death to discuss. Jasmine Stone."

I vaguely remembered Jasmine, but only because she was a tough case: older, divorced, and with children.

"How'd she die?" I asked.

"I can't give out any other specific details while the investigation is still ongoing," he said, tilting his head and gazing intently at me. "You don't seem surprised by this news?"

Heat crept into my cheeks at the accusation.

"It's quite the opposite," I replied, now nervous because of the judgment in his tone. "I'm too stunned for words. We've had very few violent deaths in our community, much less a death of one of our clients."

"I see."

He didn't expand further. Instead, he let the silence between us linger.

When I couldn't take the silence any longer, I asked, "What information do you need from us?"

"We need to know when your last communication was with Ms. Stone, whom you set her up with, and contact information for those people and any others that have knowledge of her personal information."

"Do you have a warrant?" I asked.

"No. Are you going to make me get one?" he asked, eyebrows raised.

"Unfortunately, Detective… I mean Jack… unless you have a warrant I can't give you anything. I'll need to reach out to my attorney first to check what TAFT can and can't give out, in this scenario," I said.

I had nothing to hide, yet I continued to feel anxious under the weight of his gaze.

"So," I continued, "You can either leave me your card with contact information and I can call you as soon as I get an answer, or you can get your warrant. The only information I can give you right now is relative to TAFT in general, not our clients."

He reached up and pinched the bridge of his nose before sighing and mumbling something under his breath. I *thought* he said, "Why can't anything be easy?" but I wasn't certain.

"I really am sorry. I know this makes your job more difficult. However, I must ensure that I don't violate my clients' rights. I promise you'll be my very first phone call after I have an answer."

I felt the urge to reach up and smooth the lines that now furrowed his brow, but I resisted.

"I'll hold you to that," Jack said with a cold stare. "And, if you don't call within the next 24 hours I *will* return. With a warrant."

"Understood," I replied, once again resisting an urge. This time it was the urge to give a smart-ass salute. "Are there any questions I *can* answer for you right now?"

Jack removed a well-worn, palm-sized notebook and a pen from his front shirt pocket. He flipped through it for several moments before returning his attention to me.

"Can you please tell where you get your male selection pool candidates?"

"It varies. Sometimes they respond to flyers we have posted, sometimes—"

"Where do you post these items?"

"Flyers are posted at Love Bites, Runs with—"

"What is 'Love Bites'?" Jack asked, his attention never leaving the paper where he was making notes.

"Are you going to let me answer a question before you interrupt?" I snapped, unable to control my irritation any longer.

His gaze moved up to meet mine. "Love Bites? What is it?" he asked, completely ignoring my question.

I took another deep breath and clenched my teeth, "Love Bites is the nightclub Julia, my business partner, manages."

"Do you have a copy of the flyer you post?"

"Not printed. But I can get you a copy."

"Good. And Runs with… I didn't catch the rest."

"You didn't catch the rest because you cut me off!"

Did his lip just twitch up at the corner? He said nothing, just waited.

I tried to outwait him, but patience wasn't my best quality.

"Runs with *Scissors*," I finally said. I knew he was going to ask what that was, but two could play the waiting game.

"And that would be?" he finally asked. A small crinkle at the outside of his eyes gave his amusement away.

"The hair salon that my other partner, Sara, works at. And before you ask, no, I don't have a copy, but I can get you one."

"Anywhere else?"

"The pro-shop at McClellan's. I can also get you a copy of that flyer."

"Is that all?"

"Yes. The rest of our business is received through word of mouth."

"Good," he said, flipping the page on his notebook. "Can you get those flyers for me now?"

"Can't we email them to you?" I asked.

"I'd rather not forget," he said.

I stood up—more abruptly than was probably necessary, reached over the desk, and angrily punched the button for Eva's desk.

"Yes, Callie?" Eva said.

"Can you please print out copies of the flyers we post at the club, pro-shop, and the salon and bring them to me?"

I stabbed the off button and sat back down.

"Eva will bring them in shortly," I said. "Now, what other questions do you have? I have an appointment soon, so I would really like to get this wrapped up as quickly as possible."

"How did you start TAFT?" he asked.

"I'm sorry, but how is that relative to this conversation?" Now he was starting to annoy me. I didn't have time for useless questions.

"It's relative because I say it is. I'm trying to get background information."

I crossed my arms, leaned back in my chair, and let out a huff.

"Several years ago, we were asked by the wife of McClellan's chairperson if we could set up her daughters with some 'nice boys' in town. When it turned out well, she put the word out. It didn't take long before we had a long list of women asking to be set up."

Eva knocked on the doorjamb then made her way into the room. She handed me the flyers.

"Thank you, Eva," I said.

She nodded before she quickly turned and left.

"Here you go," I said, handing the flyers to Jack.

Jack took them and looked them over. I could tell when he reached the portion of the flyer where we mentioned the "negative references" because his eyebrows rose, which was not an uncommon response.

The flyers had started out on a whim. When we'd first started TAFT, we'd only reviewed and made suggestions on suitors we currently knew about. However, it wasn't too long after that we'd run out of men to recommend. So, Julia had put up a flyer in the nightclub asking for any single males looking for love to shoot TAFT an email. She listed out the "negative references" criteria as a joke. We were not only floored to see that our inbox was flooded the next day, we were stunned to see they had, in fact, included a list of references. And, this was all without us even mentioning the looks, age, or income of our potential pool of women. From that point forward, we posted our flyers in all three locations.

"And how do you determine which men you select?"

"Why? Are you interested?" I asked, unable to stop myself.

He moved his gaze back up to me, and it was not amused.

"Sorry," I said. I knew a blush was once again creeping its way up my face. "We take all of our applicants and run them through a rigorous screening process which includes: reference checks, algorithms, background checks, and a Grandma Olive check."

"Grandma Olive? Is that supposed to be code for something?" he asked.

"No. It's my grandma. She knows everything about everyone. And what she doesn't know, she finds out from her friends."

"You're telling me, you pick men based on your grandmother's recommendation?" he asked, head tilted and eyebrows raised.

"We wouldn't be successful without her."

He let out a little snort, shook his head, and chuckled. I chose to ignore him.

"And what individual roles do and your partners play in the business?" he asked.

"Sara oversees the recruitment of men for the pool

with Grandma's help. Julia processes the reference checks, plus she is the writer of our monthly advice column. I deal with day-to-day operations, including data entry, running the matching algorithm, and managing the books."

"And who pays for your services?"

Some of these questions made no relevant sense to me, but clearly, I had no choice but to answer.

"We are paid by both the female clients looking for love, and by the men who want to be selection pool candidates. The men pay us for being given the chance to match up with one of our clients."

"Have you received any complaints from your clientele regarding interactions with one another?"

I thought about it for a minute. "None come to mind, but I'll have to check with Sara and Julia before giving you a solid answer."

The phone on the desk buzzed, which was followed by Eva's voice. "Callie, your next appointment is here."

"Thank you, Eva. I'll be right out."

I turned my attention back to Jack. "Are we done here?"

He flipped back and forth through his little notebook a few times before answering. "Yeah. For now. If I think of anything else, I'll ask you tomorrow *when* you call me."

I heard his emphasis on the last portion of his statement, specifically on the word "when." Clearly, subtlety was not his forte.

"Of course," I said sweetly, making sure to add my

own special tone to the words.

We both stood, turned, and made our way out to the lobby. When we reached Eva's desk, we stopped. Jack reached into his back pocket and extracted a business card that he handed to me.

"Thank you. I'll be in touch." He nodded and headed out the door.

My stomach churned as I digested the horrible information I'd just learned. What I wanted to do was go in the bathroom and toss my cookies and cry. However, that wasn't an option with my next appointment just feet away. So, I bottled up my tears for later, put on my big girl panties, and walked over to my next appointment.

"Good afternoon. Welcome to TAFT. How may I help you?"

***

As soon as my next appointment left, I grabbed the phone and called the girls; I conferenced them both in at once. Music was playing in the background from wherever one of them was.

"Hey, ladies," I said.

"What's up?" both said, almost in unison.

"You need to get to the office right away. We have something important to discuss."

The music faded. I didn't know if that meant a radio had been turned down, or if whoever was in the place with the music had moved to a quieter room.

"What's so important?" Julia asked.

"I'd rather not say over the phone," I said.

"Okay…" Sara said, letting the one word trail off.

"Do we need to bring anything?" Julia asked.

"Actually, yes," I said. "Our lawyer."

Chapter Three

While I waited for the girls to arrive, I pulled everything we had on Jasmine Stone. My memory had been accurate: twenty-nine, divorced, two kids—ages eight and four. Jasmine's death in and of itself was devastating news, but to know two children were now motherless was the sour cherry on top. The one piece of good news was that the father was in the picture, so they wouldn't also be orphans.

By the time Sara and Julia arrived and were seated in our conference room, I had a packet of information prepared with all the details I could find. JJ hadn't been able to attend in person, so I'd multi-tasked and spoken to him over the phone while I put everything together.

I leaned over the desk and punched the intercom button on the phone, ringing the front desk. "Eva, can you please come join us."

"Of course. Be there in a jiffy," she replied.

As always, Eva was quick and efficient and was in the conference room in no time flat, pen and notepaper in hand. She moved towards the end of the table and took a seat.

"Okay, out with it. The suspense is killing me," Julia said.

I cringed at her choice of words. I cleared my throat and took a deep breath. "We had a visit today from the police."

Everyone, except Eva, who already knew this bit of information, looked at one another.

"And…" Sara said. As was her style, she let the word linger.

"And, he wanted to talk to us about our clients. Well, more specifically *a* client, Jasmine Stone."

Sara, Julia, and Eva all donned their version of "thinking" face while they pulled up Jasmine in their mental database.

Julia was the first to answer. "She's the divorced lady with kids?"

"Yes. In front of each of you is a packet of all the information we have on her, relative to TAFT."

"Why did they want to know about her?" Sara asked.

"Because she's dead."

This time everyone in the room, excluding myself, gasped.

"Dead? When? How?" everyone asked in some order at the same time.

I held up my hand to get everyone's attention.

"What I know is that Jasmine is dead. How and when she died was not released to me," I said.

"Do they think she was murdered?" Julia asked.

"The detective did not specifically say anything about her being murdered. However, because they came to us for information I can only assume they think her death is suspicious. What they have asked of TAFT is to provide them with all the details relative to who knew Ms. Stone, including who she was set up with, who had access to her profile, and who had contact with her at our agency."

Julia—who is an amazing multi-tasker thanks to her job as a bartender—had been flipping through the packet at the same time she'd listened to my answers.

"It looks like she's only been matched twice so far. And, one of those was with Stewart. There is no way he's a murderer unless he had a serious psychotic break. He is one of the gentlest men I have ever come across."

"I would agree," Sara chimed in.

"You won't get any arguments from me," I concurred. "It's the second match I know little about. I can't even say I recall anything but his name. Sara and Eva, you two would've had the most interactions with him. What do you think?"

Eva shifted in her chair, leaning forward to look closer at the packet in front of her. While Sara pulled hers into her hands and leaned back in her chair. Each was quiet for several moments while their eyes scanned the document. Eva was first to look up at the group.

"He signed with us less than a month ago. I believe Jasmine was his first match. On the surface, the guy seemed nice enough," she said with a shrug.

"Eva said pretty much the same thing I was thinking," Sara chimed in, leaning forward and placing the packet back on the table. "He had a standard background with nothing overly juicy in his basic details or dirt profile. Just a normal, average guy. The only thing I remember that stands out is that he's a pharmacist."

"What about her ex?" Julia asked. "Do we know if there were any abuse issues while she was married to him, or any stalky stuff since?"

"Not that I know of or is mentioned in Jasmine's file. I also searched the public records database and found nothing about him except the marriage certificate and divorce papers," I said. "JJ told me we can give them all of Jasmine's information, including the names of her two matches. However, because both male clients are living, we have to get a release from them personally before we can supply any details on them, beyond their names and contact numbers."

"Sounds reasonable," Julia said.

"Eva," I said, "can you please go ahead and fill out as

much of each release form as you can and email them to me. Hopefully, this will help expedite them getting returned by the matches."

"Shouldn't you send them to the police to distribute versus contacting the men directly. They might not want to bring these gentlemen in on the case just yet," Sara—an avid binge watcher of detective shows—pointed out.

"You're probably right, Sara. I hadn't thought about that."

"Julia, since you are our in-house writer, can you call JJ and work with him to get a press statement ready in case anyone tries to tie this back to TAFT. As of now, there is no direct connection, so it should be an easy situation to diffuse."

"Sure thing, jelly bean," Julia responded.

"Eva, are you comfortable reading from the script JJ and Julia draft, or do you want to transfer the calls to one of us?"

"I think I can manage. If I get concerned, I'll either transfer the call or take down the name and number of the caller for you."

"Good. Well then, I guess we're done with today's meeting. Thank you, everyone, for rushing in to deal with this sad situation."

We all stood and I saw Julia glance at her watch.

"Looks like happy hour! Anyone interested in going with me to the club to get a drink and play 'guess the killer?'"

When the room fell silent she quickly added, "Oh, come on. You know I'm just kidding." Her face showed she'd realized her joke wasn't as funny as she had thought it had been in her head. "But seriously, this situation totally sucks and scares the crap out of me. I need a drink."

"As long as the first drink is on you, I'm in," Sara said.

"Me too," Eva said.

"Thanks for the offer but I'll pass. I have something I need to do," I said. I was never much of a drinker and being sad and drinking was a bad combo for me anyway.

They waved at me as they headed out in search of some alcohol-induced relaxation. I moved into my office and opened my laptop.

It only took me a few clicks before I finished donating on GoFundMe.com. My donation was to Jasmine's funeral fund. The amount of the donation was equivalent to all of the money she'd paid TAFT, plus some additional to help make sure the funeral could be done properly. I knew her children were too young to give condolences to, so I figured this was the next best way to show my sympathy and support.

Julia might have been joking about guessing who the killer was, but I intended to do just that. There was no way I was going to sit idly by and wait to see if Jasmine's death was connected to TAFT or not.

Chapter Four

The next morning, I headed to the police station to hand off the client release forms to Detective Brown before I went into the office. I knew the sooner I did this, the less flack I'd have to deal with from him later. I prayed this would be an open and shut case.

I flipped down the vanity mirror and did a quick makeup check. Once I was certain all was in order, I got out of my car, locked the door, and smoothed the wrinkles from my skirt. I took care to step over a puddle—compliments of last night's rainstorm—and sidestep a wad of bubble gum stuck to the pavement.

The parking lot had cops scattered around, some leaving, some going. One officer was leading a tall, slender man into the station, hands cuffed behind his back. I punched the lock button on my remote once more, listening for the telltale sound of the horn confirming my car was secured.

I would be heartbroken if anything happened to my beloved cherry-red Model 3 Tesla. Not because it had cost a crap load of cash—well, okay that too—but mostly because of what the car stood for. It had been one of the first things I purchased after the divorce that I'd paid for with money I'd earned all by myself.

Before TAFT I hadn't really worked. Not because I didn't want to, but because Mike, my ex, hadn't wanted me to. He believed in the old school southern tradition where men worked and women raised the babies and kept house.

While the babies never managed to come no matter how hard we tried, the boredom had and it had driven me nearly insane. If not for the fact that I'd been the one who managed our finances—Mike was *not* good with numbers—I would've been bald from having pulled out all my hair.

The one gift I had gotten from the divorce, besides being rid of a cheating bastard, was the chance to figure out who I was and to have the career I wanted.

It was silly, but buying the car had made me feel better about myself, more self-assured. You could say the car had turned out to be my post-divorce security blanket. The inside of the car was my safe space and the purr of the engine as I drove along always helped soothe my nerves on a bad day.

I gave it one last adoring glance across the parking lot before I proceeded forward.

I knew the moment I passed the designated outdoor smoking area, as the abhorrent smell of tar and tobacco lingered in the air like a dirty shoe. My grandfather had been a serious chain smoker. He wouldn't even put down the old cigarette to get a new one, lighting the new one with the old cigarette butt hanging from his lips. The air in the room had been so thick with smoke, my eyes and lungs both used to burn. Just getting a small whiff of the stuff now made me nauseous.

I darted past the area and into the station, stopping when I reached the front desk, which was partitioned with a Plexiglass wall. A small twelve-by-twelve window had been cut out to allow visitors to speak with the person manning the desk. Today that person was a tiny blonde woman who looked out of character for both the setting and her uniform. Her name tag read Ashley.

Several moments passed before she turned her attention from her computer screen to me.

"Can I help you?" she asked, giving me a once-over.

"I hope so," I said, giving her my friendliest smile in hopes it would warm up the chill radiating from her. Clearly, what she lacked in size she made up in scary stare factor. "I'm looking for Detective Brown."

"Jack or Larry?"

"Oh, my apologies. I didn't realize you had more than

one. I'm looking for Jack Brown."

She didn't bother to explain any further as to their association. Instead, she reached for her phone, picked it up, and dialed a number.

"Is Jack in?" Ashley asked the person who answered the phone on the other end.

"… Do you know when he'll be done?"

"… There's a lady here to see him."

"… Don't know. Hold on."

She covered the receiver and looked up at me, "I didn't catch your name?"

"It's Calla Lily Bloom with TAFT. Detective Brown is expecting me."

Her eyebrows arched at my answer. I gave her my usual "yeah, I know" shrug. My full name *always* got that reaction. I'd had a short reprieve from the "looks" when I was married. But after the divorce, I decided I would rather have the looks than keep his last name. So, I changed it back.

She turned her attention back to the phone. "She says her name is Ms. Bloom, and she's with TAFT. Jack is supposedly expecting her."

"… Okay. I'll send her back."

Ashley hung up the receiver, reached for a clipboard with a log on it, and took a visitor's badge out of a desk drawer to her right. She picked up a pen and jotted down my name and the badge number on the log.

"Detective Brown is in a meeting but should be done

in just a few minutes. You can wait in his office." She lifted up the clipboard with the pen and badge laid on top of it and handed it to me through the window. "Sign your name on the 'x' and attach this badge to your shirt. Return it before you leave."

I reached out and grabbed the clipboard. I signed where indicated and handed the clipboard back after taking the badge. I cringed when I saw that the badge had a gator clip as the method for attaching it to my shirt. I had no choice but to attach it to the chest area. This blouse had a high neck, no pocket, and no collar. That would leave a nifty little mark in my brand-new silk blouse. Normally, I wouldn't care about things like that, but this outfit was a gift from my father and I hated to see it get ruined.

When I was all situated, I looked towards the officer for further instruction. She reached down and pressed a button. A soft *BUZZ* came from a door to our right. I walked over, pushed it open, and walked through.

"His desk is down that hallway, second door on the right." She pointed her finger for the briefest of moments before turning her away from me and back to her computer screen. From this new vantage point, I could see she was in the middle of a game of solitaire.

Turning my attention back to the direction where she'd pointed, I took in my surroundings. The area was one large room crammed full of low-partitioned cubicles; a desk and a guest chair—or detainee chair, if you were there against your wishes—was situated just inside each one.

There appeared to be no standard of desk etiquette, as some were littered with papers while others were spotless. Interestingly enough, the officers and detectives seated behind each desk mirrored the state of the desk.

The noise of all the phones, walkie-talkies, people, and equipment going at once was almost deafening. Feeling my nerves fray, I swiftly moved down the hall in the direction Ashley had indicated. Two cat-call whistles and one "Hey, baby" followed me as I made my way to Detective Brown's office. I wasn't sure if these were from the citizens currently being detained, or from the officers. Not really caring which it was, I didn't look back to find out.

I opened the door to Jack's office and made my way in, closing the door behind me. I didn't know what I'd been expecting, but it wasn't this. Unlike the people in the other room who mirrored the appearance of their desk, Detective Brown did not. His office, unlike the man I saw the other day, was a mess.

Papers were strewn across the desktop and sticky notes were everywhere. How this man could find anything on his desk was beyond me. I immediately doubted his capabilities for solving a crime if he couldn't even keep a clean, clutter-free desk.

Moving over to the guest chair, I looked down. The once cream-colored chair was now spotted with stains. One small tear had been repaired via duct tape. As I had no interest in adding any of those stains to my cream skirt, I refrained from sitting down.

I stood in place for several minutes, shifting from foot to foot. Stilettoes were not the best choice for standing in one place for any long length of time. Agitated, I looked at my watch, gave my manicure a once-over, and continued to survey the room while listening for footsteps in the hall.

After what felt like an eternity, I heard someone coming down the hall and I breathed a sigh of relief. The relief was short-lived, however, when they continued past the office. I looked at my watch again. Ten minutes had passed. *Seriously! Does he think I have all day?* Patience was never my strong suit.

Unable to stand still any longer, I made my way around the room first towards a bookshelf situated along the back wall. It held a mishmash of contents. Books laid every which way and a few frameless photos were propped up against one knickknack or another; others had toppled over and were now face down on the shelf. My hands twitched to straighten up, but I fought the urge and succeeded. Well, at least until I reached his desk. Once there, I couldn't take it any longer and I tidied the papers into a stack. Below the papers a file folder appeared. On its tab, it said *Jasmine Stone*.

Instantly, my inner Nancy Drew wanted me to open the file. I shouldn't. But… maybe if I knew more, it would ensure I could keep TAFT in the clear. The less connection, the fewer media, the less bad press. I tapped my fingers on the file folder while I fought my inner sleuth. I looked up at the door and listened for sounds of someone coming my way. Hearing none, I convinced myself that was a clear sign I should snoop, so I opened the file.

The top page listed out all of Jasmine's basic demographics: sex, age, physical characteristics, address, etc. Down lower on the form was the cause of death:

<u>Combined Drug Toxicity</u>
Toxicology findings: Fluoxetine, Eszopiclone, Oxycodone, and Sumatriptan identified in blood samples (see full toxicology report for details)

A handwritten note on the side of the page said, "Victim only has a prescription for Sumatriptan." I didn't need to read any more; alarm bells had already gone off in my brain. These were all drugs of some kind. Because there was no lack of sticky notes available, I picked up a pen and jotted this information down on one. I didn't know for certain what the cause of death meant, or what most of the items in the toxicology report were, but I could connect the dots enough to make a guess it all meant one thing: drug overdose.

This was *so* not good. Our selection pool candidate was a pharmacist, for cripes' sake. I quickly shoved the sticky note into my purse. I swiped my hand over the desk to re-scatter the papers I'd stacked. At least the detective's messy desk would pay off for me in this moment. I hurriedly moved from behind the desk and out of the office. He'd given me enough of an excuse to walk out based on how long he'd made me wait, so I planned on taking advantage of it.

***

My heart was racing when I slid behind the wheel of my car. I'd made it out without bringing any attention to myself. Now I needed to get out of the parking lot. As I pulled out onto the street an idea popped into my head.

I had the files with me that gave the address of the two matches. I could just run them over and get the men to sign the release, potentially getting some questions answered in the process.

I knew Sara had said I should leave that to the police, but really, wasn't I doing TAFT a service by getting them signed by the client personally? I mean, this way we looked uber-professional instead of letting a cop show up at the door. What could it hurt? Right?

It took a few more minutes, but I finally convinced myself it was the right thing to do. I activated my Bluetooth and told Siri to dial the number for the pharmacy where Mr. Rivera, the first match in the pile, worked. After a few rings a pharmacy technician answered. She stated that Mr. Rivera was not in today and asked if I wanted to leave a message. I declined and instead at the next light, I reached over, grabbed the file, and programmed the Mr. Rivera's home address into my GPS. With luck, he would be at home, which would give me an even better chance to use my investigation skills. It should be a piece of cake.

Chapter Five

I pulled into Steven Rivera's apartment parking lot, parked, but left the car on and enjoyed a quiet moment of full A/C. As I did so, I reached over and pulled out the sticky note from my purse. I googled the cause of death to find it was exactly what I'd thought it was; a drug overdose due to a toxic mix of prescription substances. I typed in each of the drugs: Fluoxetine was Prozac—anti-depressant; Eszopiclone was Lunesta—sleeping pill; Oxycodone—schedule two narcotic pain pill; Sumatriptan was Imitrex—migraine medicine. I went to drugchecker.com and did a quick drug-interaction check. There were two major interaction warnings and two moderate ones. Clearly, these drugs shouldn't have been taken together.

After jotting down each bit of info on the back side of the sticky, I took several deep breaths, shut off the engine, and made my way into the small entry. Opening the file folder, I saw Mr. Rivera lived in apartment 305. Moving over to the elevator, I pressed the "up" button. Nothing happened. I tried again and still nothing. *Well, damn!* Grumbling under my breath, I headed to the door marked "stairs" and hiked up to level three. This was so not the day for stilettos!

When I reached the apartment, I was welcomed by a "No Solicitors" note taped to the front door. *This ought to be fun.* I knocked on the door and waited. It only took a moment before I heard someone shuffling around behind the closed door. Seconds later, the door opened. A short Hispanic man stood in the opening.

"Can I help you?" he asked.

"I'm looking for Mr. Rivera," I said.

"I'm him."

I held out my hand, "Hello! I'm Callie Bloom, from TAFT. I was hoping you might have a moment."

He looked at my hand for a split second as if it might be a trick, but then he grasped it and gave it a proper shake. "Sure… Come in."

I made my way in. My heart skipped a beat when I heard the door close behind me, and a lock click. I looked back over my shoulder and felt the blood drain from my face.

"Darn door won't stay shut without locking it," he said with a small chuckle. "Been on the super for a week now to fix it."

My discomfort must have been obvious for him to explain himself. I took a deep, steadying breath. I was being silly. I moved the rest of the way in, taking in the surroundings as I did.

The apartment was medium sized with the standard small living room/dining room combo, and a galley kitchen off to one side. The walls were the normal basic white of most apartments. It was clean, well-maintained, and clutter free. The furnishings were very minimal and bachelor-like. They included a couch, recliner, entertainment center with a TV, coffee table, and a small dinette with chairs. After I finished surveying the area, I turned back towards Steven.

"I'm sorry to come by unannounced, but I thought this was best done in person."

He cocked his head slightly. "I'm sorry. I don't follow. Do what in person?"

He motioned for me to take a seat. I sat and waited for him to also sit before continuing.

"We recently had an incident with one of our clients at TAFT… nothing for you to worry about," I quickly added, "But the police are requesting access to files of any matches who our client had interactions with."

"Can I assume you are referring to Ms. Stone? She's the only person I've interacted with at TAFT thus far." He wiped his palms on his slacks and sat up a little straighter.

"Yes, you're correct. I'm here about Jasmine."

"What kind of 'incident' are you talking about?" he asked, his tone now holding a hint of concern.

I wasn't sure what the best way was to tell him in order to get the most genuine reaction. I decided on the direct approach.

"She's dead," I said, making solid eye contact and watching him closely, ensuring I could best judge his reaction.

His eyebrows shot up. "What happened?"

I took one extra moment to try to see past the outward expression of surprise, searching for something more. I wasn't sure what else I'd expected, but shock was all I got. Both relief and disappointment ran through me at the same time. I didn't want him to be a killer, not only for the obvious reasons, but also because I was sitting in his house. However, it would have been good to have a solid suspect right off the bat that the cops could pin it to. The sooner they caught the killer, the quicker TAFT would go back to normal.

"I don't really know. The police haven't released any details. They only contacted us to get the client information." I opened the file folder on my lap and pulled out the consent form. I handed it to him. "Since you're one of the people Jasmine had reviewed, you're on our list to notify. I don't have any notes on whether or not you actually interacted."

He took the release from me.

"Yes, we spoke on the phone once and were planning to go out on a date next week," he said as he looked down at the form. "What information will you give them?"

Steven bounced his leg ever so slightly, and I thought I saw a quick flash of worry cross his face right before he'd glanced down.

"Everything we acquired while doing your application approval: standard background, reference details, who you have viewed, who has viewed you."

"Can I get a copy of the file you give to them?" he asked, looking back up and scooting forward to sit on the edge of the chair. A tiny bit of perspiration glistened on his hairline.

"Some details are proprietary information, meaning it's how we pick the best matches. So, we'd prefer not to share that with anyone. It will only be shared with the police if they get a warrant. Everything else we can give you a copy of, if you'd like it. Keep in mind it's not normal policy, but then these are not normal circumstances."

He shook his head. "That sounds fair. Where do you want me to sign?"

"Down at the bottom," I said. "I'm sorry, I forgot to bring a pen."

He stood up. "No problem. Let me get one."

I also stood up. "Do you mind if I use your restroom while you sign?"

"Not at all. Head down that hall, it's the door on the

end."

I smiled at him, turned, and headed towards the bathroom. Once behind the closed, locked door, I let out a breath. See, that wasn't so bad. He didn't seem like a killer.

Being that I really did have to use the bathroom, I did. When I was done, I flushed, then moved to the sink to wash my hands. Turning on the water, I looked into the mirror and noticed it also served as a medicine cabinet. *Should I?* Well, of course, I should; that is why I came here!

I reached for a Kleenex as to not leave fingerprints and quickly—and as quietly as possible—opened the cabinet. My eyes scanned the contents looking for any pill bottles. There were a few to choose from. I held my breath as I looked at each one. None matched. *See, there was nothing to…* I noticed one more bottle shoved behind some Nyquil. I pushed the cold medicine aside and slowly turned the bottle to see the label, Eszopiclone.

My pulse began doing double-time. Okay, no reason to panic. Those were just sleeping pills. Everyone had sleeping pills, right? I shut the cabinet door, turned off the water—which had already been on for too long—and leaned against the counter. My ears rang as my blood pressure rose. A doorbell ringing brought my attention around.

I heard Steven making his way to the door. I knew this would be my best moment to make my getaway, so I hurried out of the bathroom toward the exit. I stopped in my tracks. Detective Brown stood in the doorway. The minute his gaze landed on me, he stopped talking, raised his hand to his brow, and pinched the bridge of his nose.

Chapter Six

"Detective Brown! What a surprise seeing you here," I said, trying to hide the stutter step I'd taken upon seeing him at the door.

"I could say the same," he said, lowering his hand.

Steven looked back and forth between the two of us. "You two know each other?"

"This is the detective that came to our office asking for your information."

"Oh," Steven replied, turning his attention back to the detective. "Ms. Bloom said you needed this release form."

He handed the form to Jack, who took it, looked it over, and put it into his jacket pocket.

"Do you need anything else from me?" Steven asked.

"Not right now. I'll get your information from Ms. Bloom and then call you with any questions that come up."

"Sounds good," Steven replied before turning his attention to me. "Do you need anything further from me?"

"No, Steven. Getting the release signed was all I needed."

I turned toward Jack. "Can you bring the release forms with you when you come to my office? I would like to make a copy to keep for TAFT's files."

He nodded but said nothing. I reached my hand out towards Steven. "Thank you for your time. I apologize for any inconvenience this whole incident has caused you."

"No worries."

"I'll make sure to put your name back on the top of our available match list—" Jack grabbed my elbow and tugged on it, interrupting my sentence.

"It's probably best to hold off on using TAFT services for the moment. Until we get this issue resolved," Jack said, moving his gaze back and forth between us so we knew he was talking to both of us.

"What—" I started, but this time I was cut off by Jack pulling me toward and out the door.

I looked back over my shoulder at a very perplexed client. I gave a slight wave and shrug, "I'll be in touch, Mr. Rivera."

Jack continued to drag me down the hall to the elevator. He reached to push the button, and I started to tell him it was broken, but when he hit it, the button lit up.

Figured!

The door opened and we moved inside. We both turned to face out and Jack pushed the button to the ground level. The doors slowly closed. No sooner had the door finished closing then he let out, in just short of a yell, "You realize that man could potentially be a murder suspect?"

If Jack would have said that sentence to me ten minutes ago, I would have brushed him off with some smart-ass answer, but now, after having seen the pill bottle in Steven's medicine cabinet, I remained silent.

I removed my elbow from his hand with more force than was necessary. "So, you do think she was murdered?"

"I didn't say that."

"If you don't think she was murdered, then why are you speaking with our clients?" I huffed.

"It's my job to ensure every death is confirmed to be accidental. I'm just doing my due diligence."

We both knew he was full of horse puckey, but I'd let it go. I could sense that poking this particular bear would cause me more trouble than it was worth. The doors to the elevator opened, and we moved out. Jack led me the rest of the way back to my car.

"How did you know about Mr. Rivera if I didn't give you his information?"

"If you had waited for me at the precinct, I would've told you we were able to retrieve the last several numbers from Ms. Stone's cell phone and would be following up with the owner of those numbers. Mr. Rivera was one of those numbers."

"Well, if you wouldn't have made me wait for so long, I wouldn't have left," I said, making sure I put all of my irritation into my tone of voice. I reached into my purse, grabbed my keys, and pushed the button on my key fob to unlock the door. I lowered myself into my seat and began to pull the door closed, but Jack stopped it with his hand.

"Don't let me run into you again, Ms. Bloom. I'll handle the rest of the release statements. Once I get them signed, I'll bring them to your office."

"Yes, sir," I replied, giving him a small salute. He shook his head and let go of the door. I think we both knew I had no intention of sitting back and waiting for them to close this case.

I waited until he walked away before starting my car and heading back to the office. While I drove, I clenched and unclenched my fists several times, trying to still my shaking hands as I thought about what I'd found, and what could have happened if Jack hadn't shown up at the door. *Was Mr. Rivera a killer?*

Chapter Seven

Knowing Mr. Rivera's release had been signed, the next morning I went about the task of reviewing the file that Eva had compiled. I knew Eva's work was normally meticulous, but since it was such a delicate situation I thought it best I double check it to ensure it had everything it should, and nothing more.

As I put the final document into the file, I thought back to the way Steven had looked and acted when he asked what information we'd be giving the police. I hadn't seen anything in the file that was even the slightest bit fishy. Maybe I misread the look? In any case, his file was done and ready for the detective. So, I moved on to the next file, which was for Stewart Smith.

Stewart was a longtime pool selection candidate. He was sweet as pie and very handsome. He'd gone on a lot of dates through our service because he looked very good on paper, both in his qualities and his physical appearance. The problem was with his personality. After you finished the dose of initial sugar, you realized he was dry as dirt, sloppy as a pig, and still attached to his mother's umbilical cord.

We tried to drop hints in his profile relative to these flaws, without directly saying what they were. TAFT's goal was to be honest, but not cruel. We used "laid back" for sloppy, "extremely close relationship with mother" for momma's boy, and "likes to try new things in the workplace" for can't keep a job.

However, the women were either too dense to get the hints, they only concentrated on his picture, or they thought his looks would compensate for the flaws because they kept on coming. Needless to say, Stewart might get lots of dates, but they were never *second* dates.

That being said, he was not a killer; I was ninety-nine percent certain of that. Then again, did anyone think Jeffrey Dahmer was a serial killer? Just as I finished up, my intercom buzzed.

"Callie, that detective is here to see you again," Eva said.

"Please send him back," I replied.

I stared at the folders on my desk, trying my best to look casual. A quiet knock sounded at the door jamb.

"Ms. Bloom. Your assistant said it was okay for me to come back?"

"Of course," I said, standing and making my way towards him, arm outstretched. "Good to see you again, Detective… I mean, Jack."

He gave me a *yeah right* look but took my hand and shook it. "Good to see you again as well."

I tried my best to ignore the tiny internal zap of electricity that came along with the handshake. If only it had been a static shock from the carpet. After he let go, I motioned towards the empty chair.

"Have a seat," I said, moving around behind my desk and sitting in my chair.

He sat down and turned his attention to me.

"What can I help you with?" I asked.

Jack reached into his dress-coat pocket and pulled out some papers that were folded in half. He unfolded them and laid them on my desk.

"I wanted to bring you the release forms and pick up the files for your pool candidates."

I picked up the papers and gave them both a once-over. Everything appeared to be in order. I reached over and hit a button on my phone.

"Eva?"

"Yes, Callie."

"Can you please come back to my office? I have some papers I need you to scan into the system for me."

"Be right there," she said.

Within moments she was at the door. I handed her the releases and both file folders.

"Can you please scan one copy into the system and make two paper copies of these for me?"

"Sure thing. Be right back," she said, walking forward and taking the papers from me.

After she turned and left, I moved my gaze back to Jack.

"How's the investigation going? Are there any updates?"

"I'm sorry. I can't give out any information on an ongoing case."

I sat back in my chair, trying not to let out a harrumph.

"Of course. I apologize for the silly question," I said. "Hopefully, the files will give you everything you need."

"Do the files contain *all* of your client information?" Jack asked, eyebrows raised.

"No," I said flatly. "Some information, like how we make our matches, is proprietary. You'll need to get a warrant for those documents."

I saw his hand twitch and start to move up towards his face, but he stopped himself and instead opened and closed his fist a few times.

"I'll let you know if it appears the situation will come to that," he said.

"Good," I said, sitting forward. "I hope you understand we are not trying to be difficult. We just want to protect our company and clients. I'm confident there is nothing in our proprietary data extracts that would be important to your case."

"I'm sure you believe that," he said. "However, I'll be the judge of that after I read the files."

I knew if I responded it would be snippy, or smart-ass, so I just gave a slight nod. Luckily, Eva arrived at just that moment, helping to avoid any further conversation. She handed me the folders.

"Do you need anything else?" she asked.

"No, Eva. That will be all. Thank you," I said.

She turned and left. I stood and came around the desk, handing one set of copies to Jack.

"Here you go. If you don't need anything else, I really need to get back to work." I looked down at my watch in hopes it would help signal I had something else to do.

"Nothing else. For now," Jack said as he got up, took the copies, and headed out of the door. He reached into his breast pocket and extracted something as he went. "Here are a few more of my business cards. You can pass them out if you like. If you, or anyone else, come up with any information pertinent to the case, call me. Otherwise, I'll be in touch."

I grabbed the cards from him and tucked them in my back pocket. I waved at him as he walked towards the lobby, enjoying the view as he went. Walking back into my office, I shut the door and leaned against it, letting out a sigh. Well, at least that was over and done with. I guessed we would know sooner rather than later if Steven was the killer. The quicker this was figured out, the better.

My cell phone, which was sitting on the edge of my desk, let out a soft *DING*. This particular sound was assigned to my Grandma Olive's texts. I looked at the screen.

"Are you coming to the mixer?"

Oh crap! I'd forgotten about the mixer. It was something we did monthly to bring in new clients and new gossip. Julia, Sara, and I rotated who attended as a representative of TAFT. This month was my turn. Not that I didn't like these events, they just weren't my favorite thing. I had to do enough schmoozing during the day without having to attend the mixers. Oh, well. Duty called.

I responded back to Grandma that I was on my way, put the files in my cabinet, securely locked it, grabbed my purse, and headed for the front door.

"I've got to run. Need to get to the mixer," I said to Eva as I breezed past. "If you need me, just text or call."

"Will do," she said

***

On my way to the mixer, Grandma texted again and asked if I could stop at the grocery store to get more crackers and ice. Luckily, I hadn't yet passed it, so I didn't have to backtrack.

I took the next exit, went two blocks up, and turned into the parking lot. Being that it was mid-afternoon, the store wasn't too crowded. I parked and headed inside. For once I was able to grab a shopping cart that didn't have a wobbly wheel. Those were usually saved for the trips where I actually had lots of shopping to do.

Quickly, I made my way back to the cracker aisle and grabbed a box of crackers. On a whim, I grabbed a jar of macadamia nuts from the other side of the aisle. More and more of our clients were on one diet or another where carbs were a no-no. I turned the corner and bumped carts with Natalie Tolliver—my nemesis. *Crap!*

"Calla Lily! How nice to see you again," she said, her voice sugary sweet.

She always made certain to use my full name since she knew how much I hated it.

"Natalie. Nice to see you too." *Gag!*

"I'm so sorry to hear about the difficulties with your business."

My spine stiffened. "Excuse me?"

She lowered her voice and leaned in just a bit.

"You know…" she said, her voice trailing upward in volume with each word as some other shoppers walked past, "… the murder of your client."

I cringed inwardly as I saw the startled glances from the passersby. I wanted to ask how she'd learned about it, but being that she was an even bigger gossip mongrel than Grandma, I knew she had learned it through the black vine. That was like the grapevine, but for the hush-hush topics.

"I hadn't realized it was a murder?" I said through

clenched teeth, plastering the best smile I could on my face. "That's news to me. But, yes, it is very sad. I'm certain the police will get it all squared away soon."

"Well, of course. Wouldn't want anything to hurt your dating service," she said, reaching forward and patting me softly on the arm in a fake show of comfort.

It took all of my willpower not to shake her off or show her any hint of how much she was pissing me off.

"No," I said. "We wouldn't."

Before she could say anything further, I pulled my cart backward and walked away. "Sorry. In a bit of a rush. Talk to you later." *Not!*

Luckily for me, she didn't follow. I hurried on towards the checkout. One aisle before I reached an open lane, I passed a tower of wine that was on sale. Normally, I didn't buy alcohol but today…what the hell. I grabbed a Riesling and added it to my cart.

At the checkout, I informed the checker that I needed a twenty-pound bag of ice. After ringing out, I headed out to my car with a bag boy in tow carrying the ice.

After loading up my car—wishing I could take a chug of the wine then and there—and giving the young man a dollar for his assistance, I headed towards Grandma and the club. I sent out a silent prayer that the evening would not include my shaking hands with an unknown killer.

Chapter Eight

Cars filled almost every space of the Love Bites parking lot. Normally the mixers only filled in a quarter, to at most half of the lot. I had a sinking feeling in the pit of my stomach that the influx of cars had nothing to do with our service but more to do with the black cloud of death hanging over TAFT. No one liked anything more than gossip.

I parked, picked up my cell, and dialed Tony—Julia's manager. He attended the mixers in order to cover the bar and serve drinks when Julia was not the TAFT appointee.

"Hello," he said in his deep, sultry voice.

Everything you could imagine from the sound of his voice was reflected in his appearance. He was smoking hot:

tall, dark, and handsome. Unfortunately, for the many women who tried to pick him up during his shifts at the club, he was also married to Matt. Tony didn't give off any outward signs of being gay, probably from all his years hiding it from his parents.

This made Julia's job easier because she knew—above and beyond the fact that he was married—that she didn't have to worry about him mixing business and pleasure at the bar. Mostly only women hit on Tony, and he had no interest in that particular packaging.

"Hey there, friend," I replied. "Can you come out to help me unload the twenty pounds of ice from my trunk?"

"No problem. I'll be out there in a few minutes after I get these last drinks served."

"Great. Thanks!"

It actually took less than two minutes for him to come out the back door and walk over to my car.

"My hero!" I said as he hefted the large bag of ice over his shoulder. I grabbed the bag with the box of crackers and a jar of nuts before shutting the door—after giving the wine one last longing look. I wouldn't drink at the mixer; that wasn't my style. So, I would have to wait until I got home to indulge and cozy up to my Riesling.

Tony caught my glance and chuckled, "Sweetheart, you are gonna wish you took time to take a few gulps from that bottle when you get inside. There is a gaggle of ladies, and more than enough gossip to go around."

"Hopefully we have enough men in the mix to keep it

from being completely pointless?"

"I think so. Even a man could figure out this is as close to shooting fish in a barrel as you can get: a bunch of women together in one room drinking alcohol and gossiping. They know to take full advantage of the situation."

I felt relieved knowing we might get at least a little business from the mixer. I knew we would get the business, versus the people at the event hooking up on their own, because each of the men in attendance had signed a waiver saying they would not accept a date from any of the women here unless they went through the agency. Failure to go through the agency would ban the men from working with us as a pool selection candidate in the future. So, if the women liked what they saw, they could only get it by going through us. I shifted my purse and groceries to get a better grip, then headed in after Tony.

***

Tony was right. The club was packed, and the volume was on high as the women chattered to one another. I walked over to the snack table and deposited the crackers and nuts.

"It's about time you got here," Grandma said from beside me.

I knew the moment I turned my gaze to her that things were not going well. Grandma looked frazzled, and she *never* looked frazzled.

"That bad, huh?" I asked.

"You have no idea." She leaned against the wall and dabbed a napkin on her forehead then down her cleavage. "These women watch way too much crime TV. Every single one thinks they're some sort of detective."

I chuckled.

Grandma gave me a cross look. "We'll see who's laughing after you spend a few minutes in the lionesses' den."

"I just spent five minutes with Natalie. If I can stand that, this will be a piece of cake."

A loud, very unladylike snort came out of Grandma. She shook her head and walked away. As she did, she looked over her shoulder. "Don't say I didn't warn you."

I took note she was walking *away* from the crowd towards the manager's office, and not towards the group of women chit-chatting. I took a deep breath and headed in.

I'd barely stepped into the fold when I was bombarded by questions: Did you know her well? How long had she been with the agency? How'd she die? Do they have any suspects? Do we need to be worried?

These were just a few of the bombshells thrown my way. I decided it best to defuse them all in one fell swoop.

"As you ladies know, TAFT prides itself on confidentiality. So, I cannot give you any information on the deceased other than to say how deeply saddened we are about her death. As for everything else 'police' related, I'll have to ask you to speak with them directly. You all seem to know as much as I do," I said as I reached into my back pocket and pulled out the detective's card. "I'll leave some business cards for the detective assigned to the case on the snack table. If you have any questions or feel you know something that might be of help to them, please give him a call."

I took advantage of the comment to squeeze out of the group and move back over to the table. I laid the cards down as promised and turned back towards the group. They had already clustered back together and returned to their gossip and conspiracy theories as if I hadn't ever spoken.

As I looked around the room, I saw that virtually none of the men who had shown up at the mixer were being spoken to by any of the women. Most were lined up at the bar with a beer in front of them. I noticed that Tony had turned the overhead TVs on the football game to try to keep the men entertained. *What an angel.* I would need to thank him for keeping the men busy.

But, enough of that, it was time to get this mixer back on track. I lifted my hand, curled my fingers just so, slid them into my mouth, and let out my best loud whistle. The room went silent, all eyes turning towards the sound, and me, being I had made the sound.

"Ladies! I know you're all interested in talking about what is going on in the news, but remember this is a *mixer* and you're here to mingle with potential matches and decide if TAFT is the right place for you. Currently, you are all ignoring these nice men, some of which came a long way to meet and get to know you," I motioned around the room at all the men.

At the mention of them, they all stood a little more at attention, eagerness replacing the football and beer-induced glaze of moments before. They knew their moment was upon them. A fair number of the ladies blushed at having been called out for their behavior. The others just shuffled from foot to foot like racing horses getting set at the gate.

"Please, mingle. Get to know these gentlemen and enjoy a free drink on TAFT."

I looked at Tony who gave me a cocked eyebrow in surprise. I gave the slightest of nods, saying yes, I was aware I was doing something extremely out of character. I followed it up by lifting one finger. He understood my code to say only one free drink per person.

Tony had a knack for keeping track of faces and how many drinks they'd had. He was also good about only making available the well and house beverages during these mixers, keeping people from taking advantage and drinking up the good stuff. So, I knew all was in good hands. It would still cost me a pretty penny. But this mixer was not going anywhere without a little alcohol-induced help.

"Free drinks, huh? You must be desperate." Grandma, having appeared from thin air, clucked her tongue beside me. "I told you it was bad."

I leaned down and gave her a quick peck on the cheek. "I should've never doubted you."

"Damn straight!"

I let out a chuckle and watched as she headed towards the crowd, camera in hand.

We took pictures of the attendees for future reference. Somehow it seemed we always needed to know who was there later when all the calls came in. No one ever seemed to remember names. Normally all we got was, "Well, he was... *FILL IN GENERIC DETAIL HERE*."

I would need to remember to tell Eva to pull the memory card from today's mixer and put it with the other memory cards which were still on my desk. I hadn't had time to take them to PhotoPro for downloading and organizing.

I added the item to my mental to-do list, then headed toward the crowd to work my magic and do some matchmaking.

Chapter Nine

Returning home from the mixer, I slid into my comfy clothes: black, baggy shorts and my well-worn, white Tinker Bell t-shirt. Tinker Bell was standing sideways with her wings to the left, her head turned—face looking forward—one eye winking and her wand arm outstretched to the right. A few sparse flakes of glitter remained to insinuate bright light surrounding the tip of the wand. Underneath Tinker Bell, it said, "Tinkin' Ain't Easy."

Initially, I'd planned on eating something quick— maybe a PB & banana sandwich, drinking the bottle of chilled Riesling in the fridge, watching TV for a bit, then heading off to bed. However, when I went to turn on the TV, I noticed the DVD I had forgotten I'd rented, which was due back tomorrow. Guess it was movie night instead of TV night. The wine would have to wait.

My movie night, unlike most people's, did not include popcorn. What it did require was several other things: a movie, frozen pizza, ice cream, and chocolate syrup. I opened the freezer and pantry and saw I had none of the aforementioned food items at present. *Damn!* Well, that meant I had to do a grocery run. Lucky for me, the closest grocery store was within walking distance. The exercise would do me good; I could burn off those cracker calories.

I grabbed my purse, then slipped on my shoes and socks. Deciding it would be easier to go out the garage, I punched the button to raise the door. I hurried out, punching the code into the door pad outside the door. When the door had closed completely, I headed towards the store at a fast clip.

A heavy breeze was blowing through, but at least it was cool. Light gray clouds covered up the last of the dying sunlight. I took a deep inhale of the cool, crisp air. It smelled like we might get rain tonight. We needed it. The trees and grass were crying out for moisture as they crunched a tiny bit under my Nike tennis shoes.

It didn't take too long to get into the store and gather the first two items on my list: ice cream and frozen pizza. I made my way down the aisles until I got to the one that held the cereal. This is where I would find the Hershey's chocolate syrup. Most people preferred fudge on their ice cream, I liked syrup. Besides, when I wasn't using it for ice cream, I could make chocolate milk—which I adored.

Halfway down the aisle, I found the syrup. I added it to my hand basket and turned to leave. As I finished swiveling, I came face to face with none other than Detective Brown. He looked down at me and smiled. I hadn't realized just how tall he was before since I'd always had on my high heels—which ranged from three to six inches. He must've been close to 6'3".

Jack looked good out of his work clothes. He had on a black t-shirt. At the location where a pocket might lay, was a small logo I was unfamiliar with. He had a six o'clock shadow on his face. It made the brown in his what I now realized were deep green eyes, stand out like little specks. His hair, the same matching brown as his beard, was hand brushed and fell into his eyes just a bit. I felt my pulse jump in my throat. I itched to reach up and push the hair back out of his eyes.

"I don't think I've ever seen you in town before, and now we can't seem to stay apart," I said with a smile.

"Seems that way," Jack replied, giving me a slight up and down look.

"Did you figure out if you have everything you need from us?" I said, trying to change the subject and avoid the amused look in his eyes after he had surveyed my "comfy" clothes.

"So far. If something changes, I'll let you know."

"That would be great. And as soon as you can—"

A loud, deep rumble of laughter sounded from the

next aisle over; it radiated down my spine like the squeal of nails on a chalkboard. I knew that sound. *I hated that sound.*

"As soon as I can what?" Jack asked.

Jack's words didn't register through the haze of panic now overloading my senses. I went into fight or flight mode. My body froze as I listened to the sound of the laughter as it moved towards *my* aisle. It was too late for flight, so fight it was.

"Please don't judge me," I said to Jack as I grabbed him by his shirtfront and pulled him down toward me; locking my lips with his. Because I had to go up on my tip-toes to kiss him, I needed to leave my hand on his chest for balance. The first several seconds he didn't react; he just stood there unmoving. However, by the time the owner of the laugh turned the corner, Jack had softened and was participating fully in the kiss.

Quickly, I was lost in the kiss. Heat trailed down every part of my body, settling low in my lady regions; a moan escaped my lips. Jack's hand reached up, fingers slipping into my hair, hand cupping my neck. I relaxed and moved deeper into the kiss.

A loud *THWACK* caused Jack to yank himself from me.

"Ow! What the…" Jack cried out, raising his hand to his head and rubbing the back of it.

I looked behind Jack to see Mrs. Gerardi—all 4'11" of her—glaring at us.

"You kids get a room. This is no place for those…"

she waved her cane—which she had hit Jack with—around in the air at us "… types of shenanigans."

The look on Jack's face was priceless. He was not only stunned, it was clear he was slightly afraid of the tiny old lady. He was smart to be afraid. Mrs. Gerardi was 90 years old and came from a long line of Italians. This particular line was fond of cursing others with the stink eye.

I hid a chuckle as I replied, "My apologies, Mrs. Gerardi. I'll make sure it doesn't happen again."

"You do that, young lady. Your grandmother raised you better." She turned and left, clucking her tongue in disapproval as she departed.

I'd been so caught up in the moment I'd all but forgotten the reason for the current situation. That was until I heard it.

"Callie? Is that you?"

My spine stiffened. *Is that me? Seriously!* I hadn't changed a damn thing about me since we had gotten divorced. I turned and looked at Mike and his floozy… I mean, *girlfriend.*

"Mike. Ashley," I replied with a nod of acknowledgment.

"I see Mrs. Gerardi is as soft and fluffy as always."

I couldn't help but let a twitch of a smile cross my lips at the inside joke we'd once shared. *Damn this man!*

"Some things never change," I said.

Mike turned towards Jack and raised his hand.

"Hello there. I'm Mike. You are…?"

"This is Jack. My…" I jumped in, trying to steer the conversation in a safe direction but hesitated at my last words.

"Boyfriend," Jack finished for me. I sucked in a breath.

Mike's eyebrows rose, "Boyfriend, huh? Good for you, Cal. Way to get back out there."

I used to think Mike's shortening even my nickname down to Cal was cute. Now, I realized he was just too lazy to even say Callie.

"Geez, thanks. But, I guess I should thank you for leaving. I wouldn't have ever found Jack if you hadn't," I said, turning to Ashley and lowering my voice just a touch. "Did Mike ever get over that rash?"

Ashley's cheeks flushed and she let out a huff. I smiled on the inside.

"No need to be rude!" Mike rebuked, his gaze holding a look of disapproval that I was all too familiar with.

We stood there for a moment in awkward silence before Mike finally spoke.

"Looks like it's a movie night. You've got all of your normal essentials: frozen pizza, ice cream, chocolate sauce—"

"If you two are together, then why do you have separate baskets?" Ashley cut in, a smug smile on her face.

My brain froze. I didn't have a plausible answer.

"We usually divide and conquer at the grocery store," Jack—whose cart showed a six pack of beer, bagged salad, and ranch dressing on top of a few other items you couldn't see—said from beside me. "It's a more efficient use of time. This time Callie got the frozen items, I got the non-frozen, and we met in the middle for the chocolate sauce."

Jack winked at me—which to others was him insinuating things about the chocolate sauce. He leaned over and gave me a quick peck on the mouth. Ashley's face deflated.

"Oh," she said. It was clear she hadn't expected a logical answer.

"Speaking of time. We really need to be going," Jack said as he took my elbow and pulled me down the aisle.

I followed, not sure how to say my next words. I didn't want to go with "see you later," as I sure as hell hoped not to, but I didn't want to get a reputation for being rude. So, I went for the simplest phrase.

"Goodbye." I turned and got into step with Jack's stride, heading towards the checkout.

At the lane, I hesitated a moment at the decision of whether or not to set my items on the belt with Jack's. I didn't have to come up with what to do, as Jack reached into my basket and extracted all the items.

"No use letting them in on our little ruse at this point, no?" he said softly so the cashier couldn't hear. "You can pay me back later."

I gave him a weak, embarrassed smile and nodded my head in reply. Once we were paid for, bagged up, and out of the store I let out a sigh of relief.

"Where's your car?" Jack asked, looking at me and then around the lot.

"What...? Oh, I walked," I said, my brain slowly beginning to shed the adrenaline and think clearly.

"Well, then. Let me drive you home. It'll ensure you keep dry," he said, looking up at the now dark-gray storm clouds, "and it will make your ex think we really went home together."

"How did you know he was my ex?" The words came out before I'd thought through the stupidity of my question.

The corner of Jack's lips twitched upwards. "I'm a detective, sweetheart."

Chapter Ten

It didn't take long to reach my house, being that I'd been within walking distance of the grocery store. However, in that short amount of time the heavens had opened up, and rain poured down in sheets. Had it not been for Jack's offer of a ride, I would have been drenched through and through.

"Thanks for the ride… and everything else. I would've been soaked without you, in many ways," I said, hands folded gingerly in my lap.

"No problem. Glad I could help."

I reached for the door but hesitated.

"Mike was actually right," I said, not looking back at Jack. "I did get all the makings for a movie night, including the movie. Not sure if you are interested in coming in and joining me? It might be a little dangerous to drive anywhere, with the rain coming down the way it is."

"What's the movie?" he asked.

I turned my gaze toward him.

"*The Silmarillion*," I said, "it's the screenplay version of the J. R. R. Tolkien book."

"I didn't realize that had come out on Blu-Ray yet. I meant to see it in the theater but just ran out of time. I heard it's amazing."

"So, you in?"

"Sure, but with one rule," he said with an absolutely straight face.

"Ok…" I said, not knowing what trap I was walking into.

"I don't do frozen pizza. We eat the steaks I bought at the store."

I let out a small sigh of relief. After what I'd put him through at the store, giving up the pizza from my routine was the least I could do.

"As long as you cook them. I'm not good at doing steaks." I eyeballed the heavy sheets of rain as it poured down onto the windshield. "Especially indoors."

"Deal," he said.

"Let me run in and get an umbrella. Then we can get all the groceries out of the back. There's no use in us both getting wet," I said, grabbing the handle and opening the door, not waiting for a reply.

I raced towards the garage door and hurriedly punched in the code on the keypad. I ducked under it as soon as the door was open enough to do so. I knew my grandfather rolled over in his grave at that moment. He'd always warned me to never do what I'd just done. The reason being one of his close friends had actually died from a garage door falling on him.

He had been standing under it talking with my grandfather and some of their friends when the spring broke. The door came slamming down right into his head. He didn't die right away; he was in a coma for close to a month before the brain swelling took his life. My grandfather had been terrified of garage doors ever since.

Normally, I wouldn't have done something that I'd been trained since childhood not to do. But in this instance, I was more afraid of getting soaked by the rain than by the garage door breaking.

Looking down, I saw I'd succeeded in staying semi-dry. Only my top half had gotten soaked while making my way into the garage. Oh well, at least I was home. I could change into something dry right away.

I moved through the garage—the light from the car's headlights assisting me in my journey—to the coat hook on the wall. I retrieved the oversized golf umbrella—one of the few possessions of Mike's I still had—and made my way back outside.

I held it over the area outside the driver's door as Jack got out. We moved in tandem to the back of the car where he lifted the trunk. I grabbed one bag of groceries; he grabbed the other. After locking up the car, we hurried into the garage.

We made our way inside the house into the small mud room. I turned on the light switch and was greeted by bright white light. I'd made the error of getting too bright a bulb the last time I changed it out. Now it was like being blinded by the sun. I reached down and untied my shoes and pulled both them and my socks off. I placed them in the shoe tray to drip dry.

Standing up, I turned to look at Jack and see if he managed to stay dry. I stopped in mid-motion when I saw the look on his face. His gaze was glued to my chest. I didn't understand what exactly he was staring at until I looked down at myself. My white shirt was plastered to my skin and was ninety-nine percent see-through. I hadn't bothered to put on a bra for my "quick" trip out. Tinker Bell's wings were over one breast, while the end of her wand covered the other. Because I was now cold, my nipples were standing at attention. The one on the right was poking out in just the right spot to make the ball at the end of the wand look 3D. *Just great!*

I felt the heat rise to my face, and I fought the urge to cross my arms and cover my chest. Instead, I cleared my throat. "You can leave your shoes in here if you want."

He blinked several times but finally made eye contact. While his face showed no signs of embarrassment for being caught staring, I noticed the tips of his ears were red.

"Okay, thanks," he said quickly, before bending over and removing his shoes. I took advantage of the opportunity to walk out of the room.

"I'm going to go run and change. I'll be back in a minute. Make yourself at home."

I hurried up the stairs into my room. Once the door was secured behind me, I slid to the ground and put my head in my hands. What a night. First, I threw myself at the poor man, then I gave him a free wet t-shirt show. *Ugh!* I took a few deep breaths and composed myself. Well, what's done was done. I couldn't change it, but I could ignore it.

Opening my dresser, then my closet, I pulled out a set of dry clothes and quickly changed before heading downstairs.

Jack was at the counter pulling the groceries out of the bags when I returned. I walked over to him.

"How can I help?" I asked.

He looked up from his task, brow crinkled in thought, "I'll need some steak seasoning, or salt, pepper, and garlic if you don't have a mixed seasoning."

I walked over and slid open my spice rack. I knelt and looked through the bottles. It only took me a few seconds to locate the seasoning that Mike used to use. I very rarely ever cooked anything other than chicken and hamburger, so the bottle was still relatively full.

Standing, I held the bottle out to Jack.

"Will this work?"

He took it from me, spun it around, and read the label.

"Perfect," he said. He turned his head and his gaze went to the stove, then back to me. "Do you have a grill pan?"

"That's a good question. I don't know. Let me see."

I walked over to the cupboard, opened it, and looked through all the pots and pans. I knew it had to be somewhere in the back if I had one. Everything up front I used on a pretty regular basis. I preferred home cooking over takeout. However, I hated the cleanup. That had always been one of Mike's pet peeves. I cooked using every pot and pan in the kitchen and then was too tired to clean up right away. So, sometimes the dishes would still be in the sink come morning. He was a very type A personality, and that just didn't work for him. We had quite a few fights over it during our years of marriage.

Just when I was about to give up hope of finding it, I saw a long, flat cast-iron pan leaning up against the side of the cabinet in the back corner. I pulled out a few pots and pans, so I could crawl forward and reach it. When I pulled it free, I saw that one side was a griddle, the other was what I thought of as a "grill" pan.

"Is this what you're after?" I asked, holding the pan up so he could see it.

"Yes. That should work."

As I stood a crackle of thunder sounded, causing me to let out a tiny shriek, and tumble forward just a touch. Unfortunately, the forward motion was just as my head reached the underside of the counter and I bonked it against it.

"Ouch!" I yelped.

"Are you okay?" Jack said, moving forward and pulling me the rest of the way to my feet. Without waiting for an answer, he bent my head down slightly and examined the top of my head for any injury.

I backed away out of his reach, swatting at his hands. "I'm fine. Just being my normal klutzy self."

"Well, let me take that pan from you before you hurt yourself anymore."

"Ha-ha. Very funny."

Jack chuckled as he took the pan from me and laid it on the stovetop.

"I think the only other thing I need for the steaks are some tongs and cooking spray or olive—" he started but stopped when he saw the jar of olive oil on the countertop, "—never mind on the oil. I found it."

I reached into the utensil drawer and pulled out some tongs, then handed them to him.

"Thanks. How do you like your steak?" Jack asked.

"Medium well, please."

"So, no 'moo' left?" he asked, a smile on his face.

"Yes, please," I said, sticking my tongue out at him.

He let out another chuckle before turning back to the steaks.

As he cooked the steaks, I worked on the salad. I pulled the bag of salad and the dressing out of the bag, then bent down to another cupboard where I grabbed a large bowl and a salad spinner from under the sink. After giving the packaged salad a quick rinse and spin, I put it into the bowl. I walked over to the pantry and pulled out some sunflower seeds and croutons.

Soon the smell of pepper, garlic, and other various spices wafted through the air. Another rumble of thunder sounded. This time the lights flickered just a bit.

"I'd better go get some candles going in case the power goes out," I said.

"Good idea," Jack said, turning his gaze to me. "The steaks should be done in just a minute."

I quickly went to the various rooms and switched on my flameless candles, grabbed a flashlight out of the drawer, and pulled out my battery-powered radio. Once that was done, I quickly set the table. Just as I was finishing up, Jack met me at the table with our steaks, setting mine down on my plate.

"Cut into yours really quick and make sure it's done enough," Jack said.

I reached over, grabbed a steak knife, and cut into the piece of meat.

"Looks perfect," I said, glancing up. I noticed Jack looking around the table.

"Do you have any steak sauce or horseradish?" he asked.

"Seriously? You give me grief for medium-well and yet *you* want A1? Isn't that a serious steak faux pas?"

"I guess we all have our flaws," he smiled.

It was my turn to chuckle as I turned, went to the fridge, and grabbed some A1 and horseradish out. I was actually very happy he asked for it because that is exactly how I like my steak. I hadn't wanted to embarrass myself twice in one meal by bringing it out.

As we started digging in, the power went out. Jack reached over and switched on the radio. He tried to tune in a weather forecast but could only get a country station to come on. He started to turn it off.

"No. Don't. I like that song," I said. It was *"Crazy"* by Patsy Cline.

"You like country music?"

I stopped, my fork midway to my mouth. "That surprises you?"

"A little. I guess I didn't take you for a country girl."

"I guess in most things, no. But in music, that's what my parents always played. So, I guess it's in my genes," I said with a shrug.

"Well, I'll be! You do learn something new every day."

I chucked a small piece of lettuce at him. A sharp crack of thunder covered his laugh. It was so loud the music went to static for a moment.

I jumped a bit in my seat. "Holy crap! I haven't heard thunder like that in years."

Jack got up and moved over to the window. Even from my chair, I could see that the rain poured down in sheets and the trees were being whipped around by the wind.

"Yep. This is a rough one. I can see moonlight though to the south, so it might be moving out within the next couple of hours," Jack said before returning to his seat and resuming eating.

"Well, I would say it's a good thing we have a movie. But that isn't going to do us much good if the power doesn't come back on."

As if God heard my words, the power came back on.

"Ask and you shall receive," Jack said with a smirk.

"If only that worked all the time," I said.

We hurried and finished our dinner so as to try to catch at least some of the movie before the power went out again. I scraped the food into the trash and placed the dishes in the sink, while Jack put the rest of the salad and dressing away in the fridge.

After we were all settled on the couch, I hit play on the remote. We didn't chat much while the movie was on because we really had to pay attention in order to follow it. I hadn't realized it would be so hard to follow and so dark: tons of violence and tragedy. Luckily, however, it was a good movie in content and for the situation. I wasn't exactly certain how I would've handled watching something romantic or sexual with Jack by my side. I was fairly certain any more than a friendship would be inappropriate, with him handling the currently open case. And friendship might even toe the line.

By the time the movie finished, the rain had lessened

considerably, almost down to a sprinkle.

"It's late. I'd better get moving," Jack said as he got up and stretched. I couldn't help but watch his muscles flex under his shirt. "Thanks for the movie."

"Thanks for the steaks and for saving me. I'm sorry if I overstepped in any way. That was the first time since the divorce that I've run into my ex and clearly, I didn't know how to handle it."

Jack grinned. "I think you did pretty well. Glad I could be of help."

We walked over to the door and I opened it.

"Next time, though," he said as he walked out the door, "I get the chocolate sauce."

I slapped myself on the forehead. "Crap! How could I forget the ice cream?!"

Jack just laughed as he continued towards his car. Before ducking down inside his car, he gave me a quick wave goodbye. I shut the door and blushed at what could have been a hidden innuendo relative to the chocolate sauce. *Oh well, I guess only time will tell.* With that thought, I headed straight for the freezer.

Chapter Eleven

The aroma of coffee greeted me when I entered the Where You Bean on 4th Street. I looked around and saw Julia waving at me from across the room. She and Sara had snagged the most comfortable lounge chairs in the coffee shop.

Walking up to the counter I ordered my normal: Gimme More, no water, extra spice chai latte, almond milk, with extra foam. I'd never been a fan of coffee and only drank it occasionally. Tea was my drug of choice. I always got a good chuckle at the sizes WYB offered. They had Gimme Some—equal to a Tall at Starbucks, Gimme More, Big Boy, and Kitchen Sink.

I picked up my latte and took a sip while making my

way back to the girls. I started to sit down.

"So…" Sara said, looking up at me.

"Can I at least sit down before you start the twenty questions?" I laughed as I finished sitting down. "Please elaborate, what 'so' are you referring to this time?"

Both Sara and Julia shared a look.

"What?" I asked again.

"I don't know," Julia said, "maybe *so* what's this about you making out with some guy in the grocery store?"

My eyebrows shot up.

"How in the devil did you hear about—" I answered my own question. "Ashley."

She was friends with Natalie. If she told Natalie, then everyone knew.

"*DING DING DING*," Sara chimed. "Get the girl a prize. So…?"

"It isn't what you think. I was at the store getting some stuff to watch a movie and I ran into the detective handling Jasmine's case. While I was talking to him Mike and Ashley came down the aisle," I shrugged. "I panicked and kissed Jack. We then pretended he was my boyfriend."

"Jack, huh?" Julia said, one eyebrow raised.

"Yes, Jack. I think after I forced myself on him I can stop calling him Detective."

"So how did Mike take you having a boyfriend—" Sara started to ask.

"Who has a boyfriend?" a voice I knew all too well said from behind me.

We all turned and watched as Grandma Olive made her way towards us carrying a Kitchen Sink, which we all knew was a sugar-free caramel, triple shot espresso, with fat-free milk. Grandma lived for coffee. Her visits alone could keep WYB in business for years.

"No one," I said, as she bent down so I could give her a kiss on the cheek.

"I know you just said boyfriend. Don't hold out on your Grandma, flower."

No one, and I mean no one, besides my Grandma was *ever* allowed to call me "flower." However, she had been calling me that before I could walk, so she was allowed.

"Seriously, Grandma. No one has a *real* boyfriend."

"Real boyfriend?" she asked as she got settled into the chair next to mine.

I repeated the story back to her up to the point of Sara's question. "…Mike gave me an 'atta girl' and told me it was great I was back in the saddle."

"What a jackass," Grandma Olive said.

I heard the lady behind me take in a startled breath at Grandma's affirmation. I don't think it was so much the words she used but that they came out of the mouth of a woman grandma's age.

"Yeah, something like that," I murmured.

"At least tell us the kiss was worth it?" Sara asked.

"I heard you two left together?" Julia chimed in.

"Yes, to both." I felt myself blush. "He drove me home because I'd walked and it was about to rain. By the time we got to my house, it was pouring. I couldn't send the man home in dangerous conditions."

"Of course not!" Julia said with a chuckle.

I gave her a cross look. "All we did was have dinner and watch a movie."

"What movie?" Grandma asked.

"Why does it matter what movie?" I looked at her head cocked and one eyebrow raised. "It was *The Silmarillion.*"

Julia choked on her drink of coffee. "Dear Lord. If he sat through that movie, then he deserves even more credit than I first thought."

"Hey," I said indignantly, "That was a good movie."

All three of the women around me just stared at me without a word. I huffed and slouched back in my chair.

Grandma reached over and patted me on the knee. "Don't worry. I'm sure he'll call you again."

I straightened. "I don't need him to call me, Grandma. It wasn't real and didn't mean anything. He was just being kind and helping me out of a jam."

"Whatever you say, flower."

I need to get off this topic now.

"If you're all done giving me the third-degree, can we move on to another topic?" I asked.

"You're no fun," Sara said, as she slouched back in her chair

I rolled my eyes.

"What other topic did you have in mind?" Julia asked.

"How are we going to deal with the…" I lowered my voice to a whisper. "… murder?"

"I don't think I understand your question. What do we need to deal with?" Julia asked.

"For starters, getting new clients. All the women did at the mixer was talk about 'it.' I had to buy them off with alcohol to get them to mingle with the men."

"That isn't going to be a problem," Grandma said.

"What do you mean?" I asked, turning my gaze to her.

"After you left nearly half of the ladies asked about booking appointments to sign up for TAFT."

My eyebrows rose. "Seriously? Why in the world would they want to sign up to a potential death agency?"

Sarah laughed. "What is the one thing women love more than men and money?"

I thought about it for a second, which was apparently one second too long for Sarah because she answered for me.

"Drama."

"Drama?"

"Yes, drama. Joining TAFT gets them one step closer to having an 'in' on all the details," Sara replied. "I don't think anyone really believes the murder and TAFT are connected. But they do believe if they are part of TAFT they'll get the dirt first on the current situation, and on anything that might happen going forward."

I sat back in my chair. "Hmm. I guess I didn't think of it that way."

"Granted, if anything else happens and it's tied to TAFT, then we are thoroughly screwed," Julia added.

I looked around the now very silent, pale group and nodded my agreement.

Chapter Twelve

When I finally made it back to the office, I found the door was locked. Eva must have gone to lunch. I dug my keys out of my purse and let myself in. I made my way to my office and flopped down into my chair. Surprisingly, my voicemail light wasn't flashing on my phone. That was a first, but I would take it. Right now, I just needed some peace and quiet.

I flipped open my laptop, opened my email, and went through my inbox. The first several emails were invoices, so I loaded our bookkeeping program. It only took a few minutes to enter the charges and send the invoices over via email to the client. Our bottom line had been looking very nice so far this year. I loved numbers, they never lied. I just hoped this current cloud would soon pass by and wouldn't have any lasting effect.

I felt unbelievably callous at the thought. A woman had died and two children had lost a mother and I was worried about my bottom line. How could I be worried about our bottom line? I decided to give myself a break—I was only human—and moved on to the next item.

The next thing I came upon in my emails was Julia's next advice column article for the newsletter. I picked it up, leaned back in my chair, put my feet up, and began reading.

TO RABBIT OR NOT TO RABBIT…
THAT IS THE QUESTION

In last month's column, I spoke about the value of carats. In this article, we'll discuss the value of the other type of "carrot" as it pertains to our lives as women.

How many times have you gone on a date in a fancy restaurant and only ordered the salad? This is what I say to that, "Let them eat cake!"

Do not, I repeat, do NOT start your relationship out on a falsehood. If you're a natural salad lover, and it's your go-to for any meal, then rabbit on, sister. Rabbit on! However, if you prefer a little more "cluck or moo" in your meal, order it. You should never pretend to do, or love something that you will not love later. It isn't fair to you, or your potential mate.

Avoiding these simplest of pitfalls—known as white lies—will save you from having arguments in the future. It also ensures no fight will ever contain the phrase, "Well, you liked it while we were dating. Or, was that a lie too?"

I promise you, the fewer disagreements you have over the long haul, the longer the haul will be.

This public service announcement is brought to you by TAFT

Another great article. I'd never been a salad girl when on a date, but I had to admit I did order lighter than my normal fare. My biggest fault was letting Mike order for me and pretending I loved what he picked. It was as if Julia had been a fly on the wall in our house the day we had the "Well you liked it…" conversation.

After I finished reading the article, I put my feet back down on the ground, leaned forward, and replied with a big "thumbs up" emoji to show I'd read and approved of the article. Julia didn't need our approval to publish, but we always tried to give each other input on items we published on behalf of TAFT.

A message popped up on my screen. It was a reminder to take Steven Rivera his copy of the file we'd shared with the police. Thank goodness for the reminder because I'd totally forgotten about it. I glanced at my watch and saw it was just after two. I still had time to make it to his apartment and back before rush hour, if I hurried. I hesitated for the slightest of moments when I heard Jack's voice in the back of my mind telling me to stop snooping and stay out of police business.

Well, I wasn't really doing any snooping. Dropping of papers was completely innocent. If it just so happened to give me another chance to talk to Steven, then so be it.

I reached into the bin behind me and picked up the folder with his copies in it. I slipped on my shoes, grabbed my purse, and headed out—locking the door behind me as I went.

Chapter Thirteen

I made it to Steven's apartment in record time, only catching a few lights. I parked and walked into the entryway. This time when I punched the elevator button, it lit up. I got off on the third floor and made my way to his door. I wasn't certain if he would be home yet, but even if he wasn't I could slip the papers into the crack at the bottom of his door. Easy peasy.

I reached up to knock on the door, but before I had the chance it swung open. I froze. *Well, damn!* Standing in front of me was none other than Detective Brown.

He stopped in mid-step, face frozen. As it defrosted,

a clearly not happy look took its place.

"Detective Brown," I said, pasting my most brilliant, innocent smile on my face.

"Ms. Bloom," he said, smile free. "What are you doing here?"

Before I could answer I heard Steven clearing his throat. "Ms. Bloom?"

Not given much choice, Jack backed up a step, so the smaller man could see around him.

"Hello, Mr. Rivera," I said. Thinking it best not to hesitate and give Jack room to talk, I quickly continued. "I wanted to swing by that copy of papers you asked for."

Jack eyeballed the file folder that I was now handing towards Steven.

Steven took it, flipped it open, and gave it a quick once-over. "Thank you. I appreciate it."

"No problem," I said.

"Is that all you needed?" Jack said through clenched teeth.

I ignored his tone.

"Yes. That was it. Since I have an appointment in the area, I thought I would kill two birds with one stone and drop the file off." I looked down at my watch. "Speaking of appointments, I really need to run. Let me know if you need anything else, Mr. Rivera."

"Will do," Steven said.

"Let me walk you out." Jack stepped forward, took my elbow, and turned me towards the elevator.

"No need, Detective," I smiled sweetly. "I don't want to interrupt."

"It's no problem, Ms. Bloom. I'm all done here," Jack said. He looked back over his shoulder at Steven. "I'll be in touch."

Jack didn't let go of my elbow until we were in the elevator: *déjà vu much?*

"I thought I told you to stay out of police business," he growled.

"Don't get your boxers in a bunch. All I did was drop off some paperwork I promised."

"What exactly was in the file folder?"

"I don't see what business that is of yours."

His glare said it all.

"Fine. If you're going to be like that," I huffed. "It was a copy of the information I gave you the other day. He requested it when I first told him I would be providing it to the police."

Jack's eyebrows rose. "Was there anything in it *I* didn't get?"

"Of course not," I rolled my eyes.

The elevator door opened, and we walked out. This time, now that he knew which car was mine, he steered me directly toward it. He opened the door for me and I slid inside. I started to pull the door shut, but Jack stopped it.

"Let me be very clear. If I ask you for information about one of your clients, that means you stay away from that client until our investigations are over," he glared down.

"But—"

"No buts. If you need to make contact with them, go through me. Understood?"

"It was just a folder of papers," I mumbled.

Jack opened the door just enough to kneel down, so that he was face to face with me. He reached up and took my chin in his hand, moving my face so that we were gazing into each other's eyes.

"I'm trying to make sure you don't get hurt," he said, his voice much softer than before.

Heat raced through my body and all the anger I'd been holding fizzled out. I fought every urge I had to lean forward, close the distance between us, and kiss him on the lips. I remembered just how good that grocery store kiss had been.

"Callie?"

"What…?" I lifted my gaze. I realized I'd been staring at his mouth and hadn't heard a word he had been saying.

"I said, please don't make me worry about you," Jack repeated, lowering his hand but keeping his gaze locked on mine.

"I'm sorry. I guess I didn't really think about how dangerous it could potentially be speaking with Steven. I promise I'll stay away." I crossed my heart to emphasize my point.

"Good," he said, standing. "Be safe driving home."

He shut the door and walked away.

I slowly put on my seat belt and got the car started while I got my hormones under control. *Damn that man!*

Chapter Fourteen

The following day started off with a visit to see Mrs. Virginia Thompson, who lived in a large, six-bedroom estate. It had been in her family for three generations. My window rolled down, I stared in awe as I drove under a canopy of trees towards the house. My tires crunched over the tiny gravel that made up the circular driveway. The gravel was composed of only white rocks and looked as if it had been freshly washed. The white glistened in the sun.

In the middle of the circle was a large marble, three-tiered fountain. Water flowed down with a soothing waterfall sound. In the bottom tier, large white lilies lay atop green lily pads. Seeing these flowers in the flesh was usually one of the few times I appreciated my name. They were lovely flowers.

After pulling to a stop and turning off the engine, I got out of my car and made my way over to the fountain to enjoy the sound and scenery for just a moment. I leaned over and stroked the smooth, soft petals of a lily. Straightening, I turned in a circle as I took in the rest of the estate. The canopy of trees I'd traveled through turned out to be giant oak trees. Everything surrounding the driveway and the house was lush; green grass, manicured bushes, and flowers in a myriad of colors completed the landscape. Hummingbirds and butterflies darted around the lawn, going from flower to flower in search of nectar. The grounds had been kept up in grand fashion. I closed my eyes, enjoying the sounds and smells. The moment was serene.

"I don't want to wear that dress!" came a scream from one of the windows on the second floor of the house.

My eyes flashed open and I peered toward where the noise had come from.

"Me either," another young female voice joined in.

My calm broken, I moved to the front door and rang the bell. It took a few moments before the door was opened by a young, frazzled-looking woman.

"Can I help you?" she asked.

"Yes. I have an appointment with Mrs. Thompson," I said.

When all I got was a blank stare, I continued, "I'm Ms. Bloom from TAFT."

"Of course. I apologize for forgetting. You must excuse us, we're in a bit of a dressing crisis," she said, motioning for me to come inside. "Please follow me. Mrs. Thompson is in the library."

I followed the woman through several rooms, decorated in a revamped colonial-era-style décor. Everything was polished and sparkling to perfection. I needed to get the business card of whomever Mrs. Thompson used as her maid service. You could white-glove this place and not find a speck of dirt.

We ended up in a large, oval room with hardwood floors. Most of the walls were covered in bookshelves; which were filled with books and knickknacks. The one wall that didn't have books held a fireplace with a grand marble fireplace. All the wood in the room was a rich, golden maple. Or, maybe it was oak. I wasn't a wood specialist. Besides the color, most of the wood looked the same to me.

"Mrs. Thompson," the woman said. "Ms. Bloom is here for you."

Mrs. Thompson, who was sitting in a reading chair, lifted her head. She closed the book in her lap, removed her reading glasses, and gave me a warm smile. Mrs. Thompson, as it turned out, was an older woman in her mid to late seventies. When she'd called, I'd mistaken her for what I now believed was her daughter.

A screech ripped through the room as the voices from upstairs began arguing over who got to wear what color of dress.

"You'll have to excuse me. I need to get back to the girls," the younger woman said.

"Of course, Maggie. Please make sure they are ready to go in forty-five minutes. Their father will be furious if he has to wait for them."

Maggie did a short nod and hurried off back towards the way we came.

"Have a seat," Virginia said, motioning to the couch across from her. "I apologize, but I must say you do look a bit confused. Is everything all right?"

I sat down and shook my head. "Based on the name I was given, I was expecting your daughter?"

"Oh. I see," she said. "That happens quite often. Her given name is Virgie. People tend to think that is a nickname for Virginia. It's not."

"Well then, my apologies for having incorrect information," I said. "But, in any case, that doesn't really matter. I'm here to help, regardless of who I thought I was coming to see. What can I do for you?"

"I've heard from my ladies group you run a very well-respected matchmaking agency. I'm interested in seeing if you can set up my girls with matches?"

"I think we should be able to manage. Which 'girls' are you referring to specifically?" I reached down and grabbed my notepad and a pen from my bag.

"Well, my great-granddaughters, of course."

I flipped open my notepad and made a note of the

details. "What are their names?"

"Josephine, Marie, and Rebecca," she said.

I wrote down the names; each on their own line—with several lines in-between in order to have space to write down details.

"And how old are they?"

"Let's see… Josie is ten, Marie is twelve, and—"

I dropped my pen on the floor. The *CLUNK* sound it made when it hit the floor cut off the rest of her answer.

"I'm sorry. Did you say ten and twelve?"

"Yes. And fifteen."

I leaned over, picked up my pen, closed my notepad, and straightened in my chair. "I'm sorry, Ms. Thompson—"

"Please call me Gin," she interrupted.

"Ok, Gin. We don't do matches for children. Only women over the age of eighteen can enroll for our services."

"Oh. I see," she said, brows attempting to wrinkle but not quite. I suspected Botox was involved. "I guess I'm jumping the gun a bit. I just don't want these girls to get stuck with the leftovers."

"Ew gross, boys!" cried a voice from the doorway.

We both turned our heads.

"You are such a baby. Boys are wonderful," another voice said from behind her.

That voice got closer and a much taller girl walked in the room. If I'd had to take a guess, I would've said the first speaker was the ten-year-old, Josie. And the other was probably the fifteen-year-old, Rebecca. Each girl was outfitted in a colorful dress and Mary Jane shoes.

Pushing her way in-between and through the two girls in the doorway, another girl trotted in and plopped down beside me on the couch. While this sister—who could be none other than Marie—had on a dress, she did not have the same shoes. The shoes she had on her feet were combat boots. Clearly, she was the tomboy of the group.

"Becky already has a boyfriend," Marie said with an eye roll. "If you need to set anyone up with a boy, it should be Grandma Gin. She's the one who's lonely."

I heard an intake of breath from Gin. It was so well done that I would have actually believed she was shocked by the words. However, I'd caught the oldest girl out of the corner of my eye giving her dear Grandma Gin a wink.

This was all an elaborate setup!

Gin wanted to get signed up with our agency and was using the ruse of trying to set up her great-granddaughters as an excuse to start the conversation. She wasn't as daft as I originally deemed her; she knew children couldn't be set up with an agency. This was a new one indeed.

Maggie, who was flushed and out of breath, rushed into the library. "Girls! I told you to stay put. We need to finish getting you ready before your father gets here."

When none of the girls moved, Maggie put one hand on her hip and pointed the other towards the staircase. "Move!" Her voice held a clear "don't mess with me" tone.

"Ah, man," Marie said before she slumped off the couch, a sullen look on her face.

We sat quietly for a few moments while the girls left. Maggie pulled the doors shut behind her. "I'm sorry, Gin. I'll tie them up this time if I have to."

I would've laughed, but the look on her face made me question if, in fact, she was joking. I turned my attention back to Gin. "Well, Gin. It appears the young ladies might have come up with a great idea. Would you have any interest in trying out our service?"

Gin blushed a bit and wrung her hands together. "Well. It might be fun to give it a go. Do you have clientele my age?"

"I have to be honest, Gin. We only have a handful of men in your age range and they have all been with us awhile..." I said with a shoulder shrug, "... so you can take that however you like."

"Can I get set up with younger men?" Gin asked, her blush deepening.

"Of course. I have to warn you, though; a lot of the younger men will be more interested in your wallet than you. However, at TAFT we pride ourselves on weeding out those that apply who clearly fall into that category. Our matches will only be with men who have the most compatibility with your profile results."

"I see," she said. "And if I wanted to try it, what would I have to do?"

I reached down into my carrier bag and grabbed out a

file folder. I handed it to Gin.

"Inside our packet you will find a pamphlet about TAFT along with all of our general paperwork. In a nutshell, we'll collect all of your profile data, a setup fee, and profile pictures. Then, we'll load all of that information into our system and come up with three matches."

"Only three?"

"To start. We like to take things slow," I said. "Once you've reviewed those matches, you can decide if you'd like to go ahead and communicate with them. If you do, then we'll charge you a monthly membership fee."

Gin opened the folder and thumbed through the papers. "And what if I get matched, talk to them, and then am interested in meeting them in person?"

"You can go ahead and ask them out, or they'll ask you out," I said with a gentle smile. "If you are too nervous to go out alone, we can also look at helping you set up a double date. Or, if that doesn't work, either myself or one of my partners can make sure we eat at whatever restaurant you are going to. We won't intrude on your date, but you'll know we are there as your backup if you need us."

Her eyebrows shot up. "You would do that?"

I reached forward and patted her on the hand. "Of course! We want all of our clients to feel comfortable with their experience."

"I'm not very good with filling out forms, and I don't have any profile pictures," she said, the glow on her face fading away.

"If you are certain you want to try it, I can go ahead and process your setup fee right now and we can work on the paperwork together," I said, reaching down and pulling my iPad with the credit card swipe out of my bag. "As far as the profile pictures… I can either give you a card for a local photographer, or we can try to take a few photos here on my iPad. We can always change the pictures later."

The light returned to her features, and she even clapped her hands together with giddiness. "Yes. Yes, let's get started. Let me go get my pocketbook."

She got up, and headed out, returning a few minutes later with a large navy purse. After she was settled back in the seat she had vacated earlier, she extracted a matching wallet. Flipping it open, she pulled out a credit card and handed it to me.

I scooted over on the couch, laying my iPad and the credit card down on my lap.

"How about we quickly go through our packet once, just so you can see what all we offer? We can also go through the prices and terms," I said, patting the seat right next to me.

Gin wordlessly got up and moved over to the spot I'd indicated, bringing the folder with her.

We spent the next few minutes going through the pamphlets, FAQs page, the terms and conditions, and discussing pricing.

"Do you have any questions?" I asked when we'd finished.

"Only one, dear. How long will it take to get back results for my first matches?"

"The turnaround should be relatively quick since your pool of men will be smaller due to the age range. I would think around two to three weeks at most," I said, pulling out the signature page of the contract and grabbing the TAFT logo pen included in the packet. "If you can just initial these top three spots and sign at the bottom, I can run your card and we should be good to go."

I handed her the pen and paper. I was glad I'd booked the time for the potential of three client sign-ups, as helping Gin was going to take that much time and then some. Luckily, I didn't have any other appointments this afternoon.

Gin initialed and signed the form where I'd indicated and returned it to me. I put the form into my briefcase. Grabbing the credit card from my lap, I turned on my iPad and went into our payment app. After a few clicks here and there, I reached the charge screen. I swiped the card and waited. When the signature page came up, I turned the device to Gin.

"If you can just sign here, we'll be all set."

She looked at the iPad, then at the couch, then at me. "Where did that pen go?"

"You don't need a pen, Gin. Just use your finger."

She gave me an "oh really" look but shrugged, reached forward, and signed with her finger. I took the device back, clicked a few more buttons, and navigated to the login screen.

"Alrighty then. We are all set. Now, let's get to work on that profile," I said, reaching into the packet and pulling out the profile form. "We can do this online. It will make it much easier and allow us to only enter the data once. Do you mind if I go sit at the desk? You can follow along with the paper packet. It has the same data as I'll see on my iPad."

"Of course," she said, motioning to the desk.

I reached down into my bag and pulled out my snap-on keyboard. Standing, I made my way to the desk and got situated.

We spent the next hour getting Gin set up with a login and profile. Gin seemed to be enjoying herself and worked very carefully to put just the right information into her profile. When we were all done, I clicked save.

"One more task checked off the list," I said. "Now, what did you decide on the pictures? I can either take a picture of a picture you have here and upload it, we can take a picture on my iPad and upload it, or I can give you a card for a photographer."

She thought about it for a moment before answering. "As long as we can go up to my wardrobe and I can change into different outfits, then let's just take pictures here and now."

"Sounds good."

I followed her up the stairs and into a large, square master bedroom. It was done in burgundy paisley patterns.

A queen-sized bed with a beautiful quilt on top of it sat against the far wall, a bench at the foot of the bed. A makeup table, dresser, and side table were the only other items in the room.

"You can sit on the bench. I'll be out in just a moment." She disappeared into a closet for a moment before poking her head out. "What kind of outfit should I wear?"

I thought about it for a moment.

"Let's do three shots: a professional/formal, fun/casual, and a flirty/sexy," I said.

"Okay. I'll throw on a suit," Gin replied.

Because Gin already had her hair and makeup done, and the only thing she had to do was change clothes, it only took a few moments to be ready for her first glamour shot. The first outfit she chose was a fitted, light gray pantsuit. It was perfectly tailored, and the gray worked beautifully with her hair color.

We walked back down to the library, and she leaned against her desk, arms crossed—very lawyer-like. The light filtering in from the window was perfect for the scene. I took four shots, positioning Gin a little bit differently each time. Once done, we reviewed the pictures and Gin selected the one she liked best.

Next, Gin put on a casual top and a pair of Capris. The top was plain white with a braided collar and sleeves. Her Capris were also white, but they were covered in bright, primary-colored flowers. She pulled her hair out of its tight French twist and instead did a low loose bun at the nape of her neck. Wisps of free hair framed her face.

We went out to her front yard and took a picture in front of her fountain. The flowers behind her complimented her outfit. I looked down at the images on my iPad and realized the first two shots looked too stiff.

"Gin. We want these to be a little bit more fun. Less formal. How about you give me the smile you have when you think about your family?"

It only took a few moments, but the next smile she shared with the camera was genuine. Her entire face lit up with the smile. It was clear from the photo that she was happy.

"Perfect!" I said. "Keep the smile but move around a bit. I'll snap a few free-form photos."

Gin did as I requested and I snapped away. We ended up with several great shots and actually had a hard time picking only one to use.

For the next shot, the flirty one, we made our way back up to her bedroom. We decided on having her sit at her makeup table. While she was getting ready, I turned away from the closet and straightened the table a bit to better work with the shot. I turned when I heard her come out of the closet.

"Holy Mary mother of God!" I stumbled and fell back, missing the stool and landing on my butt with a *THUD*.

Gin was standing in front of me, hair down and

fluffed, wearing a cherry-red and black teddy. Thank God all of her main bits and bobs, or should I say boobs, were covered by silk. The rest was all lace. A black cat I hadn't known was there shot out from beside her and ran under the bed.

"Oh, dear. Let me help you—" Gin started to rush forward to help me up off the ground. I waved her away, hands high in the air. I wasn't only trying to tell her I could get myself up, I was also trying to hide my eyes from what was in front of me. I knew it was pointless, however. I would never be able to remove the image from my mind.

"I'm fine, Gin."

"I'm so sorry. Did I do something wrong?"

I didn't want to embarrass her or hurt her feelings.

"No. Of course not. Your cat just startled me. I didn't see it there and I haven't had the best experiences with them," I said.

This was only a partial lie. It wasn't what had startled me, but I'd neither seen it nor had I ever had good experiences with cats in the past. I tried to maneuver my gaze so I was looking enough at her when I responded to not be rude, but *not* enough to continue seeing what was before me.

"Oh, my. Don't you worry. Henry wouldn't hurt a fly. He is more scared of you than you are of him," she replied. "Should we continue?"

"Why don't you go throw on something a little bit..." I struggled for words, "... more. We don't want this to be quite as sexy as what you were going for. Think flirty, not sexy. Like a little black dress, or a low-cut top and a skirt."

I slowly made my way to my feet, dusting off what I now knew was cat hair from my slacks.

"Silly me. What was I thinking? Of course, this was too much," she said, shaking her head, turning, and heading back into her closet.

I felt it best to just stay quiet.

It took a few minutes more for Gin to come back out. This time she wore a short, semi-low cut black dress. The dress was the perfect amount of flirty.

"That looks great!" I said. "Do you have any pearls or a nice necklace? I think that would work well with it."

She went over to a drawer, opened it, and pulled out a long set of pearls which she put over her head. Turning, she looked at me for approval.

"Perfect!" I said, giving her a thumbs-up.

Gin and I switched places, and she sat down on the stool I'd missed when I had unceremoniously fallen on my ass. We took several pictures, then selected the best one.

"It looks like we are all set. We've got some great shots here."

"Yes. They did turn out quite well," she replied as she swiped back and forth on my iPad viewing the pictures.

She handed me back my iPad, and we headed to the foyer. I picked up my bag, which I'd set there earlier, gave her one last handshake, and headed for my car. All I could think of on my way out was the bottle of still-unopened wine in my fridge. *I really needed to hit that!*

Chapter Fifteen

I sighed as I exited the highway and turned onto the residential streets. Almost home, only another ten minutes or so. My mouth watered at the thought of the wine I was about to consume. Boy, did I need it!

Turning right, I headed down Dover Street, which was situated on a very long, steep hill. As I neared the halfway point of the road, I pushed on the brake pedal to slow down the car, knowing there was an impending two-way stop sign at the bottom of the hill. Nothing happened. I tried again, pushing harder.

The only thing that happened this time was the car accelerated with the slope of the hill. I pumped my foot on the brake repeatedly. With each press, my blood pressure rose. The stop sign came closer and closer and I watched in horror as cars whizzed past on the cross street; no stop sign posted to make them brake.

My brain went into emergency mode, listing out all of my options. As I neared the last few car lengths of distance, I did the only thing I could think of. I held my breath, said a prayer, and using my right hand, pressed and held the park/emergency brake button on the shifter. I had a death grip on the steering wheel with my left hand and tried not to close my eyes. A loud squeal echoed from my tires and the smell of burning rubber came in through the window, coating my throat and making me cough.

So much smoke built up from the tires burning I couldn't see where I was going. My last glimpse had been of a single car parked on the right side of the road. I turned my wheel sharply and aimed toward where it had been.

Seconds later, I screamed as my entire body was jarred forward. I assumed from the impact of slamming into the parked car. The seatbelt crushed my chest, and the airbag exploded in front of my face, my face slamming into it, airbag dust flying into the car.

The world stopped for a second as I silently recoiled from the impact, my head smashing into the headrest. My ears rang and my eyes watered. I blinked back the tears as I tried to focus and stop the coughing the airbag dust was causing.

"Ma'am?" came a voice from somewhere in the distance. "This is Tesla-Assist. We've received an alert that your vehicle has been in an accident. Are you okay?"

"Ma'am?" it repeated. "Are you okay?"

The haze in my brain cleared enough for me to connect the dots.

"I'm…" I coughed, "… not sure."

"It's going to be all right," the voice said. "Stay still. Emergency services have been notified and are on the way."

"Okay," I said shakily. I took several deep breaths, trying to calm myself. All I managed to do, however, was increase the pain, as the inhales made the seat belt dig further into my chest.

I pushed at the airbag, deflating it out of my way so I could breathe and see better. I wiped the tears that streamed down my face as I waited for help. As my eyes cleared I noticed the burst from the impact had parted the black smoke. In front of me, the parked car I'd run into had moved forward several feet, coming to a stop just shy of the intersection. *Dear God. That had been close.*

The back side of the car was dented in. The hood of my car was non-existent. It had collapsed in on itself into a nice tidy square chunk of metal. The sounds of sirens tore my attention away from the twisted metal in front of me. I watched as a fire truck, police car, and an ambulance all pulled into the intersection almost simultaneously. The firemen were the first to reach me.

"Miss. Are you okay?" asked a sandy-haired young fireman.

"I think so," I said.

"Hang in there. We'll get you out of there in a jiffy," he said, giving me a warm smile.

He reached for the door handle. The door gave a little *POP* and then opened with a loud *SQUEAK*. He crouched down, reached over, and pushed on the seat belt latch. The seatbelt didn't click or release. He pushed it a few more times before backing away.

"Looks like we'll have to cut you free."

I let out a sob as I watched him take scissors to the seat belt. I don't know why *that* was the moment that made me sob. I mean I'd already seen the front of the car smashed in like it was in a trash compactor. But something about cutting the seat belt did me in. *My beautiful car!*

"Are you okay? Did I hurt you?"

"What...? No. I'm—" I started to say before pain crashed over my chest. I took several short Lamaze-like breaths through my nose, "—fine."

He reached in and gently placed a neck collar around my neck, pulling the Velcro straps secure.

"This is just a precaution," he said as he finished. "We're going to lift you out and put you on a gurney board. Try to stay as still as possible."

I nodded and took in as shallow of a deep breath as possible. My chest burned with pain, but my breathing was somewhat easier now that the belt was removed.

He and two other firemen maneuvered me out of the car and onto the board. After strapping me in, they hoisted me up and onto a gurney, wheeled me to the ambulance, and slid me in.

An EMT hopped in and took a seat beside me as the door closed. The EMT, whose nametag read "Alice," proceeded to insert an IV into my arm. Once it was placed and taped down, she injected something—which I assumed was pain medication—into the IV.

"This should make you feel better," she said, smiling down at me.

It was less than thirty seconds before I felt the effects of the medication. The pain reduced from a ten to a three and the shaking subsided to close to nothing. I closed my eyes and savored the feeling.

"We're good to go." I heard Alice say to the driver.

Seconds later the engine started, the emergency sirens turned on, and we drove away. We had barely moved before I drifted off into a drug-induced slumber.

Chapter Sixteen

I woke to the sound of beeping. I blinked my eyes several times trying to get my bearings and figure out what exactly was making that annoying noise. At the same moment my gaze landed on the beeping hospital equipment, a body moved between me and the equipment.

Startled, I moved my gaze upwards and focused on the face.

"Thank God you're awake. How are you feeling?" Jack's smooth, deep voice said. Frown lines burrowed across his brow.

"Jack? What are you doing here?" I asked, his question forgotten.

"I had my radio scanner on in my office when the call

came in about a car crash. I heard your name mentioned, so I headed over to make sure you were okay."

I smiled up at him. "That was sweet of you."

"Yep, that's me. A big sweetheart," he said smiling. "So, how are you feeling?"

I thought about it for a second, wiggling my toes and flexing my muscles to test them out. Three things seemed to hurt: my collarbone, chest, and knee.

"Sore. My chest and knee hurt the worse, but they're still not too bad. Granted, I don't know how much pain medicine I have in my system right now," I said, glancing over at the morphine drip machine. "Since I just woke up and haven't seen a doctor, I have no clue what other things might be—"

As if on cue the door opened and a woman in a white doctor's jacket came in the door, interrupting my questions.

"Miss Bloom. Good to see you are awake. I'm Dr. Plaxico. How are you feeling?"

I recounted for her the details I'd just given Jack. The doctor flipped through a chart she had been carrying when she walked in and jotted down a few notes.

"It appears from the physical exam, scans, and x-ray slides that you have bruised ribs, a mild concussion, a micro-fracture in your collarbone, and a lightly sprained knee. Well, that and minor bruises and abrasions," she said, not looking up from the chart in her hands.

My brow wrinkled and without really meaning to, I got

instantly annoyed.

"I thought you weren't supposed to let someone with a concussion sleep a long time?" I said.

I saw the doctor give Jack a look before looking back at me.

"We've been waking you up about every two hours. Do you not remember?"

My wrinkled brow turned from one of anger to one of worry and deep thinking.

"No. Actually, I don't."

Dr. Plaxico moved forward and gently patted my hand. "Don't worry. We don't wake you up all the way, just enough to make sure you can regain consciousness. It's not unusual to not remember."

"If I wasn't all the way awake, how are you certain I was truly conscious?"

"Believe me, sweetheart," Jack said. "Based on the language you used in those two seconds of being woken up, it was clear you were with us."

I saw the doctor try to hide a small smile that crossed her face.

I gave Jack my best cross look. "Ha-ha. Very funny."

Jack opened up his mouth to respond but was cut off by Dr. Plaxico clearing her throat.

"It's best to try *not* to raise the patient's blood pressure," she said.

I turned and saw that her back was to me and she was clearly directing the statement at Jack. When Jack's gaze turned back to me, I stuck out my tongue. He let out a short chuckle that brought the doctor's gaze back to me as well, a quizzical look on her face. She didn't ask, and I didn't offer to fill in the blank.

"The nurse will be in shortly to get your vitals one more time. Where's your pain on a scale of one to ten?"

I thought about it for a moment before answering. "I'd say a four and climbing the more I'm awake."

"Okay. I'll also have her give you a small dose of painkiller to keep the worst at bay. We don't want to give you too much while we're still doing the concussion protocol."

I nodded my head in agreement and instantly regretted it. My brain felt exactly as it should—like it had just recently been tossed around like a football. Maybe I should have said a six instead of a four.

The doctor left the room, and I turned my attention back to Jack.

"I'll need to take a statement from you about the crash. I can do it now and get it over with, or you can talk to a regular officer later if you like."

"They let you take traffic reports?"

"In special cases, and when it'll save the department time," Jack said, crossing his arms and widening his stance. "What, do you think I'd be too good to take a report?"

I laughed, "Nah. Just didn't think you'd be able to find a pen and paper based on how clean you keep your office."

He glared and me before sticking out his tongue, "Ha-

ha. Very funny. I know how to find things when the right time warrants."

A blush crept up my face as I thought of the various implications of the words. I cleared my throat.

"You can take my statement now if you like. There really isn't much to tell."

Jack made a show of it as he reached into his breast pocket and extracted his staple pen and notepad before moving over to the nearest chair and taking a seat.

"Okay," he said, "start at the top."

"I'd just finished up with a client and—"

"What client?"

I flashed back to my first interview with Jack and recalled his incessant need to cut me off mid-sentence. *Not this again!*

"A 'client' is all you're going to get for now. If more becomes necessary later I'll get a release signed."

Jack grumbled something under his breath but let it go.

"As I was saying… I was finishing up and was on my way home. I'd just gotten off the highway and turned onto Dover Street."

"Which way were you going on Dover Street?"

"Down."

Jack's gaze snapped up at me and his one eyebrow rose. "Down?"

"Yeah. I was heading down the hill towards home."

"So, *North.*"

"Sure, whatever. If you say so. I'm what they call 'directionally challenged,'" I said.

Jack chuckled and shook his head but didn't look up from his notepad.

"Hey! You're not allowed to laugh at peoples' disabilities."

Once again, Jack moved his gaze up to me. He opened his mouth, closed it, opened it again, closed it. Then, he just opted for shaking his head again.

"Why do you always make things harder than they need to be?" I asked, annoyed.

"Me? You're joking, right?" Jack pinched the bridge of his nose.

"Anyway…" I continued, "… About halfway down the street, I applied my brakes so I would stop at the stop sign at the bottom of the hill. Nothing happened. I tried again several times and nothing worked."

"How'd you manage to get the car stopped?"

"I pushed in the parking brake button. Well, that, and I aimed for the only parked car on the side of the road." I said. "I figured if one didn't stop me, the other one would."

My stomach sank as I relived the moment in my mind.

"That was really brave of you," Jack said, as he reached forward and took my hand in his.

"Thanks," I mumbled. I felt the moisture of a tear slide down from the corner of my eye.

Jack stood up, leaned over, and gently wiped the tear away. "I know it was scary. But you did good and you're safe now."

I smiled up at him and gave a slight nod, unable to speak for fear that the tears might overcome me. Jack's finger lingered on my face for a second before he moved it downward and stroked my bottom lip for the barest of moments before slowly lifting his finger away.

My breath held as I felt the movement of his fingers. I looked at him and saw his gaze was locked on my lips. Without consciously meaning to, I licked them. I heard more than saw Jack take an inhale of breath. His gaze snapped back up to mine. I'm not sure what would have happened next because the door to the room opened and a nurse came in wheeling a cart. Through the open door, I could see the nurses' station in the hallway, mere feet from my room.

"Good afternoon, Ms. Bloom. I'll be taking a quick vitals check, if that's okay with you?" the nurse said before she was even all the way into the room.

Jack quickly retreated to his chair and cleared his throat.

"That's fine," I said, also clearing my throat and sitting up a little straighter. I gazed back at Jack and noticed the tips of his ears had gone pink.

"Is there anything else you remember, Ms. Bloom," Jack asked.

The nurse grabbed my arm and checked my blood pressure. The cuff was too tight, making me squirm a bit in place.

"Nope. That's it. Like I said, there isn't much to tell."

The machine beeped, and the nurse jotted down the results before putting the O2 clip on my finger. A few seconds later she removed it and made another note on the chart. At the same time, Jack made another note in his notebook and shifted slightly in his chair before looking up at me again.

"I'm all done for now," the nurse said, smiling at me. "I'll be back in a few hours for dinner."

I nodded my thanks and watched as she walked out the door.

"Have you had any problems with your brakes in the past? When was your car last serviced?"

I turned my attention back to Jack.

"No, no problems. I'll have to check with Eva, but I think it was serviced a week or two ago. She is the one that took it in for me."

"Where do you get it serviced?"

"At the Tesla dealership on Grange Drive."

Jack jotted down a few more things in his notebook.

"That's where I'll also have my car repaired," I added as an afterthought.

Jack looked up at me, eyebrow crooked. "I'm sorry to be the bearer of bad news, but there's no way they can repair your car. It was totaled."

My heart sank.

"Oh," was all I could think to say as I thought back and recalled the one glimpse of the hood. I guessed it was possible it would be irreparable. "Well, I can have the shop at least pull any spare parts. That way if I need them on my new car I'll have them."

"I'll make sure to tell the Forensics' team to transfer the car after they are done with it."

"Forensic team?"

Jack flipped his notepad closed and returned that and his pen to his pocket.

"Yes. We're going to have it looked over to confirm what exactly happened."

"Why would you do that? Normal car accidents like mine don't get looked at in that detail. Do they?"

"No. Not normally. However, given the recent series of events, we need to make sure that this isn't somehow tied to them."

"How in the world would this be tied to Jasmine's death?"

"Since the client *was* one of yours, it's best to make sure the incidents are not somehow connected."

I sat up in the bed. "You think someone tried to kill me?"

Jack was quiet for a moment, which was one moment too long for me.

"Jack?"

"I can't say for certain. I don't want to scare you, but I think it's important you know it's a possibility."

The door to my room burst open and the nurse who just recently vacated my room came rushing in.

"Are you okay, Ms. Bloom?" she asked, concern etched on her face.

"I'm fine," I said a little too aggressively. It was clear from my tone I was annoyed by her interruption.

The nurse took a step back and raised her hands.

"I'm sorry to interrupt," she said, looking back and forth between me and Jack. "Your heart monitor alerted me that your heart rate just jumped significantly."

"Sorry," Jack said. "That was my fault. I had to give Ms. Bloom some troubling news."

The nurse's brow furrowed, and she pointed a finger at Jack, "We need the patient to stay calm and rest. Is that clear?"

The tips of Jack's ears turned pink yet again. "Yes, ma'am. My apologies. I'll do my best not to let it happen again."

"You'd better, or you'll be asked to leave. Understand?"

Jack made a cross over his heart and gave the nurse a very nice smile, "Promise."

It was the nurse's turn to blush. She huffed once before leaving the room. I waited until I heard the last squeak of footsteps fade away before I turned to Jack.

"Better be careful or you might get a spanking," I warned.

"I'll pass. At least unless it's coming from you." He winked.

I took an inhale of breath, my pulse doing a little jump

step. Almost immediately the loud squeak of footsteps returned and my door swung open. The nurse held the door open with one hand and with the other she pointed outside.

"You. Out!"

Jack looked at the nurse, "But—"

"Out!" she repeated.

Jack looked at me and I shrugged. There was no way I was going to argue with the nurse; she was a mean one. He stood and shuffled towards the door. Just before he passed the threshold he stopped, lifted his head, and looked back at me.

"We'll finish this conversation later."

He did one more wink before sashaying out the door. I saw that the nurse couldn't help but watch along with me as he made his departure. That man sure had some good *ass*ets.

Chapter Seventeen

Shortly after one o'clock, two days later, I was cleared to be released from the hospital. The doctor had held me a little past the concussion protocol timeframe just to ensure that my blood pressure was under control. After Jack informed me I could've been potentially targeted by a killer, I'd had a hard time keeping it down.

"You ready to go, Lily?" Dad asked as he made his way into the room. My father had resorted to calling me by my middle name when he couldn't call for one of us—my mother's name was Bella—without the both of us answering. Our names sounded too similar when yelled by Dad's deep baritone voice.

"I think so. Just waiting for the wheelchair. Nurse

Ratched said I couldn't leave without them taking me down in the chair," I huffed and crossed my arms as I sat on the hospital bed.

Dad walked over and gently kissed me on the forehead.

"They know best, honey."

I leaned into him and wrapped my arms around his thick waist, my head laying on his belly. My father was not thick as in fat, he was thick as in solid. As some mountain folk might say, he was built like a brick shit house: tall, big-boned, and made up of solid muscle. The muscle earned from working hard every day of his life prior to retirement. He had spent his life in construction; mostly constructing log houses in the mountains. It was never uncommon to see him hauling a forty-pound bag of concrete or a piece of large timber over his massive shoulder.

His aftershave, original-scent Old Spice, lingered on him from his morning shave. I inhaled deeply, enjoying the childhood scent of him.

"Thanks for coming to get me, Dad. I know you were planning on going fishing this weekend."

Dad put his finger under my chin and lifted my face. "There's nothing I wouldn't reschedule in order to be here for you when you need me. I'm just glad you're okay. I don't know what I'd do if I lost you too."

"I know. That's why I love you," I said with a smile. I wasn't sure if the pain reflected in his eyes—remnants of losing my mother—would ever go away. I knew I still missed her each and every day. *Damn cancer!*

"That's the only reason?" Dad said, putting his hand on his heart and pasting a fake hurt and surprised look on his face.

I leaned back, stuck out my tongue, and punched him playfully in the gut.

The door opened and a young male nurse walked in pushing a wheelchair. Thank God, I didn't have to deal with that other nurse again. She had been a serious pain in my ass.

Dad moved out of the way so the man could maneuver the chair closer. I stood up slowly, got my footing, and then moved to get into the chair. Luckily, the room no longer spun when I moved. I lifted my feet and watched as he bent over and put the footrests down.

"Ready to go?" he asked.

"You betcha!" I said. "Dad, can you grab my bag?"

"Sure thing, sunshine," he said as he grabbed it and followed us out the door.

When we got outside to Dad's work truck, he had to help lift me into the passenger's seat. Even on my best day, I'd had to use some effort to hop into it. He had put a lift kit on it in order to help him more easily get in and out of the mountain terrain. My dad's regular truck, a 1955 Ford F100, only came out to play on special occasions. It was his pride and joy. Well, next to me, that is.

Dad walked around to the driver's side, and with much more ease than I'd ever had, slid onto the bench seat.

The truck started with a deep growl.

"Dad, I really don't need to stay at your house. I'll be fine."

"Sorry, kiddo. I want at least twenty-four hours with you to make sure I feel comfortable sending you home alone." He reached over and patted my hand.

"Fine. But you better keep Grandma from smothering me to death while I'm there!"

Grandma had moved in with Mom and Dad when Mom had gotten sick. Mom's own mother had died a few years previous, so Olive was really the only choice to help care for Mom. Luckily, the two got along better than most in-laws. Grandma's biggest flaw was that she liked to smother. It was good for a day or two, but after that, it became *very* annoying.

"I'll do my best," he said with a grin. "Granted, you could always stay home if you ask your boyfriend to stay with you."

"Boyfriend," I croaked. "What boyfriend?"

Dad chuckled, "Your Grandma said you were seeing someone."

I rolled my eyes. "You know better than to listen to your mother. She's the queen of gossip, regardless of how true it is."

"So, no boyfriend?" Dad glanced at me, a frown now on his face and his gaze serious. "I was hoping you were finally over that piece of shit you used to call your husband."

I started to reach over and pat Dad on the knee, but my ribs cried foul when I tried to bend. So, I stayed where I was.

"I'm over him. Completely. I'm just too busy with work to bother with looking for someone else."

"If you say so," Dad said, turning his attention back to the road.

"Promise."

Dad hit a rut in the road.

"Yikes!" I squealed, taking in as deep breath of a breath as the bandage on my ribs and the bruising would allow.

"Sorry! I'm trying my best to avoid them. This damn road is a minefield!"

Dad wasn't joking. It was nearly impossible to avoid the potholes given the state of the road we were on. Complaints to both the City and the County had been ignored. Dad had even come out once himself and filled them all, but once was all he could manage. He had neither the money nor the energy to do it again.

"I'm writing each and every one of them another letter," I said through gritted teeth.

"That would just be a waste of a stamp. If you really want to give them hell, there's a council meeting next week."

A large, full grin spread across my face.

"Grandma and I would love to attend," I said, laughing aloud.

"Lord, help them all," Dad said with an echoing laugh.

***

It wasn't too much later that we pulled into the driveway. I always loved my childhood home. Far enough away from town to hear all the sounds of nature, but not so far that I couldn't talk Dad into going for an ice cream every now and again.

My parents' house was a large two-story Victorian. It was painted buttercream yellow with white shutters. The front had a large, open wraparound porch. The back porch was enclosed to keep the bugs out. I noticed it was a tiny bit worse for the wear. I really needed to talk to Grandma and find out what was up. I guessed my dad's back was getting the best of him again. If that was the case, I was going to pay to get him some help. Whether he liked it or not.

Dad had refused to sell the house when Mom died. Every time I brought it up, he had a new excuse as to why he wouldn't: *I'm not ready yet to leave the memories. What else would I do with my days if I didn't have the house to piddle around in? Where would your grandmother go?* And my personal favorite… *I didn't buy that riding lawn mower to just up and sell the house before I've had a chance to wear it out.*

Well, regardless of if he wanted help or not, he was going to get it if Grandma confirmed my suspicions. This place was just too big for one old man to take care of. Not to mention that Grandma was not the best housekeeper, so she wasn't much help indoors. She was famous for saying, "I'll get to it later." Later rarely came.

At least the two old folks kept each other company. I wasn't sure what they'd do if they didn't have one another to bicker and gossip with. Dad, at times, could be as big of a gossip as Grandma. I knew Grandma took credit for a lot of the TAFT information that was actually compliments of dear old Dad.

After a couple painful moments, Dad had me out of the truck and on my own two feet. I stood still for a bit until I was certain I had my feet under me and the world was not spinning. Slowly, I moved forward—arm wrapped in Dad's—into the house.

The smell of beef stew, fresh bread, peaches, and cinnamon—most likely attached to a peach cobbler—filled my nostrils as I entered the living room. While Olive might not love to keep house, she loved to cook and bake. And she was AMAZING at it.

"Thank goodness you made it home safe and sound, flower," Grandma said as she rushed forward. "Are you feeling okay?"

I quickly raised an arm to block the oncoming assault.

"Easy, Grandma, I have bruised ribs. Remember?"

Grandma slammed to a halt inches from me.

"Oh, my. You're right. Silly me," she said, blushing.

She leaned forward and gave me a gentle kiss on the cheek.

"Smells great, Mom! When's it going to be ready? I'm starving," my father asked as he licked his lips and headed towards the kitchen.

"You keep your big mitts off the food, George. It'll be ready in just a bit."

The sound of metal on metal gave away the fact that my father was disobeying and trying to see for himself exactly when the food would be ready.

"George!" Grandma yelled but with a grin on her face. She turned her attention back to me.

"Do you want to stay upstairs or downstairs?"

I thought about it as I looked around the room. The house had changed little since my childhood. Composed of three bedrooms, a living room, family room, dining room, kitchen, three and one-half baths, laundry room, and a sewing room. The living room—the room where we currently stood—had changed the least over the last decade. It still had the same cream-colored matching sofas, dark oak coffee table with a glass top, a Thomas Kinkade Autumn scene painting, and a dusty fake tree. The most colorful item in the room was the twelve-by-ten rug on the ground. It had colors that matched those in the painting: gold, yellow, red, brown, and dark green.

Personally, I thought Mom had never changed it because everything in the room had been a gift from my father during one of their milestone anniversaries—tenth, twentieth, etc. Unfortunately, she hadn't made it to their fiftieth. I doubted the room would ever change again. At least not as long as Dad lived here.

"I think I'll stay downstairs. Not sure it'll feel very good to go trudging up and down the stairs. Even if it's only for one day."

"Whatever you think's best," Grandma said as she started off towards the bedroom. "Do you want to take a shower before dinner to get that 'hospital' smell off you?"

"Actually, that sounds perfect. I'll need help, though. My ribs are still wrapped up. They said I could take off the bandages, but it might hurt a bit more without the compression."

"I'll be happy to help you with that and your shower if you need it," Grandma said as she placed my bag on the bed. "I think I might have a solution for the compression. I have a front hook corset that will do the trick. It should be just tight enough to help, and you can put it on and off yourself."

"That would be great, Grandma," I said as I sat on the bed and slid my shoes off my feet—using my other foot on each shoe to accomplish the task. I took advantage of the quiet moment to close my eyes and take a deep breath. The room was a little musty smelling from lack of use, but the scent wafting in from the kitchen helped to lessen the odor.

I always referred to this white and blue painted room as the marshmallow room. The reason was the queen-sized bed was like a marshmallow. It was firm at first, but as you lay still in it, you sank in. I wanted nothing more than to lean back and sleep, but I knew I needed to wash the last few days away and get some food. I let out a tired yawn and listened to the frogs ribbit outside.

Grandma was back a few minutes later with a corset, i.e. Spanx, with hooks going up the front, and some other garment I couldn't identify. She laid them down on the bed, then walked around to me to help me with the bandages.

I slowly reached my arms up overhead and let her take off my shirt. Once that was gone, I stood, removed the rest of my clothes, and moved more into the center of the room so she could walk around me in a circle to remove the bandage. It took several trips around me, but finally, the bandages were gone. Initially, it felt like heaven to have the hot, tight object gone. However, the relief was short-lived as the pain crashed down on me when I lowered my arms.

The onslaught was so bad I had to lean against the dresser for support, several explicit words flowing freely from my mouth.

"Dear heavens," Grandma said.

I tilted my head and looked at her through a haze of tears. What the…? Grandma used worse language than mine on a regular basis. How could my words have upset her enough to say that? That's when I saw she wasn't speaking *to* me. She was saying the words in general as she gazed *at* me.

Picking up my head and wiping away the tears, I gazed into the mirror that was on the back of the door. I immediately knew why she said what she said. My chest was covered in deep purple and blue bruises. The worst of them were covering three spots on my chest, and one spot on my collar bone—the collarbone bruise I'd seen before I'd left the hospital.

"I wish I could say it looks worse than it feels, but I can't," I said with a sigh.

"You poor thing," Grandma clucked. "Don't you worry, I'll take care of you."

The bottom of my stomach dropped. What I wanted to say was, *lucky* me! Instead, I went with, "Thanks. You're the best."

I walked slowly into the attached bathroom.

"Do you want a shower or a bath?" Grandma asked. "I can throw some Epsom salts in the bath, that should help with the bruises."

"I'll start with a quick shower just to get clean. Maybe before bed, I'll do the soak."

Grandma nodded, reached into the shower, and turned it on. After a few minutes, she nodded, indicating the water was at the right temperature. I stepped gingerly into the tub/shower combo and leaned into the stream of water. I closed my eyes and let the warmth cascade down my aching body.

The sound of something squeaking brought my gaze around. Grandma was walking into the room donning the earlier unidentified item—one of Dad's camo raincoats. It was so large it covered her from her head to almost her ankles. She zipped up the front as she moved nearer.

"You don't need to come in. I can handle it from here."

"Nonsense. You just lean there and relax. I'll do everything else."

I gritted my teeth. I really did appreciate her help, but I also *really* needed to talk to Dad about getting her to learn some boundaries and not smother me the whole time I was here.

Grandma pulled the hood up over her head and stepped into the tub. She reached around me and grabbed the body wash puff and the strawberries-and-cream scented body wash—my mother's favorite scent. The familiar scent made me smile. I steeled myself for the pressure of Grandma's touch.

I only had to grimace a tiny bit, Grandma's touch was light as a feather. The light, circular motion lulled me into a peaceful coma.

"Okay, flower. You can turn around now," Grandma said gently from behind me. "You're not dizzy, are you?"

I regretfully opened my eyes, "No. I'm okay."

Turning around as instructed, Grandma washed me from head to toe in the same feather-light manner. My breath only caught twice: at my collarbone and my ribs.

Grandma offered to wash my hair, but I shooed her away and did it myself. Once done, I turned the water off, grabbed a towel, and wrapped my hair. I grabbed another towel and wrapped it around myself before getting out.

After drying off and finger combing my hair, I moved back into the bedroom. I walked over to the bed and rummaged around in my bag until I found my pajamas.

Before putting them on, Grandma helped get me into the Spanx. She'd been right, it was something I would be able to get in and out of by myself once I got home. The pressure felt good, and I could once again take a normal breath without pain. I tossed on my PJ's and headed out to the kitchen.

Dad was at the counter pouring a glass of iced tea.

"Feel better?" he asked as he motioned to the tea asking if I wanted any.

"Yes, and yes," I said.

Dad reached up into the cupboard and grabbed out another glass, which he filled with both ice and tea. He picked up both glasses and moved them to the table.

"Can we eat now, Mom?" Dad pouted.

"Yes, George. Now that Calla is done with her shower we can eat."

Dad eagerly went to the stove, picked up the stew, and brought it to the table. He placed it on one of the trivets situated on the table. Grandma took the rolls and put them in a basket before also placing them on the table. All the other fixings: butter, salt, pepper, salad, salad dressing, bowls, and utensils, had already been placed earlier.

We all took our normal chairs and dug in. After eating the hospital food, Grandma's cooking tasted even better than normal, which was hard to do. I savored every bite.

Halfway through my meal, I remembered I needed to take my medicine.

"Dad. Can you go into my room and grab the pills out of my bag? The doctor wants me to stay on the anti-inflammatories and painkillers for a few more days."

Dad got up and retrieved my pills. I was glad I only had to take the pills for a couple more days. I hated the way painkillers made me feel. I was a serious lightweight when it came to booze and medicine.

"Thanks," I said as I took the pills from him.

I popped open each of the bottles, extracted one pill, then downed them with my iced tea. The clock was now ticking on when I would pass out from a pill-induced coma. Quickly, I finished eating my main course.

"Grandma, I know the cobbler is still cooling, but I don't think I'll be awake later to enjoy it. Do you mind if I steal some now?"

Dad's eyebrows went up in anticipation. He knew if she allowed me to get some that would mean the door was open for him as well. He never waited patiently for dessert.

"Of course. Just be careful, it's hot," Grandma said. "Do you want some ice cream to go with it? I have some in the freezer if you want to add some."

"Yeah, that would be great!"

Grandma walked over to the freezer, grabbed out the ice cream, and put two scoops in a bowl before adding a large scoop of cobbler. She sat the bowl down next to me and gave me a quick kiss on the cheek before returning to the counter to prepare dad a bowl. By the time I was done eating I could feel the numbness rolling over me from the pain pill. I knew I would have to prop myself up a bit in the bed to sleep. I never did well going to bed right after eating. I walked over to the sink and put my bowl and spoon in.

"All right, folks. I think that's all for me today."

"Goodnight, honey. Just shout if you need anything," Dad said between spoonfuls of the cobbler. "I'll come down once and check on you."

"Thanks," I said as I headed to the bedroom and marshmallow.

Chapter Eighteen

The smell of bacon greeted me the next morning when I woke. I started to sit up in bed but stopped dead in my tracks when my torso screamed out in pain. During the night I'd woken and considered taking another pain pill but had been too tired to get out of bed to take it. Now, I regretted the choice. A lot.

I wiggled out of bed and headed for the bathroom. I knew the quickest way to get things limbered up was a good soak in hot water and Epsom salts. I reached over, turned on the faucet, and let my fingers linger under the stream of water, turning the handle until it reached the right temperature. I moved over to the vanity, bent down, and extracted the strawberry-scented salts. Moving back to the tub, I poured in a generous amount.

While the tub filled, I stripped off my pajamas and removed the Spanx. With great care, I slid into the bath water. After several moments my muscles relaxed. I slid down into the delicious warmth and closed my eyes.

"Everything okay in there?" Grandma said through the door.

I opened my eyes and blinked several times. With a start, I realized I couldn't recall just how long I'd been in the tub, but the water had cooled to lukewarm. *Yikes!*

"Yes," I replied, "Just getting out now."

"Well, be as fast as you can. Your father is going to eat all the bacon!"

I chuckled as I got out of the tub and wrapped a towel around me. Feeling much improved, I strapped back into the Spanx and put on some clean clothes out of my bag.

Grandma was smacking Dad's hand when I entered the kitchen.

"I said enough, George. Leave some for your daughter!"

Dad's face changed to one of embarrassment when he saw I'd entered the room; like a child caught with his hand in the cookie jar.

"Sorry, honey," he shrugged. "You know how much I love bacon."

I gave him a smile as I sat down at the table. Before I even had the chance to put my napkin in my lap Grandma had grabbed my plate and filled it with all the items on the table: eggs, toast, hash browns, and last but not least, the last three slices of bacon. After placing my plate down in front of me, she filled my glass with orange juice.

"Thanks," I said, as I pulled my pills out of my pocket and laid them down next to the juice. It was best to get food in my stomach before I added them to the mix, so I picked up my fork and dove in.

Grandma sat down and sipped her coffee. When I looked up, in between bites of food, I noticed a mischievous grin had appeared on her face. *Uh-oh!*

"So…" she began.

I immediately swallowed and put my fork down. Best not to be holding it when she said whatever it was she was about to say. No need to have a sharp object *already* in my hand.

"So…" I repeated, one eyebrow raised.

"Opal told me the detective came to check on you while you were in the hospital. I thought you said you two weren't seeing each other."

I let out a sigh.

"He wasn't there to see me the way you mean it. He was there to take an accident report," I said with an eye roll. "How in the world did you know he was there, anyway?"

I picked up my juice and took a drink.

"Opal's sister, Judy, was your nurse. She told her."

I coughed a little on the juice. "You mean, Nurse Ratched."

Grandma let out a huge laugh.

"Nurse Ratched, huh? I guess that about sums her up."

"Well, it's the nicest thing I can think to call her. She was a serious pain in my ass."

"Why would a detective be taking an accident report? Wouldn't a traffic cop do that?" Dad asked from beside me.

I looked at him and debated whether or not to tell him the truth. I really didn't want to worry them about what could be nothing.

"Don't even think about lying to me, young lady!"

"But… how do you—"

"How doesn't matter," he said gruffly. "Tell me the truth."

I looked back and forth between the two. *I really need to figure out what my 'tell' is.*

"The truth is, he wanted to take the information down so he could make sure it wasn't in any way related to the current investigation."

Dad's face went pale.

"How in the world would it be related?" Grandma asked, not quite as fazed by the news.

"Only because one of our clients is a potential murder victim," I said, shrugging my shoulders. "He wanted to confirm it was just a coincidence I was in a car accident only days after she died."

"And was it?" Dad, who was now back to his original

color, asked.

"He didn't say. All I know is they are looking my car over to see what they can find," I said. "I'll also have the dealer look it over. They know my car better than anyone."

The doorbell rang.

"Who in the devil is ringing the door this early on a weekend?" Grandma said as she headed for the front door.

Unconcerned, I turned back to my breakfast; since I'd eaten half, I took my pills. A deep, sexy laugh echoed from the next room. *Well, damn!*

"Look who came courting you," Grandma said as she came in the room. Jack trailing behind her.

Jack gave Grandma a startled look. "Courting?"

"Ignore her," I said, wiping my mouth with my napkin. I started to get up, but Jack waved me down.

"Don't get up."

"What can we do for you, son?" Dad said as he stood and made his way towards Jack. I knew he did this so he could show just how big and scary he was, towering just over six feet four inches. Surprisingly, Jack didn't look that small next to him; a tad shorter and leaner, but not the normal shadow of the man beside him that most men were.

Jack reached out a hand towards my dad.

"You must be Mr. Bloom?"

Dad nodded, shook Jack's hand, then took his seat.

"Can we get you some breakfast?" Grandma asked, her voice chirpier than normal. "We have plenty left."

"No, thank you. I'm good," Jack said, fending off

Grandma's attempt to give him a plate. "I'm just here to check on Callie and to let her know her car will be delivered to the Tesla dealer on Monday."

"Isn't that sweet of him, flower," Grandma said, giving me a look and a wink over her shoulder.

Behind her back, Jack looked at me, eyebrow raised, "Flower?" he mouthed.

I knew I blushed, but I didn't reply, least it would give Grandma an opening for some childhood story I *didn't* want to be told.

"Do you think there is any connection to the murder?" Dad asked.

Jack's gaze snapped to me for the briefest of seconds before returning to my dad's. Clearly, he didn't realize I would tell my father the extra bit of info.

"I haven't found any direct connection to Ms. Stone's death, but we won't close the case until Callie's mechanics get a look at the car."

"You let me know if there's any reason I need to be worried about my daughter's safety. You hear me?"

"Mr. Bloom. I'm sorry, but if a link is found I can't divulge that information as it's an ongoing case," he said, raising his hand to stop the words about to come out of my dad's mouth. "I promise you I'll make sure your daughter is as safe as possible."

Dad sat back, folded his arms, and let out a loud huff, "I'll hold you to that."

"Let me walk you out," I said, as I stood and moved

forward, not waiting for anyone's approval. "I need to get up and move a bit, anyway."

Jack moved slightly to the side to let me pass. I looked back over my shoulder at Grandma and Dad.

"Stay," I said.

Grandma pouted and Dad gave a little salute. Jack and I headed towards the door. I opened the door and headed out to the front porch. I needed some fresh air. I stepped to the side on my way out, to make room for Jack. I stumbled a bit in the process. Jack caught me and held on while I got my feet under me.

"Thanks. Sorry, I guess the pain pills are kicking in."

"No problem," he said. Then I heard him inhale deeply. "Are there strawberries around here somewhere, or is that you?"

"Guilty," I said, blushing. I pulled away from Jack a bit, even though I didn't want to leave the warmth of his touch.

"It's nice." He reached up and brushed a stray lock of hair from my face.

I held my breath and looked up into his eyes. His cell phone rang, breaking the heat of the moment. Jack reached down to his hip, removed his phone from the holder, and answered.

"Detective Brown."

"… About thirty minutes away. Why?"

"… Can't John handle it?"

"… Shit. Okay. I'll be there as soon as I can."

Jack turned his attention to me.

"Sorry. I have to get going."

"Is everything okay?"

"Doesn't sound like it. But that's normally the case when my phone rings."

"Can I at least get you a cup of coffee to-go?" I said, taking a step back from him.

"Actually, yes. That might be good. Who knows how long this might take?"

I nodded, turned, and headed back towards the kitchen. I hadn't made it halfway before Grandma was coming out of the kitchen with a to-go cup of coffee in hand.

"Grandma," I said, giving her the stink eye.

She ignored me, walked past, and handed the cup to Jack.

"Stay safe," she said.

"Yes, ma'am," he said, taking the coffee from her, turning, and heading out the door.

I took note that Grandma, like every female I'd watched before her, paid special attention to Jack's lower half as he left. Age clearly wasn't immunity to the effects of his backside.

Chapter Nineteen

Monday morning was spent on hold with my insurance company. Jack had been right; my car had been deemed "totaled." After close to an hour on the phone, they finally assured me that I was being transferred to the adjustor handling my case.

"Ms. Bloom. My name is Tonya and I'll be assisting you with your claim. I sincerely apologize for your wait. We've had some staffing changes of late and things are a little hectic. I promise you I'll do all I can to get your claim processed as quickly as possible," she said.

"No problem. As long as I can get this resolved I'll be all good," I replied.

"Perfect. Give me just a moment while I look over

your account," she said. The tapping of her fingers on her keyboard echoing over the phone.

"Sure, no problem."

After several moments the tapping stopped. "Our file shows the police have submitted all the necessary paperwork with the details of the accident. Now, let's see…"

I assumed she was speaking to herself with the last comment as her voice trailed off to be replaced by incoherent mumbling.

"Yes, perfect. I also see that our adjustor was able to view and deem the vehicle a total loss. This should make things super-easy."

"Thank God," I replied. "I really need to get a vehicle."

"Well, I can put the request for payment in today. You should see a check in four to six weeks."

I jumped up out of my chair and instantly regretted it as my ribs screamed out in pain. Luckily, my sprained knee had not been as severe as originally thought, so it only whimpered instead of screamed at the sudden movement.

"Six weeks!" I squeaked.

"Yes, ma'am," she said. "It should be closer to four, but I'm required to give the window and not promise anything."

I wanted to yell at her, but I knew she was just doing her job. Instead, I let out a sigh and sat back down.

"Can you tell me how much the check will be for?"

"One hundred and twenty thousand dollars."

"What the—" I choked. "How did it drop thirty thousand dollars? I have gap insurance?"

I heard some more tapping.

"I'm sorry, Ms. Bloom. I show no record of gap insurance. If you did, in fact, have that feature, the amount will be substantially different."

"Of course I have it. My agent gave me a quote specific to gap—" *Holy hell.* He had called me and I'd realized I couldn't afford it, so I'd decided to roll the dice. Guess I just crapped out. "Never mind. He gave me the quote, but I never called in to add it. I'd forgotten."

"Oh, dear," she said. "I'm sorry to hear that."

"Yeah. Me too." I lowered my head against the desk, holding back tears.

"Is there anything else I can do for you?"

I straightened and blinked several times. "No. Thank you. I think that should be all for now."

"You have a wonderful day."

"You too," was all I could manage to say as I placed the receiver on the cradle, hung my head in my hands, and tried to keep back the tears.

First, our business was haunted by the shadow of death, next I run into Mike for the first time since the divorce, and then as if the car crash wasn't the rotten cherry on top, I was out thirty thousand dollars in one fell swoop. That was most certainly not going to lead to a "wonderful day."

I started at the knock on my door.

"Are you ready to drive over to the shop?" Jack said from the doorway. His gaze softened when I lifted my head. "Are you okay?"

I pasted a smile on my face. "I'm fine, just a rough morning. How'd you get past Eva?"

"Your receptionist?" he asked. "She wasn't out there."

"That's odd," I said, my brow wrinkling as I reached over and punched my intercom button. "Eva?"

It took a moment but she answered. Her voice was out of breath. "Did you need something?"

"Just curious where you're at. The detective is standing at my door."

"Oh my," she said. "I'm so sorry. I was in the copy room and didn't hear the door chime."

"No worries, just making sure you were okay. I'm getting ready to leave. If you go into the back again for any length of time make sure to lock the door. With everything that is going on we need to be a bit more careful than normal."

"Of course," she said.

I grabbed my purse, locked my desk drawer, and then moved past him towards the lobby. Eva had returned to her place at the receptionist desk when I passed.

"Would you like me to send your calls to your voicemail, or to your cell?" she asked hurriedly before I reached the door.

I stopped and thought about it.

"Voicemail, please. I don't want to be interrupted while I speak to the dealer."

Eva nodded and Jack and I headed out the door.

It hadn't been my first choice to ride with Jack to my mechanic's. However, he wanted to confirm the details he had received from Forensics and I needed a ride, so it all worked out. I hesitated when I didn't see his car in the parking lot.

When he saw me looking around, he pointed and started walking towards a dark blue, nondescript sedan. "I'm driving a police vehicle today."

After we were inside and buckled up, Jack headed towards the dealer. Apparently, he knew where it was, as he didn't ask for directions. I took advantage of the moment to close my eyes and give my head a break. I was trying to steer clear of the pain pills, but I just might have to sneak in a Tylenol soon if the headache didn't subside.

A gentle shake woke me at some point later.

"Callie, we're here," Jack said.

I blinked open my eyes and sat up. Clearly, I'd fallen asleep. I blushed at the faux pas.

"Sorry. I didn't mean to fall asleep."

"No problem. You've had your hands full so I'm sure you needed it."

We both got out of the car and went into the shop. Even though it was the service center and not the showroom, everything was white-glove clean. To the left were three customer service stations, each with either a representative attending a customer or on the phone. To the right was a small lounge with black leather chairs, glass tables, and green plants for decoration. A side table held refreshments: coffee, tea, bottled water, mini soda cans, and a tray with muffins and bags of chips. On the wall was a large screen TV, which was currently turned off since no one was in the lounge.

"Ms. Bloom, it's so good to see you again. I'm so sorry to hear about your accident."

I turned my attention towards the person who was walking towards us and speaking, Kevin. He was my personal service consultant, and I'd worked with him the entire time I'd owned my car.

"Thanks, Kevin. I wish I could be here under better circumstances," I said. "This is Detective Brown. He is here to get an update on what you all found when you looked over the remains."

Kevin nodded. "Let's go to my office and take a seat."

We followed him past the counters to a set of offices.

Jack moved up close, leaned down, and whispered, "Fancy. You even get to go into an office."

I threw my elbow back and punched him in the gut. He let out an *OOMPH* and a chuckle.

Kevin stopped beside an open door and directed us through. Jack and I took a seat in the guest chairs as Kevin slid in behind the desk.

"Well then, let's take a look," Kevin said as he reached for his keyboard and began clicking away. "Alan Lynch, your mechanic, says there were no signs of any holes, cuts, or leaks with the braking hoses, seals, or lines. Nor were there any visible issues with any of the brake components: master cylinder, calipers, pistons, or pads."

Kevin looked at me.

"What exactly does that mean?" I said. "Clearly, something went wrong or the brakes would have worked. No?"

Kevin pushed his glasses up his nose and returned his attention to the screen. "In theory, yes. The only other thing noted is that even though there were no leaks of any kind, the brake fluid reservoir was virtually dry, which is odd."

"Why is that odd?" Jack asked, moving forward just a bit in his chair.

"It's odd because Ms. Bloom just had her car fully serviced two weeks ago."

"Couldn't someone have just made a mistake on having checked or added the fluid?" I asked, my eye twitching as it dawned on me that I could have been targeted by a murderer.

"Normally, yes," Kevin said, swerving his chair so that he was looking directly at us. "However, in this instance, Alan was the one who worked on your vehicle. He not only remembers servicing it, he remembers filling the tank and making a note of it because the cap was sticking. He had to take extra time to lubricate the seal so that it would open and close correctly."

"Maybe he got busy with the cap and forgot to fill it?" I said, making up any excuse that I could bring to mind.

"Even if he had, he recalls the tank being at least half full to start with. We do diagnostic charting on all our systems first. Then, after we are done, we go back through and note anything attended to," Kevin said, before swiveling back to look at the computer.

"On the diagnostic pass, it said the tank was half full. In the completed notes it says the tank was now full."

I started to open my mouth to comment, but Kevin put up his hand and stopped me.

"I'm sorry, Ms. Bloom, but Mr. Lynch is not only our most tenured employee, he's also our most skilled. If he wrote it down, it happened. He doesn't skip corners."

I sat back in my chair, crossing my arms and feeling both deflated and terrified at the same time.

"Can you please forward a copy of that report to my email?" Jack said, handing Kevin a copy of his business card. Kevin took it and laid it on his keyboard before turning back towards us.

"I'd be happy to and will do it as soon as we're done. Speaking of that, Ms. Bloom, what are your plans for a replacement vehicle?"

I can't believe someone might have tried to murder me.

Jack lightly touching my arm brought my attention up. I blinked several times.

"What?" I said.

"He was asking you a question," Jack said, nodding his

towards Kevin.

I blushed. "I'm sorry. I guess I was caught up in taking it all in and missed the question. What were you asking?"

"No problem. I'm sure it's all overwhelming," Kevin said with a sympathetic smile. "I was asking what your plans are for a replacement vehicle."

"Oh," I sighed. "That's a bit complicated. I'm getting substantially less on my insurance settlement than I'd expected. Which means I can't replace my car with the same set of upgrades I had before."

"You have to love depreciation," Kevin said. "What price point are you going to be looking for?"

I did a side glance at Jack. I didn't know why, but I felt uncomfortable saying aloud just how much I'd paid for the car I'd just totaled. He looked at me for a moment and must have sensed my unease.

"I need to check in with the station to make sure nothing has come up with the case," Jack said, standing up. "I'll just go outside for a bit. You can come out when you are done."

"Ok," I said, a little too quickly. "It shouldn't be too long."

"Take your time," he said as he moved out of the door and towards the lobby.

When Jack was out of earshot, I turned back to Kevin.

"I have one hundred twenty thousand coming to me from the insurance. But, to be honest," I shrugged, "I'm not sure I'll be happy if I don't get all the bells and whistles

I've been used to. I don't want to spend this much money and then get frustrated because I didn't just wait until I could replace it the way I want it. And, I don't have another thirty thousand lying around to do that."

"That is totally understandable. But, this may be your lucky day." Kevin once again turned towards his computer and typed away.

Yeah, right. I felt like saying. Luck had not been on my side as of late.

"Yes. I think it is. We are scheduled to have a vehicle come in from the showroom in Glenville. It's last year's model, same as yours; 800 miles… all from test drives. They had to replace it with this year's model. It appears to have all the upgraded features you had. The only difference is the exterior, which is Sapphire Blue Pearl."

My heart skipped a beat.

"How much?" I sat up straight and bounced my knee.

"One hundred and twenty-eight thousand dollars."

My heart deflated. I still couldn't swing that.

"But," Kevin continued, "since you are a valued customer, and because you have provided us with so much referral business, I can go to $120,000."

"Really," I whispered.

"Really," he said with a large smile.

"I… I don't know what to say."

"No words necessary. By the looks of things, it seems as if you deserve to catch a break."

I didn't know exactly what he was referring to with the

comment, but I didn't care. I felt a tear roll down my cheek. Standing, I wiped it away and reached out my hand.

"Thank you again. You don't know how much this means to me. If you can get all the paperwork ready, I will—" I stopped. "Crap."

"I'm sorry?" Kevin said, brows furrowed.

I looked at him, my happiness suddenly vanished. "I can't get it right away. My check won't come for four to six weeks. I don't think I can get a loan approved for that amount right now."

I looked down at my feet and tried not to let the tears of joy turn to sobs of sorrow.

"No worries at all, Ms. Bloom," Kevin said. "We can work around that."

My head snapped up. "You can?"

"I think we can. The car isn't scheduled to arrive until the end of next week, if that. Then, we have to do a full-service check and cleaning, which will take a few more days."

"That still leaves us a long time before I might have my check," I shuffled from foot to foot.

Kevin stood and made his way around the desk, putting his hand gently on my shoulder.

"With your loyalty status I'm sure our VP would allow us to write up a contract stating as long as you get your check, you will purchase the car. Until the check comes, I'm sure your insurance company will give you a rental car. If not, I'm certain we could give you a loaner for a low rental rate."

"That would be amazing. I can't believe how generous you are being."

"Tesla strives itself on providing the best customer service in the industry. It's my job to make sure you are happy."

"Well, I can guarantee you that you have done your job. Above and beyond."

"So, I'll see you tomorrow to sign the paperwork?"

"Absolutely. What time?"

"Is four too late?" he asked.

"No. That should be perfect," I turned to leave but stopped and looked back. "They told you I wanted to get all the parts salvaged from my totaled car? I know there is a fee involved, which is fine."

"Yes. I think they already started putting the good items aside when they were doing the review for the police. I would say it should be done sometime next week," he said. "I'm not sure how much the cost is, I think about $200."

"That sounds about right," I said as I thought back to my earlier conversation with their billing department. "See you tomorrow."

He waved and watched as I headed out to the car. The tears were once again streaming down my face. I wiped them off as I made my way toward Jack and his car. He turned towards the sound of my footsteps, hanging up the phone as he turned. His eyes widened when his gaze hit mine. He rushed forward.

"Are you okay? Why are you crying?" His gaze went from me to Kevin—who was standing at the window—and back to me. "Did he do something to make you cry?"

Jack started towards the lobby. I grabbed him by the arm.

"No! I'm fine. Kevin just went out of his way to help me out. I guess I'm so overwhelmed from the last few days that his kindness made me cry."

I felt Jack's muscle under my hand flex and then relax as he let go of the anger he had just experienced.

"You're sure?" he asked.

"Completely," I said, patting his arm once before removing my hand.

"Okay. Good," Jack said, turning towards the car and opening my door. After I was settled he closed the door and moved around to his side. He opened the door and slid in.

"So, are you the owner of a new vehicle?" he asked.

"Not yet but soon. I'll have to get a rental until I get my insurance check," I said.

"You don't need to go to all that trouble. You can just borrow my car," Jack said as he put his seatbelt on.

I cocked my head sideways and looked at him. "Seriously? How are you going to get to work?"

"That's easy. I'll just keep the squad car. It's not out of character for us to keep them at home. I'm one of a few who switches between cars for work."

I debated the idea. Seemed a little too friendly for our …. What exactly were we? Acquaintances? *Friends?*

"Are you sure that won't seem…weird to your co-workers?"

"No one will even notice. If they do, who cares? I don't."

I clipped my seatbelt and Jack turned the key in the ignition. "Let me think about it. I don't want anyone to have any reason to question your investigation."

Jack's brows furrowed.

"Damn. I totally forgot about that," he said. "Maybe—"

"Don't worry about it, Jack," I said, patting his hand. "That's kind of you, but I don't mind driving a rental car."

"Okay. But if you have any problems, we'll figure something out."

"Deal," I said.

Jack backed out of the spot and headed towards the main intersection.

"Do you want to go back to work, or home?" he asked.

"Hmm. Good question. Let me check."

I dialed my office voicemail. I had two messages which I quickly listened to. Nothing of importance. I pressed the option to reach the operator: in this case, Eva.

"Eva, it's me. Is there anything you know of that needs my attention?"

"… Okay. Has Julia or Sara come in today?"

"… Uh-huh. Well, if you need me, call my cell. I'll call it a day and head home."

I pressed the button to hang up and turned my attention back to Jack. "Home, please."

"Your wish is my command," he smiled and did a little sitting bow.

I let out a short laugh, then a sobering thought came to mind. Jack must have read something on my face because his smile faded and his face got serious.

"What?" he asked.

"Do you think someone messed with my brake fluid?"

"Honestly?"

I shook my head yes.

"It's possible. The situation is odd. Usually, 'odd' things lead me down the darker path."

"What does that mean?"

"Well, for starters, I'll check the forensic report to see if any fingerprints were recovered from the brake fluid cap. I'm doubtful they found any based on how clean everything is at the dealer. My guess is they wipe down the engine after they service it, which would've removed any prints. But I'll check just to make sure."

I nodded in agreement. "Makes sense."

"In the meantime, I would say to be careful and pay attention to your surroundings and everyone in them. Also, don't go out alone if you can help it. That goes for your partners and staff as well."

"I'll have a staff meeting and relay the information."

"Try to stick to an overview. Don't go into details. The fewer people we give those to, the easier it will be to contain the investigation."

"I'll do my best. And Jack… Thanks for everything."

"Glad to be of help."

We both turned our attention back to the road and our own thoughts as we headed to my house.

Chapter Twenty

Kevin called the next day to say he had an emergency come up and wouldn't have the papers ready until the end of the week. So, we moved our appointment to Friday at four. That actually worked out for the best as it took a few days for me to get my rental car approval.

As I slid into the musty aqua-blue rental, I sighed. Oh, how I missed my beautiful baby and all her bells and whistles. I still couldn't wrap my mind around the fact it might not have been an accident. I shuddered at the thought. I turned on the ignition and slowly backed out of the garage, careful to make sure no one was coming. My nerves were on edge and I was more hesitant in my driving since the accident.

Not only had I locked the garage door and all of the doors to the car, I'd put a piece of string in the hood and doors when I closed them. This way I would know with some certainty if someone tried to access my vehicle during the night. Granted, there would be no way to know if they had slid under and done something. But, I couldn't cover every scenario.

Luckily, traffic was light today, and I made it to the office quickly. I noticed that Eva was not at her desk as I made my way into the conference room where I found Sara, Julia, and Grandma; JJ was on speaker phone.

"Good morning everyone," I said as I moved to pull out a chair and take a seat. "Where's Eva?"

"She has a doctor's appointment," Julia replied.

I didn't recall her saying anything or asking for time off for that matter. However, it wasn't unusual for one of us to approve it while the others were busy.

"Did you guys approve the time off?"

Julia and Sara looked at one another, and almost the same time said, "I thought you did?"

"Well, apparently none of us did," I said, rubbing my fingers over my temple in annoyance. "I'll talk to her about it later."

"With all that has been going on I'm sure she asked one of us and we just forgot," Julia said.

Sara nodded in agreement. "It's possible."

"Well then. I guess we'll just start without her."

"I'm glad to speak to you all again, but I'm not sure

exactly why I'm needed?" JJ said.

Everyone turned their attention to me.

"As part of today's meeting I wanted to give an update on Jasmine's case, and my car accident. I felt it important for you to stay in the loop."

"You make it sound as if they're connected, flower?" Grandma replied.

"Actually… they might be," I said, pointing my finger at Grandma. "And don't you tell Dad. He has enough to worry about."

Sara sat up straight in her chair. "Seriously?"

"Seriously," I said. "Both the forensic team and my mechanic said the accident has some oddities that can't be easily explained. So, for now, they are not saying it is for sure tied to Jasmine's death, but they aren't ruling it out either."

"What does that mean?" Julia asked.

"It means we need to be aware of our surroundings, be vigilant about locking our vehicles, and try not to go out alone until Jasmine's case is closed."

"Oh, my." Sara slouched back into her chair. "This is kind of scary."

"I agree," I said. "We need to tell Eva as well. Is she still riding the bus to work?"

"As far as I know," Sara said.

I turned my attention to Julia. "You're going to the store to get supplies today, aren't you?"

"Yeah. Going to leave here as soon as we're done."

"Why don't you swing by the sporting goods store and pick her up a can of pepper spray. It'll make me feel better for her to have it while she waits at the bus stop."

"Will do."

"Any other comments or questions before we move on to the next topic?" I asked.

When no one said anything, I looked at the phone. "JJ, you should be able to drop off now, the rest of what I have to say you don't need to bother yourself with."

"Perfect. Thanks, ladies. If you need me for anything else, just give me a ring."

With that, he hung up. Julia reached over and hit the "end call" button on the phone.

"What's next on the agenda?" Julia asked as she returned to her seat.

"I had a chance to load Virginia Thompson into our system and run matches. Thankfully, we were able to get three matches," I said.

"That seems too easy. I thought it would be super-hard to match her," Julia said.

"Well, I had to tweak the parameters a bit to include men in their sixties, but we found some good matches. Gerald, 78; John, 75; and Benjamin, 67."

"It's hard to believe people in their late seventies would even be interested in dating," Julia said.

"I'm old, not dead," Grandma interjected.

"Yeah. I agree with Olive. I hope to date until I die," Sara said with a chuckle.

"In any case," I continued. "I shared Gin's matches with her and she's picked her first date to be with John. She's a little nervous, so she asked if we can set her up on a double date."

I turned my gaze to Grandma.

"I was hoping you could go with her. You can take Gerald," I said. "You two already know you just want to be friends, but it'll give Gin a chance to be introduced to him and get a general idea what he is like. Kill two birds with one stone."

"Um…" Julia said, "is that really the best analogy to use?"

I thought about it and then recognized the humor in the statement.

"Yeah. Maybe not."

We all had a group chuckle.

"That sounds fine, as long as you're sure she is on board," Grandma said. "Granted, if Gin has any polish on her at all, I doubt she'll be interested in Gerald. He is a little too 'country' even for my taste."

I nodded as I agreed one-hundred percent with Grandma. However, the program had said they were compatible and we learned long ago never to doubt the machine. It had been right more often than not.

"Yes, she's on board. I explained your situation with Gerald and she feels comfortable with it. Why don't you reach out to her and get things scheduled?"

"Will do," Grandma said.

"Well, gang. If there's nothing else, let's get back to work."

Chapter Twenty-One

On Friday, after I had signed on the dotted line, I went to pick up Grandma. I'd told her about the City Council meeting and she was all for going to give them a piece of our mind about the state of our roads, especially the one towards Dad's house.

The meetings were held at town hall, so it only took us a few minutes to reach it. Grandma was coifed to perfection, and she'd worn an outfit from her paralegal days: a gray and dark blue business suit. Grandma looked so good even some younger men—meaning in their sixties—gave her a second glance. A few were also married, so I gave them a "shame on you" look as I passed.

Grandma had come prepared with our case

professionally outlined and supported by all the necessary rules and regulations. If we didn't get the roads fixed tonight, we never would. We made our way into the gallery and were about to take a seat when someone tapped me on the shoulder.

"Hello again, Ms. Bloom," Steven Rivera said with a friendly smile.

As I turned I attempted to reign in my surprise as a shiver of fear raced down my spine. I prayed I'd been quick enough that he hadn't noticed.

Glancing down I saw his arm was outstretched and awaiting a handshake. It took all the bravery I had to reach out and shake it. I knew it wasn't for certain he was the killer, but would anyone really want to touch something if they thought for even a moment it had cooties? Same premise.

"Hello, Mr. Rivera," I said. "How are you doing this evening?"

"Not sure yet. We'll see after I've had my turn talking to the Council. Their asinine rules are about to drive me insane."

Grandma, who had clearly not yet connected the dots in regard to who we were speaking with, let out a light-hearted laugh and placed her hand on his foreman. "Touché to that! We're here to give them a piece of our mind as well."

"Best of luck to both of us then, I guess," Steven said, patting grandma's hand before returning his gaze to me.

"Is that detective still bothering you? I haven't heard from him for a while, so I'm hoping they're done giving me the third-degree."

I felt grandma stiffen beside me. His words must have triggered something in her brain that allowed her to finally realize just who we were speaking to.

"I'm sorry to hear they gave you such a hard time. We're all hoping they'll catch the killer soon, so we can feel safe again and Ms. Stone can rest in peace."

"Here, here," he replied.

Grandma gently grabbed me by the elbow and pulled me toward the front row of benches. "We'd best get our seats if we don't want to have to stand. I expect it's gonna be a full house tonight."

I looked around and immediately knew grandma was exaggerating a bit. There weren't *that* many people lingering about. But, I gathered she was using this as a ploy to move us away from the potential killer in front of us.

"It was good seeing you again," Steven said as we moved away. "Hopefully TAFT can get me a few new matches soon?"

"We'll do our best," I said, as I followed grandma to the front. I knew full well we wouldn't be giving him any more matches until the killer was caught. However, he didn't need to know that.

The gallery was split into two sections with space down the middle. This was done for two reasons. First, so people could more easily get in and out of the rows of bench seats and second, so if there was a meeting where two opposing sides were debating an issue, each side could sit separately from one another.

Tonight's meeting was an open agenda for any town business, including street maintenance. In the middle, slightly in front of and between the two sections sat a podium where attendees would speak.

"Why'd you let me touch a killer?" Grandma hissed before we'd even slid all the way onto our bench.

"What was I supposed to do? Slap your hand away and tell you, 'No, grandma. Don't touch the killer?'"

She let out a loud sigh, "I suppose you're right. He seemed like a pleasant enough fella. I can't believe he's a killer."

I agreed with her assessment. Steven was friendly and personable. I would've never thought there was anything evil or wrong about him if I didn't have knowledge of the current situation.

"We don't know for certain he is. He's just a suspect."

"Well, either way I plan on staying as far away from him as possible going forward," she huffed.

"Agreed," I said with a nod.

The crack of a gavel striking down brought our attention around to the front where the council members sat. The meeting had just been called to order.

As it so happened, Steven was up first. He proceeded to explain, in a very calm and friendly manner, that he was upset with a city law which forbade him from putting metal bars on his pharmacy windows. He felt it was a necessity he be allowed to have ample security to ensure no one attempted to steal any of the pharmaceuticals they stocked—especially the schedule two narcotics.

. The council quickly denied his request, saying there were other methods for him to protect his pharmacy *internally* without marring the appearance of the community externally.

I was personally thankful for their decision, as I wasn't one hundred percent certain if he wanted the bars to keep people in, or to keep people out. It was awful to assume his intentions were those of a malicious killer, but really— as Jack had pointed out numerous times—for my own safety what other choice did I have?

"Does anyone have anything they wish to say regarding street maintenance?" Dottie King, the head council member, said.

Dottie was Grandma's nemesis the way Natalie was mine. Dottie had always had a thing for my grandfather and had even pursued him after it was clear he was in love with my grandmother. From the stories I was told, Grandpa finally had to embarrass Dottie in public, denouncing any feelings for her, in order to get her to back off and leave them alone. Dottie blamed the whole thing on Grandma, and they had been sworn enemies ever since.

A few different people took their turn at the podium. All of them had the same basic complaint; their issues were not being addressed. The Council had the same answer as always, "We only have so much money in the budget and so many employees. In the future, you should approve the ballot measures to increase funding."

When the last person sat, Dottie raised the gavel, "If no one else has—"

"We have something to say," Grandma said, standing up and moving forward.

Dottie paled. I smiled—on the inside, as I followed Grandma to the podium.

"My name is Olive Bloom," Grandma said. Everyone in the room knew exactly who she was, but Grandma stood on formality when it had anything to do with the law. She wanted to make certain that the records noted she was the one speaking.

"Yes, Mrs. Bloom," Dottie replied with an eye roll. "We all know who you are."

Grandma's faced scrunched up in annoyance. She didn't like being disrespected or made fun of. *Oh, was Dottie screwed!*

"My granddaughter and I would like to discuss our requests to have road repairs done to County Road 34 and Miers Street. To date, no response has been received nor has any work been done," Grandma said.

Dottie let out a sigh. "We did receive your letters. As we've already said more than once this evening, we only have so much—"

"I have a copy of your budget right here," Grandma cut in, holding up a stack of papers. "Along with the documentation of what it has been used for so far this year. I show you still have more than two-thirds of the budget remaining."

"The remaining balance is allocated for projects."

"Not according to the public records. They say there is only one open project remaining, and all costs for that project have been paid out."

"I'm sure that's just a mistake," Dottie said, turning her gaze to Martha.

"As far as I know, Mrs. Bloom is correct. We only have one project left, and it's been paid for," Martha said.

If looks could have killed, the one Dottie shot Martha would have left her dead on the spot. The rest of the council members tried as hard as they could to hide in the shadows of their chairs and become invisible. None of them wanted anything to do with what would happen next.

Dottie cleared her throat and turned her attention back to us at the podium, a smile on her face cold enough to freeze someone to death.

"Well. It looks like *someone* will get their wish, then. Doesn't it?" Dottie said. "Thomas please go back through the records and see who submitted the first request that would be within the remaining budget."

"That would be us," Grandma said, standing taller. "I already looked at our request, submitted on January first. It is within budget, with room to spare."

Dottie's neck turned bright red as an ugly sneer slid over her face. "I would love to just take your word for it,

Olive. But I can't do that. As I said, Thomas—"

"I have all of the documents right here if you would just look at them," Grandma held out the documents with a look that dared them not to come get them.

"We can go back to the office and review our own—" Dottie started to say, but Thomas broke under the weight of that look and moved out from his desk, towards the podium. He took the documents and returned to his seat.

"You can keep those. They're just copies." Grandma smiled sweetly. A few snickers could be heard from behind us.

Dottie gave the gallery a death stare and everyone immediately went silent. Everyone remained quiet as Thomas looked over the pages and compared them to another folder he had unearthed from papers in a stack to his side. After a few moments, he flicked his gaze back and forth between us and Dottie.

"Her documents appear to be accurate," Thomas said. "The Blooms' request was the next item submitted and does fall within the remaining budget, with a bit of room to spare for any unforeseen costs."

Dottie clenched the gavel, her knuckles going white. Her gaze moved to Thomas. He nodded but didn't dare say a word. *Smart man!*

"Why don't you go ahead and double check all the paperwork tomorrow and then call us to—" I started to say.

"Why don't you worry about your business instead of

telling me how to run council business? My business doesn't have people dying," Dottie snapped.

The entire gallery, including myself, sucked in startled air. A few audible gasps filling the rest of the silence.

"You no-good whor—" Grandma started.

"Grandma. Don't!" I said with a swift yank on her arm, turning her around, and heading out of the room before she could finish the word.

Once outside I leaned against the building and took in a few shuddering breaths.

"I'm so sorry, flower," Grandma said patting my arm. "That was even beneath that old bitch."

I let out a small chuckle. "It's fine. I'm sure they are saying worse."

"How about we get out of here," Grandma said.

"Sounds good to me," I replied. "Do you really think they will fix the road?"

Grandma turned and gave me a wink. "Damn straight they will!"

Chapter Twenty-Two

During the next several days TAFT was all the buzz. News from the Council meeting had spread fast and furious through town. Lucky for me, most people in town hated Dottie, so I was winning the sympathy vote. Better they feel sorry for TAFT than be afraid of us.

"You got a minute?" came a voice and a knock on my door simultaneously.

I looked up from the papers I'd been reading. "Sure, Grandma. What's up?"

Grandma moved in and took a seat in the guest chair across from me.

"A couple of things. I just got off the phone with the City. The Council has approved the work on the roads."

"Dad must be thrilled," I said, leaning back in my chair and giving Grandma my full attention.

"I haven't told him yet," she said. "I thought I'd give you the honor. It was your idea to go to the meeting."

"Yeah, but you were the one who had all the paperwork researched and talked them into it."

"Don't be silly," Grandma waved me away. "You just let your daddy know."

I took a closer look at Grandma. She was being awfully shifty and not meeting my eyes. There was clearly something more to this. "Grandma. Tell me the truth. What's up? You normally love letting Dad know when you accomplish something he couldn't."

Grandma blushed but still didn't meet my eye.

"Well…" she began, but my intercom buzzed.

I held up a finger.

"Hold that thought. Yes, Eva."

"Callie, I have a Mr. Thompson here to—"

"Where is she?" I heard a man's voice yell into the intercom followed by heavy steps, which were headed my way.

A tall, thin man pushed my door open. Eva came rushing in behind.

"I'm sorry. He walked right past me," Eva said nervously.

"It's fine, Eva," I said quickly before turning my

attention to the man in the doorway.

"Mr. Thompson, is it? How can I help you?"

The man didn't bother to apologize, he just started yelling.

"Where on God's green Earth do you get off signing my 78-year-old mother up for a dating service? How dare you take advantage of the elderly!"

I motioned towards the empty seat next to Grandma.

"Why don't you take a seat and we can discuss this further." I waited until he sat down and calmed down a notch before I began. "Can I assume from the last name that your mother is Virginia Thompson?"

"Well, at least you have the decency to remember the name of the old lady you're scamming," Mr. Thompson scoffed.

"Hey, buddy," Grandma said. "I take offense to that. Your mother and I are the same age!"

The words that had started to come out of his mouth ceased and a blush crept across his face.

"I didn't mean to…" he stuttered. "What I meant to say was…"

When it was clear he was at a loss for the proper words, I stepped in.

"I can assure you, in no way are we taking advantage of your mother. She approached us," I said.

"That doesn't matter! It should be clear she has no business signing up for a dating service."

"And why's that?" Grandma asked.

I gave Grandma a look telling her to zip it.

"I'll have to second my grandmother's question," I said. "I'm not seeing why your mother shouldn't be able to sign up for our service. She is clearly of sound mind and body."

"Says *you!*" he snarled.

I sat back in my chair and crossed my arms. "I'd have to disagree. I would say there are probably more people who believe your mother is of sound mind than not."

It was his turn to sit back and cross his arms.

"I promise you. I went over all the paperwork with her very carefully and asked questions to ensure she knew exactly what each clause meant," I said.

"Well…" he stammered, "… she may have the sound mind to do it, but that doesn't mean she should. No seventy-something *lady* should be out on the prowl for men."

Grandma sat up straight in her chair. "Excuse me?"

He looked from Grandma to me and back again, immediately realizing he had once again stepped on a landmine.

"I'm sorry if you are uncomfortable with the idea of your mother dating, but that's really a discussion you should have with her, not me," I said.

"I *did* talk to her, and she refused to see reason!" He pounded his fist on the arm of the chair. "I'm here asking as a courtesy that you refund her money and tell her you cannot help her."

"And why would we do that?" I asked, now getting angry myself.

"Because if you don't I'll tell the world the story of the agency who took an elderly woman for her money."

"Nobody will believe that load of horseshit," Grandma said.

"Really?" Mr. Thompson said, looking at Grandma with contempt. "With your current situation, who do you think they'll believe?"

That stopped Grandma dead in her tracks. Her mouth opened, then closed.

"I will not be privy to threats, Mr. Thompson," I said, standing and pointing towards the door. "Get out of my office now, or I'll call the police for harassment."

He stood and stomped out of the door. "You'll regret this. I promise you!"

His heavy footsteps echoed down the hall and out the front door. I moved over to my desk, sat in my chair, and put my head down.

"Well, damn!"

Chapter Twenty-Three

We all held our breath waiting for Mr. Thompson to spill his version of the beans. None of us were quite sure what people would believe, given the recent circumstances. JJ had a statement all primed and ready for us in the event we needed it. Luckily, we hadn't needed it yet, and it had been nearly three weeks.

Gin, unaware of her son's visit, called to say she had thoroughly enjoyed herself the other evening and was looking forward to another date. The fact that surprised us was not so much that she enjoyed herself, but that the date she wanted was with Gerald. We had known better than to doubt the data.

Grandma said the dinner had gone well, and that Gin

had gotten along with both men. She also said that both she and Gin had a marvelous time getting to know each other and were planning to get together for tea sometime soon. I was glad Grandma had found a friend, but I warned her, given the situation, to do it all on the down-low for now. No need to ask for more trouble. They both promised to be as inconspicuous as possible. I knew Grandma would keep her word. The last thing she would do was hurt TAFT, much less me.

So, for now, it was business as usual. I checked the mailbox eagerly each day hoping my check was in there. My car had arrived at the dealership and the only thing they were waiting on for the deal to be finalized was me, or more precisely, my check.

The car was a beauty, almost exactly like the one I'd lost. There had actually been two differences, though; the color and the fact that the new one had cooled seats in addition to warmed, which was a bonus. It was nice to have something go better than expected for a change.

I'd determined the most annoying thing about the rental car was not the car itself, but the fact that I had to spend so much time putting gas in the damned thing. I'd forgotten what that was like since I'd gotten an electric vehicle. I salivated at the thought of getting my car and never having to pump gas again. Well, at least into a car.

Since I was having such a great day I decided to stop off and treat myself by picking up a Bronx Bomber from Heidi's Deli. This monstrosity of a sandwich had pastrami, egg salad, sprouts, mustard, and tomato on a French roll. It was uber-messy but so good. Sitting at my desk, I unrolled the gigantic sandwich. It was always a chore to not only finish the sandwich but to get my mouth around it. Opening as wide as I could, I leaned over, picked up the sandwich, and took a bite. It was at that moment that Julia rushed into my office.

"Oh. My. God," she said breathlessly as she dropped down into one of the guest chairs. "Did you hear? Wendy Krenick was found dead at the bottom of her stairs. They say someone might have pushed her."

My head whipped up and a large chunk of wet, mustard-covered egg salad fell out of the sandwich in my hand and landed onto my favorite white Marc Jacobs silk top. *Damn!*

"I'm sorry. What did you say?" I said, after quickly chewing and swallowing the bite I'd just taken.

"Wendy Krenick, *one of our clients*, was just found dead in her home," Julia repeated.

"Damn!" I grabbed my sandwich, rolled it up, and threw it in the trash. *There goes my appetite.* I picked up a napkin and dabbed gently at the stain.

My intercom rang.

"Yes, Eva," I said, unable to keep the annoyance out of my voice.

"Detective Brown is here to see you."

Double damn!

***

Eva didn't bother to lead Jack back to my office; he knew his way around since he had been here so often. When he walked in his gaze went from me to Julia and back, lingering on the yellow spot on my shirt.

"So… I guess you heard about Ms. Krenick?"

"Yeah. Julia just filled me in," I said. "I need to go get some club soda. Be right back."

I got up and headed to the staff kitchen. Julia could handle Jack for a bit. In the kitchen—well really, it was better described as a "kitchenette," I went into the small refrigerator and shuffled through it for a club soda. As luck would have, there was one left.

Taking it out, I moved over to the sink and grabbed a paper towel. I twisted open the top and poured some onto my shirt. A few drops went straight through, the cold making my nipples harden. I was glad I hadn't done this in front of Jack. *Or was I?* A tiny evil voice said in the back of my mind. *Dear Lord, get a grip!*

I dabbed at my shirt with the paper towel; feeling some tension ease when the stain lightened. Hopefully, this bit of pre-treatment would allow my cleaners to get the stain all the way out at a later date. Once I was satisfied it was all done, I chugged the remaining club soda, tossed it into the recycle bin, and turned to head back to my office. As I was clearing the doorway, I saw Julia and Jack heading toward the lobby.

Turning, I followed them. I reached the lobby as the door closed behind Jack. A wave of disappointment washed over me. *Wasn't he even going to say goodbye?*

"He's leaving already? What did he want?" I asked Julia.

"To ask for us to compile records on Wendy and all of her matches."

I pinched my shirt and fluffed it up and down to try to get the spot to dry quicker. "You reminded him we needed releases?"

"Didn't have to," Julia said, raising a piece of paper in her hand. "He had a warrant this time."

"We should still give JJ a call and confirm how we should handle it."

"Agreed," Julia said as she turned towards Eva. "Can you please pull all the necessary documents for this? I'll go call JJ now and talk to him before we finalize the file."

"Sure thing," Eva replied, taking the warrant from Julia. "Do you need me to drop it by after it's ready?"

"No," Julia replied. "Detective Brown said we could just scan and email it all to him."

I proceeded to my office and read emails. A few minutes later Julia knocked on my door, walked in, and plopped down on one of the guest chairs.

"I talked to JJ. He said to follow the same procedure as before. He also recommended we make a note of any gossip our clients give us and forward it to the detective."

"Thanks for following up on that," I said.

"What a mess!" Julia said with a sigh. "I need a drink. How about we call all the girls and head to the club after work? Drinks are on me."

I thought about it, and for once, the thought of a drink to soothe my nerves sounded good to me "I'm in. What game are you in the mood for this time?"

"I'd say, 'guess the next victim,' but I think that would be in even worse taste then the last game I recommended."

"Yah think?"

Chapter Twenty-Four

Because none of us wanted to deal with the public, we ended up having drinks in Julia's office in the back of the bar. Julia had a beer, Sara an Apple Martini, Eva a red wine, Grandma a Margarita, and I splurged with a Moscato D'Asti; sweet bubbles would help take the edge off.

"I can't believe someone else was murdered," Julia said. She sat behind her desk looking all country chic in her fitted flannel shirt, jeans, and cowboy boots. She was every guy's dream with her long, flowing blonde hair, crystal-blue eyes, and long to-die-for legs—which were currently propped up on the desk, the beer balanced on the armrest of the chair.

"Not to mention the fact that it was another one of

our clients. I mean, what are the odds?" Eva said.

"It's really creeping me out," Sara said. "I wish I had my own personal 'detective' to protect me."

I rolled my eyes.

"I like to see that guy try something with me," Grandma said. "I'd wipe the floor with his ass when I'm done with him."

Grandma always got tough when she had a Margarita under her belt: liquid courage.

"I hope whoever it is stays far away from all of us and our clients. I'm not sure how we are going to overcome this most recent hiccup."

"Yeah, I agree," Eva chimed in. "I already had a few calls asking about suspending their accounts and Wendy's death isn't even officially public knowledge yet."

"The best we can do is stick with JJ's script," Julia said. "It'll blow over. Let's hope."

The door to the office opened and Tony peeked his head in. "Sorry to break up the party, ladies. George is here to collect his mother."

I smothered a laugh when I saw the look that crossed Grandma's face.

"What does that boy think he's doing. I'm the parent!" she huffed.

"Come on, Grandma. You know he's just looking out for us both," I said. "If he takes you home, it keeps me from driving out of my way."

"I know. I just don't understand why he had to come

so early. I've barely finished my first drink," Grandma said as she chugged down what was left, wiping her mouth with the back of her hand when she was done.

"Daddy's never been a night owl. Not to mention he hates driving in the dark. Give him a break."

Grandma sighed, got up, walked over and gave me a kiss.

"Good night, everyone. Be safe," Grandma said with a wave as she walked out the door to meet my dad.

"I think I'll call it a night too," Eva said, standing and smoothing her skirt. "I have a feeling tomorrow will be one heck of a day."

"You're right," Sara added, also standing. "I think I'll go too. We can walk out together."

"Later," Julia and I said in unison.

"What about you?" Julia asked. "You ready to head out?"

"Not yet. I'm gonna give it a few more minutes for this drink to settle before I drive."

Julia let out a loud belly laugh as she stood and made her way to close the door that the girls had left open. "You didn't even drink a quarter of it, lightweight."

I stuck my tongue out. "Not everyone can be an Olympic drinker like yourself."

Julia did a bow. "Don't let the jealousy get to you!"

I did another eye roll before leaning back and letting out a sigh. "But seriously, Julia. What are we going to do? This could be a business crusher."

Julia leaned back against her desk instead of sitting down. "Hey now. Knock that crap off. It might be rough for a bit, but it will get better. We have a great reputation and even if they leave for a while, they'll come back when the police close the case."

"I sure hope so."

The door to the office opened again. Tony looked in sheepishly.

"Sorry, boss," he said, looking at Julia. "Need you out here. Mr. Fuller is putting up a stink again about his tab. I know you have it memorized."

Julia shook her head in agitation.

"I'd like to knock that man over the head," she said, standing and moving towards the door. "I'll be back in a jiffy."

"Don't worry about it. I'm good," I replied.

Julia followed Tony out the door.

***

A "jiffy" turned out to mean something other than what I expected. It had been over twenty minutes and Julia had not returned. I decided I was fine to drive now, so I would just go see if Tony could walk me out. I was careful to make sure I shut the office door behind me as I exited the room.

The bar was packed wall-to-wall, and the volume was maxed out. Between the music and the conversations, I didn't know how anyone could hear a thing. I looked around the bar searching for either Julia or Tony. I found Julia first. She was still in what appeared to be a heated discussion with Mr. Fuller. He had always been a pain in the ass. I never understood why Julia continued to let him come in her bar to drink. I'm guessing it had to do with the fact that even though Julia was the manager, Mr. Fuller had a longtime friendship with the owner. Owner trumps manager.

Knowing I wasn't about to interrupt that discussion, I looked for Tony. I found him in the far corner. I headed in his direction. When I was about halfway to him, a little brawl broke out between two patrons. Tony stepped in to handle the situation. I knew it would be a few minutes. I also knew I really had to pee. From here I could see the line to the ladies' room was super-long. That meant it would take me longer in line than it would take to drive home. Oh well, I could just walk to my car alone. It really wasn't that far, or that late.

I swung my jacket on and headed outside. A rush of cold, crisp air greeted me. I stopped for a moment and took a deep inhale to clean my lungs of all the stale bar air. Turning I walked towards my car, passing a couple laughing and kissing up against a car parked at the curb. I smiled at the young lovers.

As I moved away towards the parking lot, I heard the club door open and close and a deep voice yell something incoherent into the night air. I ignored it, assuming whatever was said had been directed at the couple making out.

When my exhale of breath produced a swirl of steam to indicate just how oddly chilly this spring evening was, I worked my zipper upward, to seal in my body heat. As I passed under the broken-out street lamp on the corner, I noticed simultaneously that it was both very dark out here with the light out, and that there was the sound of heavy footsteps following behind me. I gave a tentative glance over my shoulder and saw a large figure coming my way.

I looked forward and hurried my pace up just a tad. When the larger, heavier footsteps closed in, I moved even faster, my heart rate increasing with the speed of my feet. Turning right, I headed into the parking lot. I didn't see my car right away. I'd sworn I'd parked closer to the door. Maybe that was the other day?

I heard the footsteps turn up the aisle I'd just gone down. Whoever it was, was clearly following me. Panic bubbled in my chest. At long last, I spotted my car at the very end of the row, in the back of the lot. I almost ran to my car, letting out a small cry of relief when I touched the cool metal with my hands. I dug my hand into my pocket to get my keys. They were gone.

Frantically, I checked my other pocket. Nothing. The footsteps behind me were getting closer and closer. *Shit!* Where were my keys? A large, cold hand grabbed my shoulder and spun me around. I yanked away and let out a scream. The man jumped back.

"Fuck, lady. Calm down!" he said. "I was just trying to give you your keys. You dropped them. I tried to yell at you?"

I looked at him, blinking. My mind too frozen with fear to comprehend the words he had said.

"What?" I asked.

"I said, I have your keys." He reached out his hand and dangled my keys in the air.

I reached up slowly and took them as my mind registered what had transpired. "I'm sorry. I didn't realize you were yelling at me. Thank you."

"Sure. Whatever," he said with agitation. He turned and stalked off towards the other side of the parking lot.

I quickly unlocked my car, scrambled inside, and locked the doors. It wasn't until I heard the reassuring click of the locks that I let out a breath. In that moment I realized what a stupid mistake I could have just made. There was a killer out there. I needed to take that more seriously.

Turning the ignition, I idled in the parking spot until my nerves calmed. I backed out of the parking spot and headed home. Shivers of what could have been were running down my body all the way home. How I managed to make it there and to the bathroom without an accident was beyond me.

Chapter Twenty-Five

Eva was wrong about the next day being "one heck of a day." It ended up being so much worse than that. From the moment we opened the office until the closed sign went up, we were bombarded by both phone and in-person visits: clients, media, attorneys, and those just looking for gossip arrived at our doorstep.

We did the best we could to follow JJ's script. While the majority of the clients who called or showed up ended up suspending, or straight-out canceling their accounts, most did so with a sympathetic word or smile. We were confident that once the murder cases were solved, they would come back to us. There were a select few who we knew were just taking advantage of the opportunity to cancel the account without penalty. To be honest, we weren't all that upset to see those people go.

The only good thing about the day was that it was a Friday, which meant we had two days of reprieve coming. Julia and Sara had already left for the day. I walked over to Eva's desk as she was getting ready to close up shop and head home.

"Here," I said, handing her an envelope.

"What's this?" she asked, taking it from me and flipping it back and forth. "Do you need me to get this ready to mail or something?"

"No. That's for you. It's our way of saying thank you for all your hard work lately, including handling today's fiasco so professionally."

Eva turned the envelope over, opened the flap, and pulled out the paper within.

"Oh my gosh, a spa gift certificate. Thanks so much!" she exclaimed, her eye did a weird little twitch when she answered. I didn't know what the twitch was about, so I just waved it off as just a facial spasm.

"It's our pleasure. The spa is open all day tomorrow, and we went ahead and booked you in starting at nine am. You'll get a full day of pampering including a pedi/mani, facial, and a massage."

"That sounds wonderful."

"If tomorrow doesn't work for you, just call and reschedule. They have been warned that's a possibility."

"No. Tomorrow is perfect. Just what the doctor

ordered," she said, moving out from behind the desk and giving me a hug.

"Glad you like it. You earned it. Now get out of here. I can finish closing up."

Eva didn't hesitate or waste any time grabbing her purse and heading for the door.

"Have a good weekend," she called as she let the door close behind her.

I moved over to the front door, flipped the sign to Closed, and locked the door, then headed to my office and grabbed my own purse. After getting my keys in my hand—didn't want another repeat of the night before—I headed out the back door to my car, making sure to lock it behind me.

Grandma had called earlier on the phone and invited me over for dinner. I was happy to accept not only because I could use some home-cooked food, but also because I felt like I needed the company, too nervous to spend the evening alone.

I was halfway down Miers Street before it occurred to me that both County Road 34 and this street had been repaired. *Well, I'll be damned!* I bet Dad was thrilled. That reminded me… I never figured out why Grandma hadn't wanted to be the one to tell Dad she had accomplished the feat.

As I pulled into the drive, I saw Grandma on the front porch. She wasn't alone. Standing next to her was none other than John Snow. It was the same John that Virginia and Grandma had gone on a double date with. Because Grandma wasn't a paid employee of TAFT she wasn't really crossing any lines by dating a client, it just wasn't something we liked her to do too often. It might send the wrong message to our clients.

I watched as the two snuggled up to each other. A light bulb went on. I bet *that* was why she was avoiding Dad. They must've been fighting over her new beau and she hadn't wanted to rub in the fact that she'd gotten the roads fixed. I pulled into the drive and parked behind a... motorcycle. The "calm" dinner I had envisioned just got flushed down the toilet. Well, at least it would be memorable.

***

Grandma had gone all out for this meal. Whether or not that was for me, or John, I didn't know. Didn't know, didn't care. We had prime rib with au jus, fresh ground horseradish, homemade rolls, mashed potatoes, sour cucumbers, and green beans. To top it all off, I saw a strawberry cheesecake in the fridge when I got a glass of iced tea to have with dinner.

Dad did not make eye contact with anyone, head down, stabbing and cutting at his meat as if he were imagining John's body. We could cut both the silence and the tension with a knife. I dared not bring up the topic of the roads, work, or the murders. The last thing I needed was to end up taking Dad to the ER for a heart attack. So, I filled up my plate and concentrated on enjoying the food.

"This is wonderful," John said, breaking the silence.

I looked up at Grandma, who blushed, Dad gave John a cross look and grunted.

"Yeah, Grandma. It's great."

"Thanks, honey," Grandma said. "With the day you had, I was sure you would like a nice home-cooked meal."

Dad stopped cutting, put his balled fists down on the table—utensils still grasped like deadly weapons in each hand—and looked up at me.

"Everything okay, Callie?" Dad asked.

I wanted to give Grandma a kick under the table, or a choice look thanking her for the can of worms she just opened, but I didn't. She probably didn't even realize what she had just done.

"Nothing I can't handle," I said, trying to avoid details.

"What exactly made your day bad?" he persisted.

I sighed, put my fork down, and prepared for the onslaught of questions to follow.

"We had a lot of clients calling to suspend their accounts," I replied.

Dad's eyebrows rose as he set down his utensils. "Why would they want to do that?"

"Because of the second murder," John said between bites of the food he was shoveling in his mouth at a rapid pace. "All the ladies are scared silly."

John jumped a bit and I knew, because I felt the breeze under the table, that Grandma had just kicked him. Let's just say I was glad I'd put my fork down and was on the other side of the table, or he would have gotten much more for his *help* answering Dad's question.

"Why would the murders have anything to do with your business or clients?" Dad's neck slowly reddened.

"She was a client of ours."

"You mean they *both* were clients of yours?" Dad asked, his red neck going pale.

"Yes, Dad. But it's nothing to worry about. The police will figure it out soon and it will all blow over."

He took in a deep inhale. "It better. And nothing had better happen to you, or I'll visit that detective and give him more than just a piece of my mind. He promised to keep you safe."

"I'm safe," I said, reaching over and taking Dad's hand in mine. "Promise."

"Don't you worry, Georgie Boy. I'll take special care of your ladies. It will be easy now that Olive and I are spending so much time together."

I saw Dad eyeballing the steak knife so I "accidentally" knocked it to the ground.

"Oops! Sorry, Dad. Let me get you another."

I stood, picked the knife up off of the floor, and took my sweet time getting to the knife drawer. I opened it and then closed it without getting a knife.

"Grandma, do we have any more knives clean?"

"Well, I swear there were more in—" Grandma made eye contact with me and immediately stopped her sentence. "Sorry, flower. If there aren't any in the drawer they're all dirty. Your father already cut up all of his meat, so he should be okay with a fork."

Dad flicked a look between the two of us, huffed, grabbed for his fork, and stuffed a huge chunk of steak in his mouth.

I tossed the dirty knife in the sink before sitting back down. We ate the rest of the meal in silence. Dad stalked out of the room as soon as his plate was empty. That was a bad sign. A *very* bad sign. Dad never left without at least attempting to get some dessert. Oh, well. It was probably for the best he went to get some air.

"So, Grandma. What are your plans for the weekend?" I asked, as I also finished off the items on my plate. I would have picked it up and licked it clean, but I decided to save that trick for the cheesecake. It wasn't ladylike to lick more than one plate per meal.

"John here is going to take me for a ride on his new motorcycle. Did you see it when you pulled in?"

"Yeah, I saw it all right," I said, leaning back in my chair.

"Isn't it a beauty," John chimed in. "It's a Harley-Davidson."

"Have you ever driven a motorcycle before?" I asked.

"This is my first one. I've wanted one my whole life, but never had enough savings until recently."

"Grandma, are you sure it's a good idea to ride around with a newbie driver?"

"Oh, don't worry. John took all of the safety courses. Didn't you, John?" Grandma said, patting John on the arm.

"You betcha. I wouldn't risk this pretty lass's safety."

"Hey, Grandma. Would you mind if I have dessert now? I want to get home before it gets dark."

"Sure thing. Let me go get you some."

"Two slices to go too," I hollered after her.

As soon as she cleared the doorway, I leaned forward and looked at John.

"Here's the thing, John. You'd better be damned careful driving my grandma around on that death trap. Because I promise you, if she gets hurt, it won't be my father you need to worry about. Do you get my drift?"

John paled several shades, which was quite a trick since he was very pasty already. He didn't answer, he just nodded.

"Three slices of cheesecake, all ready to go," Grandma said, coming out of the kitchen with a plate in one hand and a Tupperware container in the other. She laid both items down in front of me. She glanced at John.

"Are you all right, sweetie? You look like you've seen a ghost."

He turned his gaze to her. "I'm fine, Olive. Do I get some dessert?"

"Of course. You and George can have some later."

John pouted a little but let it slide.

I quickly scarfed down the dessert, and yes, licked the plate clean. After helping Grandma clean up the food and dishes, I used the restroom, grabbed my Tupperware, said goodbye to Grandma and John, then went out in search of Dad.

I found him in his workroom. He was pounding a nail into a new dresser he was making for Grandma. Making furniture had been his hobby as long as I could remember. You'd have thought he would have been over handling wood after dealing with it all day at work. However, he said that was how he found his best pieces. They were usually the ones rejected by the builder due to defects. Those defects were what made Dad's creations beautiful.

"I think that nail is in as far as it's gonna go," I said, trying to hold back a smile.

Dad looked at me then looked at the nail. He shrugged and put the hammer down. "You're probably right."

"You know she'll get tired of John. Right?" I asked, coming up to stand behind him and give him a backward hug.

He leaned back into me.

"I know, but I just can't stop worrying," he said. "And now I have to worry about you too."

I moved back and looked him straight in the eyes. "I'm fine. You don't need to worry about me. Jack—I mean Detective Brown—is making sure I'm safe."

Dad smiled at my faux pas but let it go. He leaned forward and gave me a kiss on the forehead.

"I don't know what I would do without you." As he pulled back, his gaze landed on the Tupperware of cheesecake in my hand. His eyes lit up. "Is that for me?"

I hadn't really planned on it being for him, but I just couldn't take away his joy. Especially knowing he still had to deal with John later when Grandma gave them their dessert.

I nodded and handed it to him. He greedily grabbed it and popped it open. Without putting it down he reached behind him, opened a drawer, and pulled out a plastic fork. The man was always prepared. I left him to devour his sugar in private and headed home.

Chapter Twenty-Six

The door chime went off when I entered Runs with Scissors on Monday morning. Sara had been on me for a few weeks to get a trim and to freshen up my color. In the last couple of years, I'd sprouted a few gray hairs at my temples, but not enough to warrant a full-blown color routine. Instead, Sara used her skill to cover and blend in the gray by weaving in low lights. We had tried highlights first, but the lighter color had washed my pale skin tone even more: not an attractive look.

"Hey, you," Sara called from her station at the back. She was removing the cape from the client in the chair. "Let me sweep this up and I'll be right with you."

"No rush."

I walked over to the waiting room chairs and plopped down, leaned forward, and thumbed through the stack of magazines on the table. Nothing caught my attention, so I sat back and instead watched Sara. Like a robot who had done it a million times before, she grabbed the broom and swept up all the recently cut hair. I watched as her client moved to the front desk to be checked out by the receptionist.

My gaze went back to Sara. I was always amazed at how such a large personality and free spirit could reside in such a tiny person. She was barely five feet tall and had a slender frame that was reminiscent of a ballerina. The only exterior hint that gave away the wild girl on the inside was her hair color. Today, she was cotton candy-pink.

"Come on over," she said, motioning me towards the chair.

When I was finally settled in the chair, Sara tossed a chemical cape around my shoulders.

"I'm gonna whip up your color. Be back in a jiffy," Sara said as she moved towards the back.

Hair color was always put on dry hair so, no need to shampoo first. I nodded, closed my eyes, and enjoyed the moment of silence with no other clients around. I opened my eyes when I heard Sara wheeling her color tray into the room. She rolled it to a stop beside me.

"I'm changing you up a little today; more chocolate, less red," Sara said as she picked up a comb and sectioned off my hair.

"Good. I wasn't all that fond of the color last time. It was great in the beginning, but it turned brassy too quick."

"Yeah, that's what I found too," she said as she twisted and pinned a section up. "You sure you don't want to change up your cut?"

This was a question she asked *every* time I was in. She said my "just below shoulder length" hair was boring. I liked it. I could wear it up, down, or in a braid. Granted, most times it was in a French twist at work, and a ponytail at home.

"Nope. Still can't talk me into it." I chuckled.

Sara shrugged and continued on with her sectioning. When she was all finished, she added the lowlights, alternating colors on each layer of hair. Sara had a very steady rhythm and a light touch. It didn't take long before my eyes were closed and I was lulled into a calming trance. After roughly thirty minutes she was done applying the color. Moving around me she set a digital timer for forty-five minutes before rolling the cart away to clean it up and shed the smock.

A couple of minutes later she poked her head out of the back.

"I'm going to grab a quick bite of breakfast. I ran late this morning and didn't get to eat," she said. "Do you want anything?"

"No. I'm good."

I knew Sara would be back right on time to wash out my color, she had an internal clock that never failed. I also knew that if she didn't eat, she would get very cranky. Because I had another hour before I was done and gone, it was best to feed the beast.

***

As expected, Sara was back with five minutes to spare. After confirming my color met her expectations, we went over to the sink to wash it out.

"I had the funniest thing happen yesterday," Sara said, as she massaged the conditioner into my hair."

"Yeah, what's that?"

"Mrs. Hammond came in with her ninety-year-old mother, Orpah, to treat her to a color rinse and blow-out."

"And that's funny?" I asked, not understanding the humor.

"No. Not that, silly. It's what happened when I took her to the shampoo chair to rinse out the color," she said, her fingers making firm swirling motions on my scalp that made me want to purr with pleasure.

"I told her that she'd have to let me know if the water temperature was uncomfortable because I couldn't feel it through the rubber gloves I had on. Do you know what she said?"

"Haven't a clue."

"She said okay. Then, out of nowhere she said—at full volume I might add, 'don't you feel so bad for the fellas having to wear those rubber thingies on their wieners. I bet they can't feel anything either.'"

I burst out laughing, "Are you serious? She sounds just like Grandma Olive."

"Yeah, but I expect it from Olive. Orpah was as quiet as a church mouse before the shampoo bowl. Come to think of it, she didn't say anything at all after we got back to the chair either. You should've seen the look on her daughter's face. I swear, I almost peed myself I laughed so hard."

"That's too funny. You gotta love old people!"

By the time Sara finished her story I was cleaned, conditioned, and rinsed out. We made our way back to the chair, changed into a haircutting cape, and she did my normal quick trim and blow dry. As she switched off the dryer and turned on the flat iron, the chime for the front door went off. I glanced at the door and noticed that not one, but two women entered.

I groaned inwardly as Brenda and Donna made their way in. The two women were both queens of gossip and pampering. Because of this, I knew the rest of my time in the salon would not be quiet. The number of cuts, colors, blowouts, and up-dos those two had done regularly would keep RWS in the business for years to come.

They were such regulars they didn't even check in at the front desk. Instead, they headed back to their respective salon chairs. I heard the back door open and close, giving off its own special chime. Two stylists appeared from the hallway and headed towards the stations where the women had just seated themselves.

As the two women were caped and washed—apparently today was only a cut, no color—Sara sectioned my hair and started the process of flat ironing it. My hair always had a slight wave that had to be erased when I blow dried it straight. If I added product when it was still wet, I could get the wave to set and look nice and bouncy. However, Sara always did the blow out after a color so she could go through my hair and ensure everything turned out the way she wanted.

She dropped one of the two final top sections and straightened it as Donna, Brenda, and their stylists returned to their stations. It didn't take more than a minute for the gossip to begin.

"Did you hear about Wendy?" Brenda said, her voice loud enough to carry across the room to where Donna sat.

Sara and I immediately made eye contact in the mirror at the statement. Not the topic we preferred to hear discussed. Sara picked up the pace, wanting to get us out of the room as soon as possible.

"I did. Isn't that just awful? Tina said Barb told her Wendy's maid told her, she found her at the bottom of the entry staircase; her head burst open like a watermelon from hitting the stairs."

"Really? I didn't think Wendy ever used the front stairs since she had the elevator put in for her Yorkie."

"That's what I thought too. I mean, who puts in an elevator for a dog?" Donna scoffed.

"I'm just shocked they were able to teach the dog how to use it. Yorkies aren't the most intelligent breed," Brenda added.

I started to let out a sigh of relief at the direction the conversation was taking.

"True, but anyway..." Donna began again, "... I heard her fall down the stairs wasn't an accident. Joy, who works in records at the police station, said the ME's notes indicate the fall was a result of a push, not a stumble. And, the detective noted that she had Valium in her system."

I sucked the sigh back in. Jack would *not* be happy someone was leaking information. At least none of it tied TAFT to the murder.

"Oh, my. Who would do such a thing?" Brenda exclaimed. "To think we aren't even safe in our own homes!"

Sara was almost done with my hair, one top section to go. She dropped it and hurriedly worked.

"The scariest thing is Karen, a tech at the pharmacy, told me when I told her about the report, that she didn't have a prescription for Valium. *But...*" Donna added with emphasis, "...both Jasmine and Wendy not only used their pharmacy, they have the same dispensing pharmacist. Some guy named Steven."

I froze and the room spun. I grabbed the armrest and took several deep breaths. On the last inhale the smell of something burning grabbed my attention. I opened my eyes and looked at Sara, who was also frozen in place. Her mouth was open and the look of shock covered her features. That's when I saw it; smoke swirled up right behind my head.

"Sara!" I yelled, yanking my head forward.

She jumped back and blinking several times. In her hand was not only the flat iron she had been using but a wide, long, smoking section of my hair.

"Shit!" She jumped back, dropping the flat iron.

I watched as it clattered to the ground, fell open, and my now melted remnant of hair fell out.

"Oh. My. God," she said, moving to grab the iron off the floor, unplug it, and put it in the holder. She bent down again and came up with my hair in her hand. She looked at her hand, then up at my hair.

Looking in the mirror, I saw the reflection of myself pale noticeably.

"How bad is it?" I whispered.

Sara took a step back. Donna, who was closest to me and able to see my hair, let out a gasp, "Oh, she's in trouble!"

My gaze met Sara's in the mirror.

"Callie… I'm so sorry!" Tears welled up in her eyes.

"Get me a mirror," I said quietly.

"I swear, I can fix it—"

"Just get me a mirror," I said again.

Sara moved to her drawer and handed me a mirror. Ever so slowly, she turned the chair around. I took a deep breath, raised the mirror, and saw what remained of the section of my hair. The four-inch-wide section, which had previously reached just below my shoulders, now lay at my occipital bone. Roughly half an inch of that was melted together in a clump. I blinked back tears that mirrored the ones I saw in Sara's eyes when our gazes met.

"Well," I said. "I guess that's one way to get me to try out a new hairstyle."

Chapter Twenty-Seven

Parking the car in the police station lot, I flipped down the visor and took another look at my new hairdo. I ran my hands through it and shook my head from side to side, watching as the short layers tumbled back into place. I tucked the strands around my face behind my ears.

Not what I'd planned on when I entered the salon that morning, but it would have to do. Sara had done her best to cut off as little as possible. However, even at that, my hair now sat just below my ears in the front and was layered generously in the back, from just above my occipital bone down to my neck. The feel of air on my neck made a shiver run down my spine.

All-in-all, for a short hairstyle Sara had worked wonders. I knew she felt just awful about what had happened. The good news was it had caused both Donna and Brenda to forget about the earlier topic they'd been discussing. The bad news, besides now having short hair, was both Sara and I would be the newest topic of gossip on the street. I let out another sigh and got out of my car.

I made my way to the front desk, where the same tiny blonde officer, Ashley, was on duty. She looked up and did a double take. "New haircut?"

I reached up and touched my hair, "Yeah."

"It's cute."

"Thanks. I'm still trying to get used to it," I said, dropping my hands back down. "Is Detective Brown around?"

"I assume you mean Jack," she asked, an eyebrow raised.

"Oops. Sorry. I forgot there were two 'Browns,'" I replied. "Yes, Jack."

She nodded in response, picked up the phone, dialed his number, swiveled in her chair to look towards Jack's office. After a brief moment, she had a mumbled conversation which I could not hear with whoever had answered.

"He'll be right out," she said, swiveling back around.

"Thanks."

Noise from the door behind me brought me around. An officer was hauling in a teenager who was clearly not wanting to be hauled. The officer moved the kid over to the bench and "helped" him take a seat, handcuffing him to ring installed on the bench.

"Where'd she go?"

I heard Jack say from behind me. I turned.

"She's right there," Ashley said, as she pointed a finger at me.

Jack turned his gaze to me and froze. He blinked a couple times before regaining his composure. He moved forward hand outstretched.

"Ms. Bloom. I wasn't expecting you." His gaze flicked between my hair and my eyes, "New haircut?"

"Wow. You really are a detective," I said, rolling my eyes.

A snicker from the Ashley floated forward. Jack stiffened for the briefest of moments before relaxing and smiling.

"What can I help you with?" he asked.

"I have some information for you regarding your most recent case," I said in a low voice. I doubted anyone around us either knew or cared about Wendy's case, but I preferred to not point out I was a gossip snitch.

Jack gave me a questioning gaze before he took me gently by my elbow and turned me towards the door at the desk. "Let's go to my office and you can tell me what you have."

Ashley, seeing we were coming her way, buzzed the door to let us through.

"I'll jot her name down on the log for you," she said, batting her eyes at Jack adoringly. The tiniest jolt of jealousy ran through me.

This time, there were no catcalls as I made my way to Jack's office, which was just fine by me. Another thing that was different from this visit than last time was the clutter on Jack's desk. Instead of it looking like a bomb had exploded, it was organized. A tidy stack of papers, desk necessities, and a cup of coffee were all that remained.

"What?" he said, the tips of his ears going pink. "I do know how to clean up my office."

He clearly had a complex about the situation, being that he offered up the answer to an unasked question.

"I didn't say a word," I replied.

He shook his head and took a seat. "So. What's up?"

"Well…" I hesitated as I took a seat. I really didn't want to be one of those women who passed along gossip with no concrete evidence to back it up, but…

"Spit it out. I have things to do," he barked.

I let out a huff, stood, and started towards the door, "If you're going to be like that, then—"

"Sit down. I'm sorry. I've just got a lot on my plate right now," Jack said, motioning towards the chair I'd just vacated.

I moved back and sat down.

"While I was at the salon, I heard some gossip that I thought you might want to hear." When Jack didn't immediately ask for details, I quickly rambled on. "Don't get me wrong, I don't think it's right to pass along gossip without anything to back it up, but..."

"For God's sake, woman. Spit. It. Out."

I took a deep breath, "One of the clients said someone named Joy, who supposedly works in records here at the police station, was giving out details of both the ME's and Detective's reports, which I presume to be *your* reports."

Jack leaned back in his chair and folded his arms, "Really? What did she say was in the reports?"

"Well, she said that the ME's notes indicate Wendy's fall was a result of a push, not a stumble. And, that the 'detective' said she had Valium in her system."

The look on Jack's face when I finished my sentence was not a happy one. He reached up and pinched the bridge of his nose. Which, by now, I knew meant he was trying his best to hold his temper.

He dropped his hand and met my gaze. "Is that all?"

"Yes and no," I said. "That was all she said about the reports. But, she also mentioned a Karen from her pharmacy said that Wendy was also a patient and she didn't have a prescription for Valium."

"Please tell me that's all the tech told her?"

I shook my head no. Jack let out a loud sigh.

"She also said both Jasmine and Wendy not only used their pharmacy, they had the same dispensing pharmacist. Steven."

Jack pounded his fist down on his desk hard enough to make coffee slosh over the edge of his coffee cup,

"Christ almighty. Is anything in this town not part of the gossip mill?"

Jack let out another string of expletives and he opened a drawer in his desk, grabbed out some napkins, and cleaned up the spill.

"Well, at least the good news is they don't know Steven is a pool selection member of TAFT," I said.

Jack stopped dabbing at the liquid and turned an icy stare my way. "You're kidding, right? I'm worried about sensitive details of not one, but two murder investigations coming out, and *you're* worried about if they can be traced back to your silly agency?"

I jerked back as if I'd been slapped. I stood, leaned forward, placed my hands on his desk, and locked my gaze with his.

"How dare you call my business silly! My partners and I work our asses off to try to make finding love an easier thing to do. But I guess as a man you wouldn't understand how hard that is," I said, straightening and glaring at Jack. "The only thing you men care about is getting laid."

I turned, walked towards the door, and slammed it behind me as I exited the room. I stalked out of the station and to my car, not paying any attention to the looks I received in the process, or Ashley's question asking if I was okay.

My hands shook with rage as I opened the door to the rental car. *How dare he speak to me like that!* I didn't have to come down to this crap hole and tell him any of what I just did. I was *trying* to help him solve the case. I climbed in, strapped on my seat belt, and took a few deep breaths. When I felt calm enough to see through the red, I turned the key in the ignition, backed out, and drove away.

About a mile down the road my phone vibrated. *Damn, I hate this rental!* My Tesla would have answered my phone with the push of one button. Instead, I had to pull to the side of the road and dig through my purse to grab my cell before it went to voicemail. I was tempted to let it do just that if it was Jack calling. However, the caller ID said "unidentified" so, I had no choice but to answer.

"Yes," I said, my voice anything but pleasant.

"Lily?" Dad said. "Are you all right?"

Shit!

"Yes. I'm fine, Dad," I said. "You caught me in the middle of something. Sorry for the tone of voice. What's up?"

He didn't answer right away. Instead, all I heard was a few deep inhales.

"Dad?"

"It's your grandmother," he finally said, "she's in the hospital."

"Is she okay?"

The phone beeped in my ear and went dead. I pulled it away and looked at it. The battery was dead.

"Fuck!" I screamed aloud, slamming my hands against the steering wheel. I looked around frantically for the phone charger, only to realize moments later that I'd forgotten it at the office.

Panic welled up in my stomach as different scenarios rushed through my mind as to why Grandma was in the hospital. At the first possible chance, I jerked the car back out into traffic and sped towards the emergency room.

"God, please let her be okay!" I prayed.

Chapter Twenty-Eight

It felt like an eternity before I pulled my car into a spot at the ER. I rushed in and frantically looked around for the nurse's station. Seeing it, I hurried forward. Luckily, there was no line. Actually, there was no one in the ER at all, which I found to be strange. But, I didn't have time to worry about it.

"Excuse me," I said to the young lady at the desk. "I'm looking for my Grandma. I was told she was recently admitted?"

She looked up and gave me a gentle smile. "What is her name?"

"Olive Bloom."

The nurse typed on the keys of her computer

keyboard for several moments.

"Olive Bloom, you said?" She looked closer at the screen.

"Yes, that's right."

She tapped a few more keys on the keyboard, then looked back at me. "You said she is your Grandmother?"

Seriously!

"That's correct," I said, shifting from foot to foot.

"Can I see some identification?"

I took in a deep breath and ate the words I wanted to say while I dug in my purse for my wallet. I pulled it out, flipped it open, and showed the ID to the nurse. Exactly how she would know we were related had I still had my married name, I had no idea. Luckily for me, I didn't.

She glanced at it a long moment, looking back and forth between it and me.

"Thank you. I needed to be certain you were a relative before I gave you the information."

I dumped the wallet back in my purse and grasped the counter. "What information?"

"It says here your Grandma is no longer with us."

The world spun as her words sank in and my blood pressure skyrocketed. I blinked several times before my gaze focused again on the nurse. I saw her lips moving, but I could no longer hear her over the ringing in my ears.

"What—"

The world went black.

***

I jerked upright when a noxious odor hit my nose. Someone grabbed me and gently pushed me back down.

"What the hell?" I yelled as I pushed at the hands. I blinked several times trying to bring the room, and my assailant, into focus.

"Ms. Bloom. Please calm down."

I knew that voice, it was the nurse I was talking to earlier. I stopped struggling and looked around. I was on the ground in the ER, the nurse kneeling beside me.

"What's going on?" I asked, as I slowly sat up. This time, the nurse did not stop me.

"You passed out," she replied. "I'm not exactly sure why. Were you feeling okay when you came in?"

"You're not sure why?" I yelped. "You just told me my grandmother was dead."

The nurse just stared at me, head tilted sideways as if she didn't understand the words I'd just said. When another moment passed with no response I tried again.

"You just told me and I quote, 'Your grandmother is no longer with us.'"

"Oh, geez. I didn't mean 'not with us' as in dead," she said, hand raising to her cover her heart. "I meant she's no longer in the ER. They moved her to a room."

The range of emotions that washed over me made me instantly nauseous. I must have turned green or something because the nurse rushed up and forward, grabbing and bringing a trash can to my side.

I bent over and heaved several times. Because I hadn't had the chance to have anything to eat since this morning, nothing came out but stomach acid. The nurse leaned over and rubbed my back for a few moments before getting up and disappearing. I didn't know how long she was gone as I was concentrating on trying to not dry heave, inhaling and exhaling deeply.

She returned with an ice pack wrapped in a towel and a bottle of water. She gently laid the ice pack on my neck before twisting off the top of the water bottle and handing it to me. I took it and drank a small sip, trying my best not to dislodge the ice pack from my neck.

After several long moments, and a few sips of water I felt more like myself. I sat upright and handed the ice pack back to the nurse.

"So…" I said. "My grandmother's fine, she's just been admitted and is in a room?"

"Yes," the nurse replied. "I'm so very sorry I wasn't clear. I can't even imagine how awful that moment must've been. Please accept my apologies."

I looked up at her and saw she was pale and had tears in her eyes. No use making her feel even worse. She'd only done something I could have—and probably had—done myself. It was so easy to say something in a way that could be misunderstood.

I applied my brightest smile and said, "Apology accepted. I know you didn't mean any harm. Truthfully, I can't image how hard your job must be trying to keep everything straight; not to mention having to be careful with what information you give out. I've heard HIPAA is a bitch to follow. Maybe just be a little more careful with how you phrase that sentence in the future."

The nurse's face regained its color and she blinked away the tears. A small smile returned as she bent down and helped me get to my feet.

"I'll definitely be more careful. You're right HIPAA is hard. People just want to know how their loved ones are, but I'm seriously screwed, excuse my language, if I give the wrong person any information. Again, I'm really sorry. If there's anything I can do to make it up to you, just let me know."

I patted her on the hand as I got my bearings.

"I believe you. Don't fret over it," I said. "Just tell me where to find my grandma and all is forgiven."

She raced around the counter and looked at her screen. "She's on the third floor, Room 327."

I nodded and looked around, trying to catch my bearings. "Where do I—"

"Head down the hall, take a right, follow that down to the end, and you will see elevators on the left-hand side. After you get off on the 3rd floor, you'll hang a left and head about halfway down the hall."

"Thank you!" I said as I hurried off in the direction she'd indicated.

It couldn't be good they'd admitted her, but it sure was better than her being dead. My heart raced, and I tried not to run to get to her. Waiting for the elevator was torture. For a building with only six floors, it seemed like an eternity before it let out a *DING* and opened on my floor. At least there was no one else getting on with me and pushing the second-floor button.

I pushed the button for floor three, and after what seemed like forever, the doors closed and it moved upwards. Luck was not on my side when the door stopped on the second floor. Not only was the wait for the doors to open painful, waiting for the elderly couple to enter the elevator and push the button—which turned out to be floor number five—was a lesson in patience. With each passing second, my blood pressure rose as I worried about my grandma. My stomach continued to churn.

Finally, the doors opened on the third level. I politely as possible shoved the old man out of the way so I could exit. I had only walked a few feet before I saw someone I knew standing in the hallway.

"Dad!" I rushed forward and into his now open arms.

He wrapped me in a hug.

"Hey, kiddo," he said before pushing me back and looking me over. "Something's different."

Dad was great at noticing something was different, or "off" as he would say. However, he wasn't so good identifying exactly what that was. It had frustrated my mother to no end.

"I just got a haircut is all," I said. "How's Grandma? Why are you in the hall?"

His facial features tightened at the question.

"She'll survive," he huffed. "I'm out here while they put her into traction."

"Traction?"

Two female nurses came out of Grandma's room. One stopped and nodded at Dad. "You can go in now."

We both walked into the room, I immediately went to Grandma's side. She was lying back with both legs up in the air, held by straps.

"What in the world?" I said, looking back and forth between Grandma and my father.

"Your Grandma's extracurricular activities caused her to dislocate her hips." My dad shook his head. "Because of her age, the doctor says it'll take a little more time and care to get them properly back into place."

"Extracurricular activities?" I looked at Grandma.

"Oh, for heaven's sake, George. She's not a child," Grandma said, turning her attention to me. "John and I were trying out some new positions in the bedroom and I slipped. In my defense, it was a very complicated—"

"Enough, Mom!" Dad said as he reached his hands up to cover up his ears like a child. "No one needs to hear the details."

"I see," was all I could think to say. Now I knew why my dad had paused when I asked him on the phone what had happened. He didn't want to admit aloud what had happened.

Grandma rolled her eyes at my father. "I'll be right as

rain in a few days, flower. They want to keep me in traction for a few hours to ensure what they popped back in will stay. I'll go home this afternoon and will only have to wear a brace overnight. Don't you worry about your dear ole Grandma."

I leaned over and gave her a kiss on the cheek. "I'm so glad to hear that. I wasn't sure what was wrong. With all that's been going on around here lately, all sorts of ideas have been running through my mind."

Grandma reached up and patted my hand.

"I didn't mean to worry you," she said, her gaze landed on my hair. "Sara finally talked you into a new hairdo?"

"Yeah. Something like that," I said, reaching up and once again touching my short locks.

"It looks beautiful. I bet that detective won't be able to stay away now."

"Grandma," I whined, blushing.

"Speaking of the detective," Dad interjected, "how are the cases coming?"

"I'm not really sure. I haven't heard anything new."

If it would've just been Grandma in the room, I might have spilled the beans on the gossip I'd learned. However, since Dad was here—and he had enough on his mind—I thought it best to leave it alone. No reason to give him any more to worry about.

Dad pointed a finger at me, "Well, you just stay safe. You hear me? I've got enough to worry about now with your grandma in the hospital."

"Of course, Dad," I said, walking over, stretching up, and giving him a kiss on the cheek.

The door to the room opened and one of the two nurses I'd seen earlier walked in.

"We really need to let the patient rest now," she said as she herded my father and me towards the door.

"Bye, Grandma. Love you," I called over my shoulder. "Call me if you need anything."

Grandma blew a kiss towards us as we walked out into the hall.

"You gonna be okay?" I asked my father.

"Yeah. I'm going to head home and get some rest."

"That's probably a good idea. Take advantage of Grandma being here. You know as soon as she gets back home she's going to be a pain in your ass."

Dad chuckled. "Don't I know it."

I said my goodbyes, went back to my car, and headed to work. No rest for the weary.

***

Both Eva and Julia were in the office when I arrived. Eva was on the phone and Julia appeared to be finishing up with a client. Since they were busy, I just breezed by and headed into my office, shutting the door behind me.

As was the norm, the red light was blinking on my phone. That reminded me that my cell battery was dead, so

I dug around in my desk drawer, found my charger, and plugged my phone in. Next, I listened to my voicemails and returned all the necessary calls.

By the time I finished, a dull thud had taken over my brain. I thought it best I curb the headache before it got too bad, so I stood and went into the kitchen to get Ibuprofen. I heard the front door open and close and guessed Julia's client had just left.

"I was getting worried about you," Julia said from the doorway. "Sara called to fill me in on all the drama and she said you were on your way in. When you didn't show I got worried. Did your cell die again?"

"Yeah. And I forgot my charger. I really need to get a new phone."

"So, what took you so long to get here?"

"Dad called right after I left the salon and told me Grandma was in the hospital."

Julia stood straight and her eyebrows rose. "Is she all right?"

"Yeah," I said. "She and John got a little too creative in the bedroom and she threw her hips out. They had to put her in traction."

"I sure hope I have your Grandma's stamina when I get to be her age." Julia chuckled.

"Don't we all," I replied. "So, how are things here?"

"Looks like they are finally settling down. We aren't having much luck with new sign-ups, but the calls to suspend or cancel have weaned off too."

"That's good," I said, leaning back against the counter. "Let's just hope the police solve these murders sooner rather than later."

"Yeah. It's super-scary to know that both of the victims had Mr. Rivera as their pharmacist."

"True, but I can't imagine they are really connected. I mean, one was an overdose, the other was a fall down the stairs. I think it's purely coincidence that the women both tie back to Steven. Besides, don't most serial killers do things the same each time?"

"Got me. I'm not up to date on how killers work. I just hope I never bump into whoever it is."

Eva came up behind Julia.

"Tony is here for you," she said to Julia.

"Thanks, Eva," Julia said before turning back to me. "Catch you later."

I gave a small wave goodbye then turned to Eva. "How was your spa day?"

"It was awesome," she said. "It was so nice of you all to get me that certificate."

Her eye did the same weird twitchy thing it had done when I'd given her the gift certificate. Since I knew she'd recently gone to a doctor's appointment I contemplated asking if she was having eye issues. However, after a moment I thought better of it, thinking it best she tell us if she was having medical issues versus us prying.

"Well, I'm glad you like it. Hopefully, things around here will get back to normal soon."

"At least the days aren't boring," Eva said, smiling. "Love the new hairdo, by the way."

"Thanks. It wasn't something I did on purpose, but I think it might grow on me."

Eva smiled and moved back into the hallway. "Time to get back to it."

I nodded and followed her into the hall, turning right instead of left to head back to my office. When I was finally situated I opened up my laptop and looked through my inbox. Because there were fewer new sign-ups then normal to process, the number of emails was low. It wasn't how I wanted to get a break from the long days, but I would take advantage of the lull.

Less than fifteen minutes later, I was on my last unread message. The email was from Julia. Attached was her article for the next newsletter. It wasn't actually due for a while, so I knew that meant her inbox was light as well. I kicked off my shoes, tucked my feet underneath me, pulled my laptop into my lap, and began reading.

WHAT TO EXPECT WHEN YOU ARE EXPECTING

You just did a double take, didn't you? No. I haven't jumped topics from dating to pregnancy. Wondering what to expect actually comes long before you see those two pink lines. The minute you first meet your prospective Prince (or Princess)

Charming you create a list of expectations, and so does he/she.

The problem is that nine out of ten times, both parties either forget to tell each other what's on the list, the list is misinterpreted, or for some unknown reason, one or both believe the other has ESP. As they say, "We have a failure to communicate."

So, instead of sitting at home wondering what the rules are, ask. This will tell you exactly where your expectations will get you. Do you want/expect to text each other daily, weekly, whenever the mood strikes? Are you casual or exclusive? Do you want to split the bill, or should he always pay? Figure it out now.

Getting these basic guidelines in place before you start down the yellow brick road will ensure you take the freshly paved path and not the one with all the potholes. Don't get me wrong, I'm not saying kill each other with rules upfront. Just cover the basics. This will keep you from either diving into ice cream or hitting his car with a baseball bat. And, if you can't agree on the rules, then don't go down either road. Make a U-turn and take the other road not yet traveled.

This public service announcement is provided to you by TAFT

Finished reading, I untucked my feet, leaned forward, and replied to Julia's email with a big smiley face.

Julia's choice of topic had hit home with me this time

more than normal. I was contemplating my interactions with Jack. Were we flirting with one another? I hadn't purposefully set out to kiss him, invite him over, or to flirt. It just happened. I guessed I wasn't sure what to expect at this point, or if I even had the right to expect anything. One thing I did know was in all reality we shouldn't get involved while TAFT was connected to the murders. The dilemma with that knowledge was, hadn't we already crossed that line?

Then there was today. I couldn't believe he had said what he did. All I'd been trying to do was lighten the mood. His outburst had been completely unnecessary. My business was not silly. I put blood, sweat, and tears in to getting it off the ground and building a clientele. We weren't the top agency by accident. Granted, I knew a lot of men scoffed at the idea of a matchmaking service. They just didn't get it. We weren't wired the same way.

I always remembered the first time a boy made me cry. Mom had sat me down and explained relationships. She had taken her hands and using them as puppets, pointed them both facing in towards one another. She then mimicked them talking. She said this was two women talking. Next, she took her two hands, faced them forward—so they were not looking at one another—and mimicked them talking. She said this was two men talking. Lastly, she took one hand and pointed it in, took the other and pointed it out, then mimicked talking. She said this was a man and a woman talking.

The point of the puppet show… men and women don't communicate in the same way. Men talk to each other in hopes of solving the problem. Women talk to each other in hopes of being heard without needing the problem to be resolved. So, when a woman talks to a man, the man will try to solve the problems, when all the woman wants is to be listened to. And, when a man talks to a woman, the woman only listens and doesn't try to solve anything, when all the man wants is to get help solving the problem. This leads to frustration all around.

I wasn't *really* sure how I could or would deal with my next encounter with Jack. Should I pretend like nothing happened, or should I expect an apology before I forgave him? I just didn't know. What I did know was he was overwhelmed with the investigations and hadn't meant to hurt my feelings, or at least I hoped he hadn't. Nonetheless, my feelings were raw. I guessed I would just have to wait and see.

Deciding to call it a day, I cleaned up my desk, grabbed my purse, and headed home.

***

I'd just gotten comfortable on the couch after changing into my Tinker Bell T-shirt when the doorbell rang. Getting up, I moved to the door and looked out the peephole. Jack was standing on my front porch with a grocery bag in his hand. It appeared I wouldn't have to wait too long to find out how I would handle seeing him again after all. I unlocked and opened the door.

"Hello, Jack," I said, putting my hand on my hip.

His gaze flicked from my face to my T-shirt and back up again. I knew I blushed as I recalled the last time he had seen Tinker Bell. By the look on his face, when his gaze looked back up, I knew he was having similar flashbacks. He shuffled a bit from foot to foot.

"I wasn't sure you would answer," he said.

Should I make him squirm? Sure, why not!

"Why wouldn't I answer?" I asked sweetly.

Jack unsuccessfully covered up a smirk. "You're going to make me say it, aren't you?"

"Say what?" I asked, this time batting my eyelashes.

Jack let out a loud sigh, stood up straight, and crossed his arms, the bag dangling from his left hand.

"Fine. I was a jackass. Okay," he said. "I should've never said your business was silly. It's not, and I would never have intentionally said something to hurt your feelings. I know how passionate you are about your business and how hard you all work to keep it going. Especially now."

I knew there wasn't an actual "I'm sorry" in there anywhere, but it was implied as much as a man possibly could. So, I decided to give him a break.

"Apology accepted," I said, as I leaned against the doorjamb. "I know you're overwhelmed at work, and you just reacted without thinking."

The lines of tension that had creased Jack's face faded away, replaced by a look of surprise.

"You do?"

"Sure. We all say things from time to time we don't think through, and I know you wouldn't deliberately hurt me," I said. "If that were the case, you've had several opportunities already where you could have done it."

"Well, that was easier than I thought. I guess you don't need this," he said, lifting the grocery bag.

I leaned forward and peered down into it. Ice cream and chocolate sauce. I licked my lips.

"Since you already brought it all this way, it would be a shame for it to melt," I said.

When he didn't answer, I looked at him and realized he was staring at my mouth. When I reached forward and took the bag from his hand, his attention snapped back to my eyes. The tips of his ears turned pink. This time it was my turn to hide a smirk.

"You want to come in and have some with me?" I dangled the bag from my hand.

Jack cleared his throat. "I'd like to, but I think it's best I don't. With the open cases, it could complicate things. Probably for the best if we avoid that."

Disappointment raced through me, the smirk vanishing. "I get it. We don't want there to be anything that keeps the psycho who is murdering women to get away with it."

Jack again looked relieved.

"I'm glad you understand," he said as he turned to head back down the driveway.

"Don't worry, I'll just write you up another rain check for the chocolate sauce," I said, unable to help myself.

"I look forward to cashing them in," Jack replied with a chuckle as he headed towards his car.

Chapter Twenty-Nine

I woke with a start when the telephone beside my bed rang. I peered at the clock on my nightstand as I reached for it; 1:45 am, it read.

"Hello?" I croaked.

"I'm sorry to bother you so early, Callie," Tony's smooth baritone floated over the line. "I can't get a hold of Julia and I'm getting worried."

I wiggled myself more upright in bed, leaning against the headboard.

"Was she supposed to come into work?" I rubbed my eyes, my mind too fuzzy to remember my schedule, let alone Julia's.

"Yeah. She called and said she was running late, but

that was over two hours ago," Tony said, the worry clear in his voice. "I've tried calling her over and over again, but it goes straight to voicemail."

The bottom sank out of my stomach. Julia *always* answered her phone, and she was the most reliable person I knew of when it came to keeping her phone charged.

"The only way it would go straight to voicemail is if it's either dead or off."

Little Big Town's *"Girl Crush"* floated in over the noise of the bar. The crackle that followed led me to believe Tony might be trying to cover the mouthpiece with his hand, and he had just shifted its position.

"I would go out and try to find her, but I can't leave the bar. It's ladies' night, so it's packed," Tony said.

"Don't worry about it. I'll see what I can do to find her and if I can't, I'll call the detective I know," I said. "If she calls you or shows up, make sure to let me know."

"Will do," Tony said.

"It'll be okay, Tony. I've got this," I said, in my most reassuring voice.

I hung up the phone. *I sure hoped I had this!*

***

My first call was to Julia. As Tony had said, it went straight to voicemail. I dragged myself out of bed, went to the closet, and put on the first set of clothes I could find. I debated calling Sara and decided against it. For now. I would give myself thirty minutes to find Julia and if I didn't find her by then I would call Sara and ask for help. If we still couldn't find her together, I would call Jack.

After putting on my shoes and jacket, I grabbed my cell phone—which I ensured was fully charged—and headed to the car. I dialed Julia once more; it went to voicemail again. I backed out of the garage and onto the street. While I'd gotten ready I'd worked on a game plan. I would drive to her house, to the office, and the club. I dug through my memory trying to recall if she had said anything about her evening errands or plans. She had not.

The good news was we didn't live too far apart. The bad news was all the lights were out, her car was gone, and she didn't answer the door. Not wanting to leave anything to chance, I used my spare key to enter her house. The alarm was armed, so I punched in the security code before entering further. The alarm being armed was a good sign that she had both left and that no one had come into her house.

I did a quick search of each room. The only thing of note I found was in her bedroom. In her closet, I saw the purse she normally used when working at TAFT, the one with the tracking dot on it. She must have changed into her smaller one for work at the club. *Well, crap. There goes our chance to track her with it!*

Not finding anything else, I walked downstairs and went over to her house phone. The light on her voicemail was blinking. I pressed it. Several generic messages from her family played, all from earlier in the day, or days before. The last two, however, were noted as having come in after midnight. Both were Tony.

Quickly, I left the house, setting the alarm and locking the door behind me. Next stop, the office.

It was also not far from Julia's house. I pulled into the parking lot and shut off the engine. I took a preliminary look around the lot to ensure there were no signs of Julia or anyone else for that matter. When I saw the coast was clear, I exited my car and headed for the front door.

After unlocking it, I made my way in. I searched through each room and saw no signs of anything out of the order, or of Julia. I picked up my office phone and tried her again, for the third time: straight to voicemail. In her office, I checked her phone for messages, but there were none. Unsure what to do next, I called Sara.

"Hello?" said a half-asleep Sara.

"Hey, Sara. Sorry to wake you up. But Julia is missing."

"Missing?" she replied, her voice immediately more awake.

"Yes. Tony called and said she never showed up for work."

"When did he talk to her last?" she asked.

"He said she called in before her shift to say she was running late. That was two hours ago and her cell keeps going straight to voicemail."

"That's odd. Julia never shuts off her phone, or lets it

die for that matter."

"Those were my thoughts too," I said, as I swiveled nervously back and forth in my chair. "I've checked her house and now I'm at the office. I haven't found her, or anything unusual. Do you have any other idea where she might have gone, or why she would have been running late?"

Sara's voice was slightly muffled as if she had tucked the phone in her shoulder as she spoke. There were also rustling noises indicating she was getting out of bed or moving around.

"She did say something about heading over to PhotoPro to get those mixer photos dropped off to be downloaded. I'm closer to them than you are, so let me stop by and see if I can find her. They wouldn't be open this late. She would've just used the drop box."

"Sounds good. I'm going to call Eva and fill her in and have her keep trying Julia's phone. Once I'm done with her, I'll drive from the office to the club, look around, and then drive from the club to her house. Maybe I'll see her car along the way."

"What do we do if none of us can find her?" Sara's voice trembled over the phone.

"I'll call Jack and see if he can help."

We both hung up and went about our tasks. I called Eva first and asked for help. She was going to start immediately trying to call Julia on her phone and call anywhere else she could think of where Julia could be in town. After I hung up, I called Tony and gave him an update.

As I slowly drove down the streets—taking the only route I knew Julia would take from the office to the club—I looked back and forth straining for any sight of Julia or her car. Seeing nothing, I turned into the Love Bites parking lot and drove up and down each row looking for her car.

At the end of the last row, having not found her car, I turned back onto the main street and headed back towards her house. When I reached it without finding Julia, my hope was replaced by fear. Tears filled my eyes. Unsure what to do next, I picked up my purse, pulled Jack's card out, and started to dial.

Before I could finish, my phone rang in my hands. I yelped and bobbled it in my hands before dropping it to the ground. I quickly leaned over and picked it up, pushing the answer button.

"Hello?" I said breathlessly.

"I found her!" Sara said.

"Oh, thank God!"

Relief washed over me and I choked back the tears that had now turned from sorrow to joy.

"Where is she?"

"She was locked in her car at the camera store."

Confused, I asked, "Would her car not start?"

"That's where it gets weird," Sara said. I heard someone, who sounded like Julia, choking up a lung in the background.

"Is that Julia? What's wrong with her?"

"Yeah, it's her. Let's meet at the Urgent Care clinic on Philmore Street. I think it best to get Julia seen. I'll explain everything when you get there."

"Okay," I said before hanging up.

I dialed Eva and Tony and gave each of them a quick update, letting them know where we found Julia and that we were going to Urgent Care. After everyone was filled in, I headed towards Philmore Street.

***

By the time I reached the medical center, Julia had already been taken back to be checked over. I found Sara in the waiting area, bent over, head in her hands.

"Hey!" I said, "how's Julia?"

Sara looked up and straightened. "They only seemed a little worried, so I think she'll be all right."

I walked over and took a seat beside her.

"What happened?" I asked.

"It's all so strange. Where to start…" She tapped her fingers on the armrest, "… I guess the best place is after Julia got back in the car from dropping off the memory cards in the drop box. She said she got in, turned on the car, the doors auto-locked, and a second later she heard something 'snap and clang' as if a metal cord had broken."

"While that isn't normal, it just sounds like something

broke," I said, raising my eyebrows in confusion.

"True, but that's not the weird part. The weird thing is when Julia tried to get out of the car to take a look under the hood, the doors wouldn't unlock when she pressed the button. She tried the windows and they wouldn't work. Then, when she hit the button to turn off the car, it didn't register either. She dug the key fob out of her purse, pulled out the key, inserted it manually, and turned it."

"Clearly that didn't work?"

Sara shook her head. "Nope. She said the key turned easily; too easily. There was no resistance at all. She couldn't get the engine to turn off."

"Again, sounds like a mechanical hiccup. Maybe an electrical short for the windows and locks, and the mechanism to turn the key and stop the engine broke?" I shrugged. "Why didn't she just call one of us?"

"She said she couldn't find her phone. She was sure she had it at the office but didn't remember ever taking it out."

"Okay. We all forget about what we do with our phones from time to time. Still, worst case she would just have to sit there and run out of gas."

Sara stood and paced.

"That's what she thought too, but this is where it gets scary," Sara said, stopping mid-stride and turning towards me. "She felt nauseous and light-headed and noticed an odor in the car that smelled like exhaust."

I knew I paled at the information. If all the technical

issues included the exhaust system backing up, that would have been deadly.

"She was slowly being suffocated by exhaust fumes," I said aloud, more of a comment to myself than to anyone else.

"That's what it sounds like." Sara plopped back down in her seat. "She was nearly passed out when I found her. I had to break her window with my tire iron to get her out."

"Why didn't she break a window?"

"I don't know, she wasn't thinking clearly enough to tell me every detail, and I thought it best to get her here and checked out before giving her the third degree."

"That's probably for the—"

The door to the waiting room opened and a medical assistant in purple scrubs came out, propping the door open with her foot.

"Is…" she looked down at her clipboard, "… Sara or Callie here?"

We both stood and made our way forward.

"You can both follow me back if you'd like," the MA said, motioning us through the doorway. We went past and waited for her to get in front and lead the way. Julia was in a room a few doors down.

I rushed in and gave her a gentle hug.

"Are you okay?"

Julia, who was seated on an exam table with oxygen on, looked awful. She had a strange, faint cherry red color to her skin. Julia opened her mouth to answer but was interrupted by another voice.

"She should be fine," a doctor, whose name tag read Dr. Arnold, said. "She was lucky that you got to her when you did. It probably wouldn't have been much longer before the gas became toxic and had lasting effects."

"Can she go home?" Sara asked.

"Let's give her another thirty minutes on the oxygen first, but then as long as one of you is with her for the next twenty-four hours, she can go. You'll want to check on her every hour or so and make sure she is stable," Dr. Arnold replied, as she jotted down some notes in her chart. "I'll send her home with an oxygen machine and tank. She needs to wear it for no less than twenty-four hours and can go up to forty-eight hours depending on how she feels."

Sara looked at me. "I can stay with her today, my schedule is light."

"Ok. I think due to recent events it's best if I call Detective Brown and let him know what happened. They may want to look over Julia's car."

Dr. Arnold turned towards Julia, reached into her pocket, pulled out a prescription pad, jotted something down on it, and handed it to Julia.

"Here is a script for some minor painkillers and nausea medicine. You'll probably develop a strong headache if you haven't already."

"I already have," Julia affirmed, raising her hand to her head.

"Poor baby," Sara said, moving over and giving Julia

a side squeeze hug.

"Make sure you take the pain pills only as instructed and with food. I don't think you will need the others, but I find if you are in the middle of throwing up the last thing you can, or want to do, is try to call me to give you some."

Julia gave the doctor a weak smile, "Thanks. I appreciate it."

The doctor nodded at us and left the room.

We waited the necessary thirty minutes, then helped Julia hop down from the table and to the checkout desk. After all of her paperwork was signed, and she was cleared to go, we led her outside to Sara's car. The night was giving way to dawn; a glance down at my watch showed that it was now coming up on four o'clock.

I made my way to my car and once I was locked inside, I picked up my purse and dug out both my phone and Jack's business card. Waking him up at this time of the morning wasn't something I was looking forward to, but I knew it was necessary. I dialed and waited.

"Hello," Jack said, picking up on the third ring. He sounded surprisingly alert for having been woken up at 4 am.

"Jack, it's Callie. Sorry to wake you up so early," I said.

"I wish. I haven't gotten to bed yet. I'm working a case."

"Oh. Well, sorry to tell you, but you might have another one."

"Okay…" Jack said. "Care to elaborate?"

"Julia just had a suspicious incident with her car and because of everything else that is going on, I thought I better tell you about it."

"Is she all right?"

"The doctor says yes. She'll just need a little downtime."

"That's good to hear," Jack said. "So, how about you define 'suspicious' for me?"

"She got locked in, couldn't roll down her windows, and couldn't get the car to turn off."

"You could for sure say that is odd, but sounds more like mechanical issues than suspicious," Jack said, "though that is an awful lot to go wrong in one sitting."

"That's what we thought, but I haven't even gotten to the worst part…" I took a breath and began again "… the exhaust system somehow failed and fumes filled up the car. Julia could have died from poisoning if Sara hadn't found her and broken her window to get her out."

Jack was silent for several moments. I was certain had I been able to hear the gears in his mind turning, I would have.

"You're right… this can be marked down as suspicious. Where is her car now?"

"It should still be in the PhotoPro parking lot."

I could hear Jack shuffling the phone. I assumed he was getting out his notepad and pen.

"I'm finishing up my current investigation, so I should be able to head over and take a look at her car in an hour or so," Jack said. "As soon as I give it the once over I'll have CSI take a look and haul it over to the garage."

"I'll let her know. I have a feeling she is going to be a little gun shy of riding in a car anytime in the near future. I was after my accident."

"If anything comes up, I'll call you," Jack said. The sound of a car door—I guessed his—slammed closed.

"Okay. And, Jack," I said. "Thanks."

"Sure thing, flower."

He hung up before the words sunk it. *Lucky man!* He would pay dearly for that later.

Chapter Thirty

Sunlight blinded me when I rolled over later that day. I'd called Eva and told her what had happened before I'd gone home, crawled back under my covers, and went to sleep. She said she would call if anything urgent came up at the office. Since the phone hadn't rung, I assumed all was good. I rolled onto my back, stretched, and took in a deep breath. *Hells bells.*

I tried my hardest to not let the fear tickling my brain settle in and run rampant over my thoughts. Why would anyone want to hurt people tied to TAFT? There was no logic. We might have a few people that didn't have the best experience, or like the idea of a matchmaking service, but we have never had any serious complaints lodged by anyone.

There were so many people I needed to check on this morning before going to work. With all the worry weighing my mind down, my head felt like it weighed a hundred pounds. First stop, Dad's house to check on Grandma's health and Dad's sanity.

Flipping the covers over, I rolled out of bed. After making my way to the closet, I picked out something that was more on the comfortable side than normal. I did not feel up to pantyhose and high heels today. Quickly, I dressed and made my way downstairs where I grabbed my purse and keys before heading out the door.

My first stop was Where You Bean. Today, I opted for the Big Boy Chai and a bacon, Gouda, and egg English muffin sandwich. I would need all the help I could get if I was going to survive the day. In addition to my order, I got both Dad and Grandma a breakfast sandwich and a Kitchen Sink; Dad's straight-up black while Grandma's was her normal sugar-free caramel, triple shot espresso, with fat-free milk. I did, however, opt to make Grandma's caffeine-free to help Dad out a bit. She would never know. Or, at least not until after I'd left!

Driving and eating were much easier in my Tesla. The steering was as smooth as butter and I could normally control the wheel with my knee if necessary. The rental, however, was extra finicky. Both an alignment and some power steering fluid were sorely needed. Luckily, everything made it into my mouth and not on my clothes.

I savored every sip of tea and bite of the sandwich. Best to enjoy them, as they might be all I had time to ingest today. By the time I reached Dad's, I'd finished both items and had a nice caffeine buzz going. I grabbed the bag holding the sandwiches with my teeth and balanced the drink carrier in one hand. I knew I needed one hand free to open the doors.

Dad was in the kitchen, head down on top of his arms, which were crossed and laid on the table. A *JINGLE JINGLE* sounded from upstairs as I closed the door behind me. I walked over to the counter and set down the coffees and the bag of sandwiches.

"Dear Lord, woman," Dad hollered. "Give it a rest already."

I couldn't help but laugh.

"Having fun, I see."

Dad's head snapped up in surprise, having not heard me come in the house. He did *not* look good. He was pale, had dark circles under his eyes, and looked like he'd lost several pounds; though I knew that was impossible being that it had just been one day.

"Hey, sweetie," he said, a smile lighting up his face. "I didn't hear you come in."

I walked over and gave him a big squeeze.

"How about helping your daddy out and go see what the monster wants?" he asked, looking up at me with doe eyes.

I laughed again, "That bad, huh?"

"You have no idea! The worst part is it's only the start of her bed rest," he said, letting out a long, deep sigh and slouching back in his chair.

"Don't you worry, I've got you," I said, moving over to the counter and grabbing one sandwich out of the bag and his cup of coffee. "Here is a nice sandwich and a hot cup of coffee to make you feel better."

Dad rolled his eyes at me but greedily took my gifts.

"You're an angel!"

The *JINGLE JINGLE* sounded again. Dad growled as he bit into his sandwich and followed it up with a swig of coffee. He had always had a talent for drinking large gulps of scalding liquids without effect. I once joked with him he should join a circus and take his act on the road.

I grabbed Grandma's goodies, trotted upstairs, and made my way to her room. As I turned the corner into her room, I saw her getting ready to ring the bell, yet again.

"I wouldn't do that if I were you. Dad's liable to shove that bell somewhere you don't want it to go."

Grandma grinned. "Serves him right. All those times I had to take care of him as a boy. Turnaround is fair play, you know."

"Well, just don't take it too far. He doesn't look so good, we don't need your teasing to take him over the edge. Please refrain from ringing the bell unless you really need something, got it?"

Grandma's grin faded. "Is he okay?"

"He's fine, Grandma. Over stressed is all. Just don't

push your luck," I said. "Here you go, I brought you your favorites."

I moved over to the bed and handed Grandma her sandwich and set her coffee down on the coaster situated on the nightstand.

"You're such a dear, flower."

I leaned over and gave her a quick kiss before I sat down in the chair by the bed.

"So, how are you doing? Getting better?" I asked.

"I'm feeling much better," Grandma said. "The doctor says only one more week of bed rest and then I should be good to go."

"He isn't going to have you do therapy?" I asked, cocking my head to one side.

"Oh, I already am. The therapist came to the house this morning, and he sure is a cutie," Grandma said blushing.

I'm sure Dad loved that. Seeing some young guy helping Grandma "work out" her hips. No matter how professional you were, the positions they would have to get into would have to look rather compromising.

"So, is he helping? Or, is he just helping your eyes?"

Grandma laughed. "I felt better right away; both my hips and my eyes. I even invited Gin over once to watch."

"Really?" I asked, eyebrows raised. "Why would you do that?"

"She said Gerald has some issues with his hip, so she wanted to see what positions the therapist used. Figured they might come in handy both to make him feel better and in the bedroom."

I had a momentary flashback of Gin in her lingerie, which led to a case of the heebie-jeebies. I shook off the chills and turned my attention back to Grandma.

"You didn't make the therapist uncomfortable while he was trying to do his job, did you?"

"I did no such thing! We all had a good laugh," she said, smiling as she gazed into nothing recalling the moment.

I sure hoped so. The last thing Dad needed was the therapist filing a sexual harassment lawsuit against Grandma. Normally, I wouldn't give it a second thought, but the luck we were having these days was not so great.

"How's Julia?" Grandma asked.

"I'm not sure. Her house is my next stop."

"Well, don't let me keep you. I'll be right as rain in no time. Besides, I have your daddy here to take care of me!" Grandma said, a devilish grin crossing her face.

"Grandma!"

"You know I'm just kidding."

I crossed my arms, "Sure you are."

"Now go on. Get out of here," Grandma said, waving me away.

"All right. But you take it easy," I said as I moved over and gave Grandma another quick kiss on the cheek.

I headed back downstairs to find Dad downing the last of his coffee.

"Grandma should be all settled for the time being," I said. "I told her to knock off the bell ringing unless she really needs something."

"I know she's just bored and is jerking my chain. I'd probably do the same thing to her if I was cooped up in bed."

"Well, just remember that the next time you want to do something ungentlemanly with the bell when she rings it," I said, leaning down and giving him a hug. "I've got to go see my next patient, Julia."

"Has the detective looked over her car yet?" Dad asked.

"I don't know. Calling him or going to the station—I haven't decided yet—is going to be my last task before going to the office."

"Just be safe, no matter what you do."

"Always am," I said as I headed out the door to my next stop.

***

I decided that Julia might like some answers about her car, so stopping to talk to Jack would get me the info to share with her. This time, I texted him before going to the police station to make sure he was there. Turned out to be a good thing because he was not. He told me to meet him at the police impound lot where he was taking one last look at the car.

The impound yard was in the middle of nowhere and took up several blocks, all surrounded by metal fencing topped with razor wire. I couldn't tell if it was electrified, and I had no urge to find out. The parking spots around the lot were limited, and all required parallel parking.

My first pass I didn't find any open spaces, so I swung around the block to try again. Luckily, when I was within a few cars from the entrance a large, black SUV was leaving from a meter on the other side of the road. I quickly whipped the rental car around in the street—not caring that I was making an illegal U-turn right in front of a police impound lot—and positioned myself to park in the vacated spot. It took me two tries to parallel park as I wasn't used to parking this car; the lack of power steering worked against me. When I was finally situated, I got out, locked up, and quickly jogged across the street. Jack was standing outside waiting for me. As I neared, he shook his head.

"You do realize you just broke at least three traffic laws?"

"Three?" I smiled sweetly, "I only know of two."

"Oh, really?" Jack laughed. "Which two would those be."

"I'm guessing an illegal U-turn and jaywalking?"

"Touché," he said. "You got two out of two, but you forgot to pay the meter."

"Ah, crap," I said. I'd forgotten to look to see if the previous motorist had any time left on the meter. "Be right back."

I jogged back across the road, dug two quarters out of my pocket, and placed them in the meter before running back across to Jack.

"Are you trying for a record?" Jack asked. "You're up to five now."

"Nope. Those don't count. You can only charge me for jaywalking once per ticket and I won't get a parking ticket now that the meter monster has been fed." I stuck my tongue out.

"You think?" Jack laughed and shook his head as he motioned me to follow. We made our way to the guard shack just inside the fence.

After logging in with the guard, we headed to Julia's car.

"So, did they find anything out of the ordinary?" I asked.

I was glad I'd worn tennis shoes as we were currently walking over ground scattered with broken car debris. It would've been super-easy to have something slip into an open-toed shoe.

The lot was nothing but dirt, junk, and cars, most covered with dust indicating that they had been there a long time. I'd heard a lot of people never got their car back because of how expensive it was to get it out of impound. Based on the volume of old vehicles here, I guessed that rumor to be true.

"Not really. The only thing they found to be inoperable was the manual key turn for the key. Otherwise, it looks like it was just an electrical anomaly. All of the wires, fuses, and such were in working order."

We stopped in front of Julia's car. The driver's side window was covered with plastic held on by duct tape. I moved forward and peered into the back-passenger's door. A layer of fingerprint dust was sprinkled around the interior.

"Did they find any unusual prints?" I asked.

"There were only two names that I was unfamiliar with. I'm going to touch base with Julia to see if she knows who they are."

"I'm actually heading over to see her after I leave here. I can take the list with me and text you her answer if that would help you out?"

Jack reached into his pocket and pulled out his notebook and pen.

"That would be great. One less stop," he replied as he jotted down the names onto the paper.

Once he was done, he ripped out the paper and handed it to me. I folded it and slid it into my pants pocket for safe-keeping.

"What about the exhaust? Did they figure out why it was backed up?"

"They didn't find any obstructions beyond a bit of normal build-up, but they noted there was a fresh set of scratch marks inside the tailpipe as if something had recently been removed," Jack said, putting away his pen and paper. "There was no residue or material found, though."

"Well, that's odd."

"Yes, it is. While we can't definitively say this was no accident, I'll classify it as suspicious," Jack said.

I let out a sigh and shook my head. "All of this has me walking on eggshells."

Jack reached over and put his hand on my chin, raising my face to look at him. "I know. I promise I'm doing everything I can to find whoever is doing this."

I moved in closer, trapped by his gaze and wanting very much to be wrapped in his comforting arms. As if on cue, Jack's cell phone rang.

"Sorry," he said with a tight smile and a sigh as he grabbed his phone and answered it.

"Detective Brown," he said, as he turned and took a step away from me.

"… The list of names should be confirmed within the next few hours." Jack turned his gaze to me and raised his eyebrows.

I nodded yes, his expression indicating the unspoken question being asked of me.

"… Yes. We'll release the car back to the owner, but with the recommendation she either gets it fully checked out by a mechanic or get a new vehicle."

"… No. We didn't find anything that would tie this to the murders."

Jack rolled his eyes as he raised his hand to pinch the bridge of his nose.

"… I understand. We're doing everything we can to find the perpetrator. As soon as we know more, I'll let you know."

Jack hung up the phone and stepped back towards me.

"I swear! As if my sergeant breathing down my neck isn't enough, now I have to deal with the mayor," Jack said, shaking his head. "They act like I'm just sitting around twiddling my thumbs."

I reached out and touched his arm. "I highly doubt that's the case. Your sergeant knows you're good at your job and the mayor is just covering his own ass."

Jack smiled, lifted my hand, and kissed it.

"Hey, Detective," came the voice of the guard from a dozen or so feet away.

Jack turned, "Yeah. What's up, Phil?"

"I'm getting ready to head out for my lunch break. You two almost done looking at the car? I can't lock up and leave until the yard is empty."

"We're done," Jack said. "We'll head out now."

Not needing any more detail, I followed Jack as he walked towards the exit. He walked me to my car and after I unlocked it, opened the door to let me in.

"When do you get your new car?" Jack asked.

"I'm hoping within the next week or two. I'm still waiting on the check from the insurance company."

Jack leaned in close and in a soft voice said, "Just think how much more you will appreciate it after having to wait all this time for it."

My heart skipped a beat and heat ran from my head to my toes. I looked up, meeting his gaze.

"Oh, I most definitely will. I can't wait to run my fingers over every inch… of the leather," I smiled sweetly and moved into the car, shutting the door behind me.

The smile spread across Jack's face said it all.

Chapter Thirty-One

On the way to Julia's house, I pondered my relationship with Jack. Was I really ready to get involved with him once the murder cases were closed? I wasn't sure. Mike had been my first and only relationship to date. Risking my heart again was not something I would do lightly. Besides the fact, I didn't know how Jack would react when he realized just how inexperienced this "master matchmaker" was in both relationships and in the bedroom. While I was great at flirting and kissing, I wasn't so sure how good I was at the rest. Mike hadn't ever complained, but he hadn't given me a standing ovation either.

By the time I pulled into Julia's drive I'd given up the

debate. If it was meant to be, it would just happen naturally. Worrying about it wouldn't do me or my blood pressure any good. I got out of my car, locked the doors, and headed to the front door. Sara answered after the first ring.

"How's the patient?" I asked as I made my way in and towards the kitchen where I sat down my purse.

Julia's house was neat and tidy as always. While the outside looked like the house was the size of a shoebox, the inside was laid out in a way that made it spacious. The first level had a living room, kitchen, breakfast nook, and powder room. All of which were painted eggshell white. Julia preferred to use artwork, décor pieces, and plants to add color to the rooms instead of painting the walls. Downstairs had pops of purple and green.

"She still has a nasty headache and is annoyed with the oxygen machine, but otherwise she's doing good," Sara said, as she pulled out a chair and took a seat.

"Glad to hear some good news," I said, also taking a seat.

"Did you talk to the detective?"

"Yeah. I met him at the impound lot and looked at Julia's car," I said, as I leaned to the side and pulled out the slip of paper Jack had given me.

"What's that?" Sara asked, motioning to the paper.

"It's the list of names that came back associated with the fingerprints pulled from the inside of the car," I said, as I slid the paper across the table.

Sara picked it up and looked at it, her gaze scanning

the list of names. "Seems to be a list of everyone Julia knows."

My eyebrows rose. "You know all the names?"

"Sure," Sara said, setting the paper down and turning it so I could see it. "This first one is Julia's Yoga instructor. She gives him rides to the bus station sometimes. The second one is her brother."

I gazed down at the paper and the light bulb went on. Of course, it was her brother. I'd totally spaced on his name. He was actually a *stepbrother*, so their last names were different, which is why it hadn't registered.

"Well, that was easy," I said, reaching into my purse and pulling out my phone. "I told Jack I would text him the answer. Give me a second and I'll go up and see Julia."

Sara nodded, stood, and went to the fridge while I texted. Once I was done, I turned my attention back to Sara, who now had a half a sandwich and a soda on a tray.

"Can you take this up to Julia when you go. I need to catch up on some calls and emails."

"Sure thing," I said, taking the tray from her and heading up the stairs to the bedroom.

Upstairs had two bedrooms, two full baths, a laundry room, and a loft that Julia used as an office. None of the rooms were very large, but they all fit her needs perfectly. Unlike downstairs where the colors were all done in purple tones, upstairs each room was done in its own color. The office had blue accents, the guest bedroom orange and yellow, and Julia's bedroom was various shades of gray.

When I reached the bedroom, I knocked softly on the doorjamb.

"You up for a visitor and some lunch?"

Julia, whose eyes had been closed, opened them and looked towards the door. She removed the oxygen mask and waved me in.

"Of course! I welcome both."

I walked over, and after Julia got situated, laid the tray on her lap.

"How are you feeling?" I asked as I made my way towards the nearest chair, taking a seat.

"Beside the jackhammer constantly pounding my brain, good," she replied, leaning forward, picking up the sandwich, and taking a bite.

"Glad to hear it. Do you need us to call the doctor and ask for something stronger for the headache?"

Julia started to shake her head no, but stopped, eyes wincing at the movement.

"No," she said, swallowing the bite of sandwich. "I'm not even taking what she gave me. It makes me feel too loopy. Would rather deal with the headache."

"Well, just be careful. We don't need your blood pressure skyrocketing because you are in too much pain. If it doesn't get better, promise me you'll take something before you go to sleep. Then you won't even know you've taken it, but your body will get a break from the pain."

Julia made a little "x" over her heart. "Cross my heart."

"Good. One less thing I have to worry about," I said.

"Speaking of worrying," Julia said, "did you get any info on my car?"

"Yes. I just left the impound lot. Jack met me there and told me that while things were 'unusual' there was nothing that made them think the three failures were related or human-caused."

Julia sat down her soda and looked at me with head tilted and eyebrows raised. "They didn't find anything wrong at all?"

"The cable to the manual key turn was broken, as you suspected based on hearing the noise. However, none of the electronics seemed to be broken or short-circuiting."

"What about the exhaust?"

"Jack said it had minor build-up, but nothing out of the ordinary. The only thing that was the least bit suspicious was some fresh scratches inside the tailpipe as if something solid had been pulled out recently."

"So, that's the 'unusual' part?"

"Yeah," I said. "I wish I could give you more definitive answers."

Julia, done with her food and drink, moved the tray over to her nightstand. "Did they say when I would get my car back?"

"By the sounds of it, sooner rather than later. However, they are going to recommend that you get it looked over one last time by another mechanic. That, or get a new car if you are afraid it might happen again."

Julia paled at the comment. I hadn't meant to scare her, I just wanted to be honest about the fact that she should consider it to be a possibility.

Julia shrugged. "It was a piece of junk anyway. I say now is as good a time as any to make a change."

"I agree," I concurred.

Julia let out a long, deep yawn.

"Looks like it's time for me to go. You need a nap," I said.

"I think you're right. Maybe I'll take one of those pain pills now too. If I sleep through it, I might feel better when I wake up."

"Sounds like a plan," I said, as I got up and walked over to the dresser where her pills lay. I picked up the bottle that held the pain pills, opened the top, and poured one out. After securing the lid back in place, I turned and walked the pill over to Julia.

"Thanks," she said, taking the pill from me. She used the glass of water on her nightstand to take the pill.

"I'll let Sara know you took the pill and you are going to try to get some rest," I said. "If you want to hand me your tray, I'll take it back downstairs for you."

Julia nodded and handed me her tray. Then, she moved the covers aside and crawled beneath them. I took one last glance over my shoulder as I left the room. Julia was already snoring softly, out as soon as her head hit the pillow. Poor thing. I noticed she had forgotten to put the oxygen mask back on. Not wanting to wake her, I quietly moved back over to the bed and placed the mask as close to her as I could to let the oxygen hit her face, without actually applying it. That should be good enough for now.

Turning I headed out of the room and made my way to the kitchen where I rinsed off the plate and put it in the sink before going to find Sara. She ended up being out front sitting on the porch swing.

"Hey, you."

She looked up from her laptop, worry lines creasing her brow as her gaze went to my hair. "Hey. Have you gotten used to the haircut yet? I can't tell you how sorry I am for that."

"Will you stop apologizing! I know it was an accident. I was as frozen in that moment as you were. Besides, I like it," I said, as I reached up and touched my hair. "It's not as easy to do as my other hairdo, but it's manageable."

The worry lines softened and her lips turned up into a small smile. "Did Julia eat?"

"Yeah. I brought the tray back down and put it in the kitchen. I even got her to take a pill."

"How did you manage that?" she said, eyebrows raised. "I've been trying since we got home from the urgent care."

"I told her if she took it right before she went to sleep, she wouldn't notice how it made her feel."

"That's why we call you the smart one!" Sara smiled.

I laughed and rolled my eyes. "Sure. That's what you call me!"

I waved goodbye as I headed for my car. My last stop for the day would be the office. Hopefully, it would be quick, painless, and uneventful.

***

The nice thing was the ride to the office was short since I was coming from Julia's house. And, being that it was mid-afternoon, there wasn't much traffic. I pulled into my designated spot, got out, clicked my key fob—listening for the telltale chirp to say the car was locked and headed inside.

Eva was at her desk painting her fingernails. She paused mid-polish when my entry caused the door chime to go off.

"Hey, Eva. Nice color," I said, nodding towards her nails as I stopped at the desk. "Anything come up that needs my attention?"

"Nope. It's been the quietest day in weeks."

"Thank goodness for that. After the last few days, I think we all need a small break."

Continuing past the front reception area, I headed to my office. After stowing my purse, I unceremoniously plopped down into my chair, closed my eyes, and spun around a few times just for the fun of it. When my stomach said enough, I stopped and took a deep breath. The *DING* of an incoming text on my phone pulled me out of the moment of solitude. I reached into my drawer and pulled my phone from my purse.

It was Jack thanking me for the information about the names and asking me if I could let Julia know her car was ready to be picked up. I replied that I would be happy to, and I also told him she would sell it and get a new one. She didn't want a repeat of her accident. He said that was a good idea and goodbye.

After shooting a quick text to Sara, in case Julia was still asleep, I put my phone away and checked my desk phone for the voicemail light. For the first time in I didn't know how long, it was not illuminated. Maybe the universe was finally giving me a break.

I hadn't even finished the thought when Eva's voice came through the intercom.

"Callie, you have a visitor. It's Mrs. Thompson…" she hesitated, "… and her son."

I straightened in my chair. *Well, damn! So much for that idea.*

"Send them back," I said.

A few moments later, Gin came into my office followed by her son—whose first name, I realized, I'd never learned. I stood and made my way over, giving Gin a light hug, and reaching out my hand to her son. He looked at it but did not act until Gin elbowed him in the ribs. He grasped my hand, did a short, quick shake, then dropped it.

I motioned to the guest chairs.

"Gin, this is a surprise. Please have a seat," I said.

"How can I help you?"

Gin and her son each took a seat, then turned their attention to me. "Well, dear. I brought Calvin in to give you an apology."

My eyebrows shot up. "An apology?"

"I just recently learned he'd come in and yelled at you regarding my signing up with your agency."

I turned my gaze to "Calvin" and saw he was fuming; his red-faced, scrunched brow, and pursed lips saying exactly how he felt about being here.

I looked back at Gin. "Your son did visit me. He was concerned about your welfare and wanted to be certain we weren't taking advantage of you."

"Nonsense!" Gin said. "He just had his undies in a twist because I was dating."

I coughed back a laugh and said nothing.

Calvin's head whipped around and he glared at Gin. "Mother!"

"Oh, don't go getting your undies in a twist again, Calvin. We both know my mind is better than yours. Don't pretend it was my welfare you were looking after, more like my wealth."

Calvin opened and closed his mouth several times, but no words came.

Gin raised a finger at him. "Now, I want you to apologize to Ms. Bloom for making those threats. You had no right to do that."

"Now, Gin," I said. "We welcome anyone who has

concerns to come speak with—"

"It's sweet of you to overlook his being a nincompoop. But he's my son and out of respect for me, he should have *never* embarrassed me like that. He owes you an apology," Gin's voice quivered, and I saw moisture building in her eyes. It was clear from her face, he had done more than just embarrass her, he had hurt her.

I raised my hands and sat back in my chair saying nothing. I knew saying anything more would be pointless and would only make the situation worse for Calvin. I watched Calvin, and I saw the moment when he realized that not only had he lost this battle, he had hurt his mother.

The angry child melted away replaced by a man who saw his mother hurting and the realization he was to blame. He reached forward and took his mother's hands in his, raising them to his mouth where he laid a gentle kiss. He put them down and turned his gaze towards me.

"Ms. Bloom, you have my apology. While I'll admit part of me did this because I wasn't ready to have her date..." he said, his gaze flickered to his mother for the briefest moment before returning to me, "...I truly was looking out for her well-being. There are too many people out there willing and able to take advantage of older people. I didn't want my mother to be added to that list."

"I completely understand that, Calvin. And you have my word, we *never* take advantage of our clients, regardless of age," I said, leaning forward and putting my hands on the desk.

Calvin gazed intently at me for a few moments.

"I believe you. I guess before I was just too angry to take you at your word," he said, leaning back in his chair. "And, I'll admit my mother does seem happier now. I hadn't ever considered how lonely she might be since my father died."

"Oh, Calvin—"

"No, mom," he said, looking at his mother. "It's okay. You were right to do this if you're lonely. I never meant to embarrass or hurt you. I swear it."

A tear fell from Gin's lashes and tumbled down her cheek. Calvin reached up and wiped it away, "Besides, I've met Gerald and he is a decent guy."

"So, you're okay with me dating?"

"As long as you take it slow and allow me to meet any of the men you feel are worth seeing more than once or twice, then I'm on board with this."

I sat back and watched the exchange. It was clear how much they loved each other. I knew if I put myself in his shoes I could understand why he did what he did. I'd never really given any thought to my dad being lonely or dating, for that matter. I doubt I'd react well to it either.

"That sounds just fine," Gin replied to her son before turning her gaze to me. "I know TAFT will watch out for me too."

"Absolutely!" I said, smiling.

"Well then," Calvin said, standing from his chair, "we'll get out of your hair and let you get back to work.

From the sounds of it, your hands are quite full these days."

"Yes," I shook my head in acknowledgment, "they are."

Gin stood, and I followed them both to the front door. This time when Calvin turned, his hand was outstretched to me. I took it and gave it a shake.

"If you have any questions, or need anything at all, just give any of us a call," I said, passing my gaze back and forth between the two. "And, Gin. Thank you so much for keeping Grandma company while she is laid up. I know she really appreciates it."

"It's my pleasure, dear," she said. "Olive is a hoot, and I definitely enjoyed the lesson from the physical therapist!"

"Physical therapist?" Calvin asked, eyebrows raised.

Gin and I both laughed as she led him out the door, the question left unanswered.

Chapter Thirty-Two

There are three things I hated in the world: spiders, sharks, and dead people. Lucky for me, we hadn't had to go to Jasmine's funeral since they'd ended up having it out of state, and Wendy's funeral was a closed casket. I knew this because we—me, Julia, Sara, Eva, JJ, and Grandma— were front and center for the viewing. I'm not exactly sure how that happened, but it did. Possibly the limelight had faded away slightly as it had been nearly two weeks since her death and it was no longer front-page news. Based on what I'd heard, it had been delayed while they processed evidence and waited for her next of kin to do the final identification of her remains.

Even with the delay however, almost every seat was

filled and Grandma was taking advantage of the limelight; everyone stopped to see how she was doing after they did the required "pass by" of the casket. Grandma loved any attention she could get and since she had been bedridden, she was due for a refill of gossip and human interaction. She wasn't the least bit embarrassed about *how* she'd gotten injured. If anything, she wore it as a badge of honor—as a woman of her age who was still getting it on should.

I, on the other hand, took equal advantage to give everyone a once-over, sizing each one up as a possible candidate for murder. The one thing on our side was a large portion of the women attending were clients of TAFT, so we already had full profiles and background checks on them. It was the men who showed up for the service I was watching closely.

We had found no connection between the two women related to TAFT. No matching profile hits, or dates were logged in our system. Granted, that didn't mean they hadn't met the same men out and about, but we hadn't been the ones that had facilitated the meeting. At least that made me feel better about how TAFT might look to the public.

The funeral itself was as lovely as it could be. Flowers decorated every possible surface. I had made certain to take my allergy medicine first thing this morning to ensure I wouldn't spend the whole time sneezing away. The casket was a dark cherry wood with black metal handles. A large, beautiful picture of Wendy sat on a tripod next to the casket.

Wendy's sister, the only family she had left, was sitting in the row across from ours. She was pale and her face was streaked with tears. I couldn't recall how much older the sister was, but at this moment it looked like decades. I knew what it felt like to lose someone in your innermost family circle. That memory, more so than the funeral I was at right now, brought tears to my eyes.

As I looked around the room, I saw Jack out of the corner of my eye. He was standing against the back wall watching everyone in attendance. I knew he was sizing each one up just as I had. Though I was certain he was doing a better job at it based on his qualifications.

Pastor Trenton Ashton moved to the podium to begin the service. His sermon was short and sweet. When he was done, he turned the podium over to Wendy's sister. Unfortunately, she was overcome with emotion and could not speak. JJ, who was used to talking in front of a crowd of strangers in the midst of emotional proceedings, stepped up and offered to read the statement she had prepared. Wendy's sister only sobbed loudly once, when he got to the part where she had quoted Wendy's favorite poem.

After JJ had read the last of the eulogy, the pastor returned to close out the ceremony. Before he could finish, the loud vibration of a cell phone echoed through the room. Pastor Ashton's glare pointed out to everyone in attendance who the offender was: Jack. Jack mouthed "sorry" and quickly exited the room as he answered his phone.

The pastor said a final prayer and everyone filed out. There would not be a graveside service, only light refreshments in the lobby. My group was the last to exit, and I immediately searched the crowd for Jack. I finally caught sight of him as he was walking back in from outside. Our gazes met, and he motioned me over.

"I'll be right back, everyone. It looks like Jack needs me," I said.

They all nodded, and I headed towards Jack. When I reached him, he took hold of my elbow and steered me back out the door he had entered. Once we were a dozen or so feet away from the chapel he turned me towards him and dropped my arm.

"Sorry to pull you away, but I have something important to tell you."

"Okay…" I said, waiting. The look on his face was not comforting.

"While the service was going on, we had some officers go back to Mr. Rivera's house to ask him a few more questions. We wanted to solidify the link between him and the two women as purely pharmacist-related and coincidental."

"So, what's the problem?"

"They just called to tell me that his apartment has been cleared out, and he is gone."

I reached up and placed my hand over my heart.

"What?"

"He's gone," Jack said again, his hands reaching out to grab hold of me when I swayed slightly in place. I felt light-headed as my mind raced with questions.

"Why... What... I mean, where...?" I stuttered, unable to complete a thought or question.

"We don't know where he went and we can only make assumptions as to why he left so suddenly," Jack said, frown lines creasing his brow.

The urge to reach up and smooth them away was strong, but I resisted.

"An APB has been issued for him and his vehicle," Jack continued. "We'd like to send each of you ladies' home with a police escort who will stay outside your residences overnight. Just to be safe."

I nodded, "Sounds reasonable. I'll go inside and let everyone know."

I turned and started to go in but stopped and looked over my shoulder. "Do you think this means he is the killer?"

"Honestly, I can't say. Everything we had to date was circumstantial and his profile just didn't add up as a serial killer. But..."

Inhaling deeply, I ingested the information before turning and heading back inside. It wasn't hard to locate my group as they were surrounded by well-wishers for Grandma. She was beaming and drinking it all in.

"Excuse me, everyone. I need to speak to my friends

for a moment." I lightly pulled on Sara's arm, who linked up with Julia, causing a chain reaction until the five of us were all huddled together in one of the empty viewing rooms.

"What's wrong, sweetheart?" Grandma asked.

"Jack wants each of us to have a police escort going home, and for them to stay outside overnight."

Sara paled and Julia's eyebrow's rose.

"Why?" Eva asked, her expression as startled as the others.

"The police went to talk to Mr. Rivera again. However, it appears Steven skipped town."

"Why would he do that?" Julia asked.

"Jack said they didn't know, but they were classifying it as suspicious and have issued an APB."

"Do you think we're in danger?" Sara asked.

"Not directly, but the police don't want to take any chances. There isn't anything solid to say he was involved with the murders or is any kind of serial killer."

Grandma moved forward and took my hand. "Maybe it's best if you come home with me tonight. You are safest if you stay with me and your daddy."

I thought about it for a moment before finally nodding. "You're probably right. Plus, it will make for one less officer they have to keep from looking for Steven."

"Why don't we all go give our condolences to Wendy's sister and then make our way outside as stealthily as possible. I'll field any questions if they throw them at us when we leave before the reception is over," JJ said.

"Thank you, JJ. Our knight in shining armor."

JJ did a little bow before motioning for us all to head back out into the lobby. We quickly found Wendy's sister and gave our condolences before sneaking out the doors where Jack was waiting. A few people asked why we were leaving so early. I heard JJ saying something about Grandma and Julia being tired and needing to go get some rest; we were their rides.

Jack was outside waiting with the officers.

"Grandma and I will go to Dad's house for the night. Spare you one set of hands," I said to Jack as I neared.

I saw a tiny fraction of the tension leave his face. I wasn't certain if it was because I was giving him one more officer for the search, or because he knew I would be safer with my family.

"Good idea," he said, as he motioned the officers to each of the others in the group. "I'll call you if anything comes up. Just make sure you ladies, and gentleman, keep your doors locked and your phones on and charged."

We all nodded, got into our vehicles, and headed home.

Chapter Thirty-Three

After sliding on some slippers, I quickly headed towards the mailbox in front of my house, all the while taking extra care to be aware of my surroundings. The police car that had been in front of the house last week was now gone. It had been determined that Steven had fled the state, by all accounts to California. Jack hadn't provided the details as to why, just that he headed in that direction. We were all still on pins and needles wondering if he would pop out of some shadow, but the police couldn't watch over us forever.

I reached the mailbox, opened it, and extracted several envelopes. Normally, I would flip through them as I made my way back into the house, but now, I waited until I was back inside with the door locked to take a look. The first two items were junk mail, the second was a coupon for Bed, Bath and Beyond, and the third was an envelope from my insurance company.

Eagerly, I rushed to the kitchen where I grabbed a letter opener and sliced open the envelope. I pulled out the paper. On top was the summary of my claim, on the bottom was my check. I did a little dance and giggled. I could get my car! Unable to contain my excitement, I grabbed my house phone and dialed the number for the dealership.

When the receptionist answered, I asked for Kevin. He answered on the second ring.

"Kevin, it's Callie Bloom."

"Well, hello, Ms. Bloom. How can I help you?"

"I just wanted to let you know I received my check today from the insurance company. I'm leaving here in a minute to deposit it in the bank before it closes at noon."

"That's great news!"

"I'll keep watch on my account and as soon as it clears I'll call you and let you know that I'll be by to pick up the car."

"Perfect. I'll get all the rest of the paperwork done saying we've received payment and you're taking possession."

"That would be great."

"I'll also let the detailing department know to get the car ready for you right away, so there will be no delay when you come to get it. Just a few signatures and you'll be good to go."

"Thanks again, Kevin. I really appreciate all of your help with this."

"No worries, Ms. Bloom. I'm just glad it all worked out."

"Me too, Kevin. Me too."

***

Dad dropped me off at the dealership in the evening four days later. As I waited for Kevin, I looked at the "Excellent Service" awards wall where they posted photos of all the service technicians who were being recognized for stellar service each month.

"Ms. Bloom," Kevin said from behind me.

I turned and watched as he neared.

"Are you ready to get your car?" he asked.

"Absolutely!" I said.

"This way," he said, as he motioned me to follow him to his office.

Kevin did not disappoint. In no time flat, I'd signed the papers and grabbed the keys to my new car. After sliding in, I took a moment to close my eyes and inhale that new car smell. As I ran my hands over the smooth leather, I thought back to my exchange with Jack about doing just that and the innuendo that followed. I felt myself blush.

I reached forward, punched the start button, put the

car in reverse, and backed out. TAFT's phones had started ringing off the hook again after everyone "assumed" the murders had been solved, the killer on the run. My schedule had been overflowing with new client meetings all day long. As much as I didn't want to go back to the office, I knew I needed to. The only way I was going to get caught up was to go in when the phones and door chimes weren't ringing.

Pulling into my spot and turning off the car, I let out a sigh. I didn't want to get out of the car yet. It felt so good to be back in luxury again. Wanting to get this over with, I got out, locked up, and headed for the office. As I unlocked the door, the light in the parking lot came on indicating that it was now getting dark outside. Closing the office door behind me, I locked it and headed for my office.

As I sat in my chair, I flipped open my laptop and began going through the items in my inbox. Not seeing anything that couldn't wait, I grabbed the thumb drive Eva had left on my desk and plugged it in. It held the mixer photos PhotoPro had downloaded and arranged for us from our camera's memory cards. The file was quite large, and I admonished myself for getting so far behind on the task. We were going to have to do a special issue of the newsletter just to catch up on showing the pictures.

Opening the photo program, I started a slideshow to view the pictures. I only recognized a third of the photos, where I'd overseen the mixer personally. Those, I scrolled past quickly with no reason to reminisce beyond jotting down the image number for the one or two best pictures to use in the newsletter.

When I got to the other photos, I opened up an email and addressed it to Sarah and Julia. When I came across a picture that I liked and felt was share-worthy, I typed the number that coincided with it into the body of the email. I would leave it up to Sara and Julia to pick which photos from their events they wanted to use.

Nearing the end of the file a specific photo caught my eye. I realized as I looked at it closer I had done so because both Jasmine *and* Wendy were in the picture. I double clicked on the image and looked at the "details" information. This information was entered by Eva after we got the thumb drive back.

I saw the photo was dated three months ago. For some reason, I couldn't recall who hosted that mixer. I scanned the list of names also included in the details. One name stopped me dead in my tracks.

I clicked back on the image of the photo and my breath caught in my throat. I clicked back on the details box again. *Holy shit!* When my brain registered the man in the picture; puzzle pieces slammed into place. It was Steven Rivera. I had to let Jack know right away. It would confirm that they were chasing the right man. He had interacted with both women outside of the pharmacy! I had photographic proof.

As I reached to pick up the phone it rang. Startled, I

jumped a bit before grabbing the receiver.

"Hello?" I squeaked, my voice still reflecting my recent activity and start.

"Callie!" Eva's panicked voice yelled in my ear.

"Eva? What's wrong."

I heard deep, panicked inhales of breath and the sound of high heels clicking at a rapid speed over pavement.

"They were wrong. It wasn't Steven…"

"Slow down, Eva. You're not making sense?"

"Alan Lynch—" Eva screamed and the line went dead.

I tried calling her back, but there was no answer. I tried again. Nothing. My blood turned to ice. Alan Lynch? What about Alan Lynch? The wheels in my mind spun as I replayed Eva's words and tried to make sense of them. As I did my gaze once again landed on the picture details window. The name Alan Lynch jumped out at me as if it was now a flashing neon sign. *What the—?*

I took a closer look. The list of names included Jasmine, Wendy, Steven, *and* Alan Lynch. But what did Alan Lynch have to do with anything? I again clicked on the photo.

This time my breath froze as I glanced at the picture, but not because of Jasmine, Wendy, or Steven. A new face registered, and it was in the exact place listed for Alan Lynch. I'd seen this face just today. On the Excellent Service board at the Tesla dealer. He was one of the service technicians.

My vision blurred as I grabbed onto the edge of the desk for support. I took several deep breaths until I calmed down enough to see. *Oh. My. God.* That's what Eva meant. It wasn't only Steven who had contact with both women, but Alan too. He had also serviced both mine and Julia's cars in the past.

As the realization settled of what this meant, panic built. I had to tell Jack and find Eva. I grabbed the phone and dialed Jack's number. It went to voicemail.

"Jack, it's Callie. I don't have time to explain, but the killer isn't Steven. It's Alan Lynch and I think he has Eva!" I said frantically. "Please call me!"

I stood and paced my office as I waited for him to call. After several minutes I couldn't take it and I tried reaching out to Eva again. No answer. My cell phone in my purse rang. I grabbed it.

"Hello," I said breathlessly.

An automated voice rambled on with a sales pitch. My heart dropped as I hung up. I shoved my phone back in my purse and in doing so, I snagged my fingernail.

"Dammit to hell!" I screamed aloud.

Angrily, I yanked open my desk drawer and rummaged around for a fingernail file. The only one I was able to find was the old metal one that more often than not did additional damage to your nail. Too wound up to calm down enough to look for another one, I paced and sawed at the snag.

The light on my desk phone's voicemail lit up. Someone must have called in and left a message while I was leaving one for Jack. Jamming the file in my back pocket I raced to my desk and punched in my code. It had just been a party rep calling me back about a reception we wanted to host for the summer. Her words were muddled as she left her number, so I was unable to write it down.

Having nothing else to do while I waited for Jack to call back, I reached for my purse to get the business card of the rep to get her number. It was in that moment that I noticed the tracker on my purse, and bells went off in my brain. Of course! I could track Eva using the tracker on her purse.

I grabbed my phone, opened the tracking app, and loaded Eva's phone. I watched in agony as the wheel turned around and around while the program loaded. Finally, a blinking blue dot showed Eva's location; it was moving east towards the harbor. I reached for my purse and raced to the car. If I hurried I could catch up to her. While I waited for Jack to call, I could at least get closer to Eva and not only find her but give Jack her exact location.

Jumping in and turning on my car, I pulled out of the lot, tires squealing as I turned the corner onto the main thoroughfare. When my car's Bluetooth picked up, the screen transferred to the dashboard monitor. Thank God, I didn't have to try to hold the phone and drive. I did my best to follow all of the traffic laws—plus a few extra miles of speed—as I followed the dot.

I made multiple turns and went several blocks. After what seemed like an eternity, the blue dot stopped in a warehouse district near the harbor, only a few streets away. I dialed Jack's number. As I pulled into the lot where the dot blinked like a beacon in the night, his voicemail answered.

"Jack, it's Callie again. I've found Eva. She's at the ware—"

BEEP BEEP BEEP

My phone disconnected and the screen went back to the radio station selections. My heart sank. I grabbed my phone from the seat beside me and frantically pushed the home button. The screen was black; the battery had died. Panicked, I dug through my purse searching for my phone charger. When my first search was fruitless, I picked up my purse and turned it over, dumping all of the contents on the seat. *It had to be here!*

Looking at all of the items and not seeing the charger, it finally dawned on me I'd left it in the rental car I'd returned earlier that day. Nausea rolled over me in a wave as the bottom dropped out of my stomach. What was I going to do now?

Not knowing anything other than I couldn't just sit here and do nothing, I got out of my car, raced to the trunk, and grabbed out the tire iron. I said a prayer as I moved towards the nearest building, being as quiet as humanly possible.

Stepping inside, I noted some of the overhead

fluorescent lights were on, but most were flickering on and off. One light was attached to the ceiling on only one side; the other side dangled, swaying back and forth in the breeze from the open windows above, causing shadows to dance across the floor.

The stale, musty smell of the old industrial building hung in the air. Footsteps echoed through the empty space from somewhere deeper in the building. A chill raced over me as the cold night air sunk in. I crept closer, hesitating at the entrance. Should I wait? I only debated for a second before I decided it wasn't worth the risk. Moments could mean the difference between life and death for Eva.

Gathering all the courage I could muster, I tiptoed forward towards the direction of the last noise I had heard. As I stepped inside—closing the door softly behind me, the building opened up into one large room, where some form of heavy equipment sat. What exactly it had produced was unclear to my untrained eye. By the amount of rust and dirt on the machine, it was obvious it hadn't been used in quite some time. On the outskirts of the room were several offices and two hallways. Listening carefully, I strained to hear which way the footsteps were going but had no luck. Silence was the only thing I heard. After a few moments however, the sound of a door opening on squeaky hinges echoed to my left.

I turned toward the noise and the hallway it had come from and moved forward. When I came to a corner, I peeked a look around it before continuing on. The next stretch of hallway was empty. At the end of that hallway, I saw a door that was partially opened. I took a deep, steadying breath and wished myself to be light as a feather as I made my way forward. I gazed through the opening and saw Eva sitting on a chair in the middle of the room.

Without another thought, I rushed forward.

"Eva—"

She looked at me and screamed, "Watch out!"

I spun, tire iron raised. My head exploded with pain and I crumpled to the floor.

Chapter Thirty-Four

I swam through a mental haze trying to break the surface and reach consciousness. As I got closer, and with great effort, I inched open my eyelids. Each one felt like it weighed a thousand pounds. The further they opened, the more the pixels of dim light in front of me focused.

When I could finally see again, my other senses kicked in. The taste of iron sat on my tongue, and pain I'd not been aware of before shot through my skull. I ran my tongue over my lip and felt the pinch of pain when it hit a split in my flesh.

What in the world?

I tried to move my hands from behind me to touch the wound on my lip but realized they were tied to the chair that I sat on. My feet were also a no-go, tied to the same chair. Slowly, and with a large amount of pain I turned my head and gazed around the room. It took several moments for my memory to come back to me, reminding me of where exactly I was: the warehouse.

I frantically wiggled and jumped—ignoring the jolts of pain this caused my head—trying to get the chair to move in any direction. No luck. The chair was bolted down to the ground. *Why would there be a chair bolted to the ground?*

Panic welled up in my belly as I tried to make sense of it all. Okay, think. Start from the beginning…

After entering the warehouse, I'd made my way through and turned left. I had looked through the open door and seen Eva sitting in this chair. I'd rushed forward towards her, and then… I didn't remember. *Oh my God, Eva! Is she all right?*

I wanted to scream out for her, but I was afraid whoever had done this to me would return. I needed to think. *What should I do?* My head pounded with pain. I took several long, deep breaths. First, I needed to free myself— as quietly as possible. I ran my fingers over my bindings and realized they were some sort of rope. How could I cut them? As I thought this question, the snag in my fingernail that I'd tried to deal with earlier, caught the rope.

My fingernail file! I still had it in my back pocket. I maneuvered so that I could squeeze some fingers from one of my hands into my pocket. It took several tries, but I was able to pull the file free. My dislike for this particular file evaporated. Today, this destructive metal instrument was exactly the tool I needed for the job at hand.

Careful not to drop it, I twisted it around and slid the point in-between two of the ropes. With great difficulty, I drew it back and forth across the fibers. Finally, after several dozen strokes the rope gave way the tiniest of amounts. I didn't think I'd cut through anything yet, but all the movement had loosened the knot and given me a little more room. This space was exactly what I needed to get a better grip and momentum.

I had no concept of how long it was taking me; I tried not to dwell on it. I knew whoever did this to me could be back at any moment and the longer they had Eva, the worse it could be for her. My hands cramped and my fingers burned, screaming in pain to stop. But I couldn't.

I let out an audible gasp of relief when I heard and felt in unison the tear of the rope. The bindings loosened around my wrists. I grasped the file, to ensure I didn't drop it, then yanked my hands in opposite directions as hard as I could. It took several tries, but finally, the ropes dropped away.

Tears of joy slid down my face as I brought my hands around and rubbed my wrists. Quickly, I started to kneel and untie the knot in the rope on my feet, but the sound of the footsteps coming my way made me freeze. *Shit!*

Knowing I didn't have time to finish the job, I grabbed up the rope from my wrists off the floor and I tucked my hands back behind me—the file squeezed tightly in one fist, the rope in the other—in hopes it would appear I was still bound.

The footsteps stopped in front of the closed door and the doorknob turned. The door swung inwards and Eva walked through.

"Oh good, you're awake," she said with a smile on her face.

"Eva!" I sighed, "I'm so glad—"

My words stopped when I noticed the gun in her hands. I looked from the gun up to Eva's face, and back down again.

"Did you get away? Whose gun is that? Untie me!" I said.

She made no move to get closer or untie me. "It's my gun, silly girl."

"What? I don't understand." The bottom dropped from the pit of my stomach. "Did you have that in your purse when he kidnapped you? Where is he? Why aren't you untying me?"

I knew I was rambling, but the multiple possibilities of why she wasn't untying me and why she had a gun were scaring the bejeebers out of me.

"There is no one here besides you and me," she said, a creepy smile lighting up her face.

"I still don't understand. If no one else is here, who hit me on the head?"

"I did," Eva replied as she walked back and forth in front of me, swinging the gun around as if it were a toy.

"But... Why?"

She stopped in her tracks and turned to stare directly at me. Tight lines of anger creased her brow. "Because I've gotten my revenge. Now it's time to tie up loose ends and give the police a murderer."

I started to speak but realized I didn't know what to say. The realization of what she was indirectly insinuating left me dazed and confused.

"Are you trying to say *you're* the killer?" I asked.

"I'm not *trying* to say it. I *am* saying it."

"But, why?" I asked, shifting my weight just a bit, in case I needed to have forward momentum to grab or push her. "Why would you kill our clients, or try to kill us?"

Eva let out a loud huff. "Because I'm sick of seeing all the spoiled, rich, 'think they are so pretty' women taking all the good men, and you helping them."

"You have a boyfriend. Why would you care about what men other women are getting?"

"I *had* a boyfriend. I lost him to one of TAFT's clients, Wendy."

Eva hadn't ever said anything about a breakup, much less a TAFT client was involved.

"Eva, I'm so sorry. I didn't know."

Eva whipped her head back at me a scowl marring her features. "Of course you didn't know. When have you ever given a damn about my personal life? All you have time to do is bark orders and throw your money in my face with your fancy cars and stupid gift cards."

"I…" I started to give examples of when we'd last had a one-on-one chat. I realized she was right; although I'd given her monetary "thanks"—which she clearly took as offensive, we hadn't had a conversation about her personal life in a very long time. "Please forgive me. I didn't realize. Why didn't you say something?"

"And give you the chance to laugh at and judge me behind my back? Or worse yet, try to set me up with one of the TAFT men out of pity. I don't think so!"

"I understand how hurt you must have been by Wendy, but to kill her? And what did Jasmine ever do to you? She had children!"

Eva frantically paced back and forth, her feet scuffing the ground as she moved. "If she loved her children, she would have worked harder to save the marriage," she said, motioning with her hands as if she was on stage. "It's her fault we didn't stay together as a family."

I noticed she had changed what should have been "they" to "we." Did she come from a broken family? I wanted to respond and keep her talking to buy time to figure out what to do, but I didn't know what to say that wouldn't worsen the situation. Then I thought of something.

"Did you kill Steven too? The police said he fled," I asked.

"I didn't have to. He hopped away like a scared little rabbit when I told him the police knew about the 'intent to distribute' charge his father had gotten rid of for him by paying off the arresting officer. He was afraid they would reinstate the charge and arrest him."

"Intent to distribute? There was nothing like that in his file."

"There wasn't because I removed all implications of it. Sara had to leave early that day to screw around with another one of her boy toys and she left me to finish up the review. Grandma Olive's notes had mention of an arrest that had been swept under the table. When I got the background and didn't see anything listed, I did my own research and found out the details."

Her hands waved around in the air as she explained how she had managed her deed.

"When I saw what Mr. Rivera did for a living, I knew he would make a perfect red herring. So, I erased Olive's notes, then used that delightful tidbit of information when I visited Steven. I told him I'd keep it off the record as a courtesy as long as he got me some Xanax. I didn't have any hard proof, but Steven didn't need to know that. I also took the opportunity while I was visiting him to steal some other drugs out of his medicine cabinet."

So, that is why he was so nervous about what was in the police files and how the sleeping pills came into play!

"He dropped by with the Xanax on the same day you gave me the file to deliver to Jasmine. I took advantage of the situation and gave her a little something extra in her shot glass when we toasted her first set of matches," Eva continued.

"But there were four drugs in her system when she died, not two."

"I added a couple of my own personal stash of Oxycodone to the mixture, left over from my root canal. The other drug was just a bonus. When I showed up, Jasmine said she had a migraine and had just taken a pill. Granted, that did almost cause me problems, though; I really had to talk her into taking the shot. But you know how persuasive I can be," Eva said with a sly smile which she aimed straight ahead at no one.

Suddenly she stopped pacing and turned her gaze to me. Something had shifted in her features as if she had come to some sort of decision.

"Enough chit-chat. It's time for you to die," she said, raising the gun to aim it at me.

"They'll know it's you! You have no alibi and I'm certain your prints are all over this place." I felt the file cut into my skin as I clasped my fists in fear.

"Don't you worry, Calla Lily, I have that all planned out," she sneered. "I was kidnapped just like you thought, by big bad Alan Lynch. You came to save me, and you did. But he caught you on the way out. I knew the only way to save you was to go get help. But I failed you."

I'd seen her fake act before when she was in a fight with her boyfriend and wanted to make him think he had really hurt her feelings. She was good, really good. The girl could get an Emmy. I was so screwed.

"He isn't going to have a story that lines up with yours

when they find him. Not to mention they won't find any trace of him here." I felt the binds on my ankles begin to loosen. I set my feet back down and shimmied just a bit to get a solid seated stance.

"On the contrary. He is all over the place. I made sure to take bits and pieces of his DNA—some hair, some skin under my fingernails—before I had him hang himself."

I scoffed, "Alan was a huge man. There is no way you could slip him enough drugs. It would take a truckload to get him to overdose. Not to mention the fact that there is no way you would be strong enough to hang him."

"Getting him to take a shot laced with some of the drugs was easy. I didn't need him to overdose, just get enough of the drugs in his system for the police to connect the dots," she smiled brightly. "And, his fetish for erotic asphyxiation helped me do the rest. We've done it so many times before he was comfortable with me making sure he was safe—"

"Erotic what? I don't understand…" I cut in, "… how could you get him to hang himself?"

Eva rolled her eyes, "You are such a prude, Callie. It was easy to convince him to do it. I told him it would be mind-blowing for him. His belt and gravity would do the work of the asphyxiation while his standing on the chair would put me in the perfect position to do some blowing of my own. He had nothing to fear; the strong, sturdy chair and I would make sure he was perfectly safe."

Dear God, she'd had the whole thing planned out! I worked

my feet with more determination, I needed the ropes looser. I had to get free!

"That might explain how he ends up dead," I stammered, as I shimmed my feet this way and that as inconspicuously as possible. "But not why he would kill people."

"Once they look at his file and see how many matches have turned him down and how long he has been single, they'll believe it. Eventually, they'll conclude he was a nice guy who was tired of being rejected. He holds TAFT accountable, so before he ends his life he ends the lives of those associated with TAFT who had a hand in his rejection.

"It will all tie together in a nice neat bow when they realize not only was he the mechanic who serviced both yours and Julia's cars, but his brother is a pharmacist—so he had a way to access all the drugs involved in the murders."

Oh my gosh, she was right about everything. That's when I thought of something.

"If TAFT closes, you lose too. I remember how hard of a time you had finding a job. You told me yourself," I said.

Before I had time to process the stupidity of my words, Eva slammed her fist into the side of my face. I both felt and tasted the split in my lip widen as the blood flowed. The other thing I felt, with much relief, was that the impact of the blow had caused me to jerk my ankles hard enough to loosen the bonds on my feet, causing the ropes to slide down the back of my shoes. I slowly slid my heels up out of my shoes, ready to jump at the next opportune moment.

She took several steps towards me. "You stupid woman. They won't have to close TAFT because they'll know who the killer is. When there is no one left to worry about, all will go back to normal. Sara and Julia won't let TAFT die. If anything, they'll keep it going in your honor."

Her anger when she spat these words at me was so intense the words sprayed on my face. Realizing this might be my only opportunity for surprise—because of her proximity to me—I lunged forward out of my shoes, swung my arms around, and stabbed the file into her chest bone-deep. She screamed out in pain; the gun slipped from her hand, clattering to the ground. I frantically looked around for its location. I spotted it near her right foot. I dove forward, stretching towards it. As I neared the ground, my breath was literally kicked out of me as Eva swung her foot up into my solar plexus. Pain ripped through my chest and recently bruised ribs.

Gasping for air I ignored the pain and reached for the gun. We both grabbed hold of it at the same time. She yanked it upwards, pulling me to my knees as we fought for control. I tried my best to wrench it from her grasp, but my hands were too tired from all the effort it had taken to free my bonds. I couldn't hold on. I watched in horror as the gun slipped from my fingers.

I screamed and raised my arms in front my face as she swung the gun towards my chest; her finger pulling the trigger. A shot rang out and the feel of hot, warm blood splattered my arms, neck, face, and chest. Pain was the last thing I recalled before it all went black.

Chapter Thirty-Five

A bright, white light blinded my eyes when I opened them. My first glimpse of Heaven would be just as people described it in stories: bright, warm, with a feeling of safety as if cradled in the arms of God himself.

I blinked several more times; the light faded away, and the sparkles cleared. I smiled and looked up to see the face I had prayed to so many times in my life. *What the…?*

"You're not God!"

"Depends on who you ask, sunshine." Jack smiled down at me, worry lines creasing his brow.

I jerked upright and patted myself down.

"Whoa there. Slow down!" Jack grabbed my hands and clutched me forward into his chest. "You're fine."

I tried to pull away, but his iron grasp held me fast.

"Fine! How can I be fine? I was just shot in the chest."

Jack loosened his grip, slid his hands down my arms, and gently pushed me from him.

"You weren't shot in the chest."

"But... All the blood?"

"Most of it isn't yours."

I stared down at my blood-covered hands before touching the cloth at my chest, which was also covered in blood spatter. I turned my gaze up to his.

"If it's not all mine, whose is it?"

"Eva's."

That was when the voices around me finally sank into my consciousness. I looked around and saw several officers taking photos. A click to my left brought my attention around and I got a quick glimpse of a gurney being wheeled away with a figure handcuffed on top.

"Eva?" I asked.

"Yes. And yes, she'll survive," he replied, also answering the next question he knew I would ask.

"I don't understand? I saw Eva pull the trigger."

"She did, but her shot went wide," Jack said, pointing at a bullet hole in the wall behind me. "It only grazed your arm."

"But how?" I asked, the pain in my arm now registering.

"I came in just as she pointed the gun at you and I got off a shot. It hit her in the shoulder."

"So..." My voice trembled, "... if you hadn't shot her."

"Shh..." Jack said, pulling me up into his arms and stroking my hair. "Let's not think about the what-ifs. All that matters is that you're safe."

I pulled back out of his arms. "How did you find me?"

"After I got your voicemail I tried calling you back. When you didn't answer, I reached out to the Tesla dealer and asked if you had a tracking device on your new car. They said you did, so they tracked you for me."

I sat up straight as a new thought hit me.

"You need to go check on Alan Lynch. Eva said she killed him, but..."

"The mechanic from the Tesla dealer?" Jack asked.

"Yes."

Jack didn't ask for more details, he just pulled out his phone and dialed.

"This is Detective Brown. I need you to have officers locate Alan Lynch. You can get his address from his employer, the Tesla dealer. It's a matter of life or death, so do it quickly."

He hung up and turned his attention back to me.

"Let's get you up and to an ambulance to get looked at. At first glance, besides the bullet graze, I don't see anything but a head wound and some abrasions and bruises. I'm guessing at a minimum you have a concussion. Are there any other injuries you know of that I *can't* see?"

I started to shake my head, but abruptly stopped when

it exploded with pain.

"No. Just the ones you mentioned. I'm not sure what she bashed me over the head with. I just know it hurts like a mother."

Jack helped me to get slowly to my feet. The EMTs rushed to our side when they saw what we were doing. They helped me onto a gurney and wheeled me outside. They did a quick vitals check. Besides my blood pressure being high, they didn't see anything that immediately worried them beyond the obvious. They pushed me inside and started to close the doors. Jack stopped them.

"I'm going to get things figured out here and find out about Mr. Lynch. I'll get to the hospital as soon as I can to check on you and get a statement."

I gave a smile and a tiny nod. Jack let go of the door and the EMT shut it.

Chapter Thirty-Six

After I was admitted to the hospital, I was taken for a CT scan to determine how severe my concussion was. Once the scan was completed, a nurse bandaged my arm and debrided the wounds on my head, arms, and feet. I'd done a number on my wrist with the nail file, but it had all been for the greater good. Without my hands being free, I wouldn't have stood a chance of getting away; instead of being here, I would've been down in the morgue. Granted, if Jack hadn't shown up, I would've most definitely had a toe tag right about now.

Shortly after the nurse had me situated in my room my dad and grandma arrived.

"Lily," Dad said, taking my hand. "Are you okay?"

"I'm fine. Just a concussion and a flesh wound."

"What happened?" Grandma asked.

"Well, the good news and the short story is that I know who committed the murders. The bad news is, if it hadn't been for Jack, I would've been the next victim."

Dad paled several shades as he lowered himself into the chair next to my bed.

"Who did it?" Grandma asked.

"Eva."

Grandma's eyebrows shot up, "Eva! As in your receptionist?"

"One and the same."

"How the hell did she pull all of that off?" Grandma asked.

"Well, for starters, she blackmailed Steven with the information you found out about his intent to distribute charge. She said if he gave her pills she would 'lose' that piece of information. That's how she got part of the drug cocktail that killed Jasmine."

"Okay. But what about you, Julia, and Alan?"

"Eva knew that Alan serviced both mine and Julia's cars, so she tinkered with both and left breadcrumbs that would eventually lead to him. It would be easy for the cops to make assumptions once they knew to look at him. No one would think to check who else had access to my car, or to Julia's car both before and after the accident."

"I thought they didn't find anything wrong with your friend's car," Dad said.

"They didn't," I said. "I think the reason is that I called Eva right after we found Julia and told her where we found her. That gave Eva ample time before the police arrived to get to Julia's car and undo what she'd done, making it all appear coincidental. The police wouldn't be able to connect the dots until she was ready to let them. The only clue she left behind was the scratch marks in the tailpipe."

"I still can't believe they could ever tie it to Alan. His personality just doesn't match up with being a killer," Grandma said, shaking her head.

"I don't know. Alan had a background of being rejected not only by people in his past but by TAFT matches. I think he was rejected by our client pool more because of how he read on paper versus his personality; he was a nice guy. The women just couldn't look past his being a lowly mechanic whose mother lived with him. Throw in the fact he apparently had an erotic asphyxiation fetish…"

"Dear God. You just can't know anyone for certain nowadays, can you?" Grandma said, shaking her head.

"Well, what about Eva? Is she dead?" Dad asked.

"Not last I'd heard," I said, turning to look at him. "Jack said he shot her in the shoulder and that she should be fine."

Dad leaned forward. "I don't know what I would have done if I'd lost you."

I patted his hand. "It's okay, Dad. I'm fine. I told you Jack would keep me safe."

He lifted my hand and kissed it gently.

I brought my gaze up and towards the door at the sound of a soft knock.

"Is it okay if I come in?" Jack asked from the doorway.

Dad dropped my hand, stood, and stalked towards Jack. Jack took a step back, panic on his face. Dad grabbed him and pulled him into a full-on bear hug.

"Thank you, son. You said you would keep my daughter safe, and you did," Dad said, releasing Jack and stepping back. "Next time though, I expect you to do it sooner. I don't like seeing her all bruised up."

"Me either, sir," Jack said, stepping far enough past my Dad to both be by my bedside and be out of Dad's reach. "I hope she never has an instance to be in danger again."

"Damn straight," Grandma said.

Jack looked at me. "I need to take your statement if you are feeling up to it?"

I looked at Dad and Grandma.

"We'll come back," Dad said.

He moved forward, took Grandma's elbow, and they walked out. Jack took a seat in my dad's vacated chair.

"Did you find Alan?" I asked.

"The patrol officers I sent over did. He had already died from asphyxiation."

I felt a tear run down my cheek. "That's just awful."

"I agree," Jack said, leaning forward and wiping the tear away.

"So, how good of a job did she do?"

"What?" Jack said, clearly not understanding my question.

"She gloated about how well she set up the red herring with Steven and framing Alan. Would you have believed it if you didn't know it was her?"

"It's hard to tell." Jack shrugged. "I haven't had the chance to do more than glance at the pictures of the crime scene. She definitely had us following the wrong path. However, I think we would have figured it out, eventually."

"Really?"

"Yeah. For two reasons." Jack held up a finger. "First, even the best murderer always leaves clues."

Jack held up a second finger.

"And second, if you would have died, I would have never stopped looking at your case until I was one hundred percent certain we caught the right guy. Or, I guess it would be a gal, in this instance."

Looking into his eyes, I knew what he said was the truth. My whole body warmed at the thought and I knew I blushed again, for the hundredth time.

"Where is Eva, by the way?"

"The bullet was a thru and thru, so the ER just released her into our custody. She is heading to the station to be booked."

I shook my head. "I still can't believe she did it. I never knew she was so unhappy."

"About that," Jack said, reaching into his pocket and

pulling out his trusty notebook and pen. "Can you fill in the blanks for me?"

I spent the next half hour giving Jack all the details I could recall, starting from the moment I got Eva's call until Jack found me. This time he didn't interrupt me once. *Who said you can't teach old dogs new trick!*

Chapter Thirty-Seven

By the time Eva was treated and released into police custody, she had already lawyered up. According to her defense attorney, she would be pleading insanity. She was insane, all right. Just not in the way the legal system determined it. I guessed it would be a wait and see. Jack said her first psychiatric evaluation would happen sometime next week.

Since she had been arrested, we had learned a lot about her that we'd never known. She had, in fact, come from a broken home. Her mother had left her father when she was just a child, the divorce papers claimed domestic abuse. Clearly, Eva did not care what her mother's reasons were; she faulted her for splitting up their family.

Eva's ex-boyfriend had also come forward and made a statement that while he had broken up with Eva, Wendy was not the only reason. He claimed Eva was unstable and had acted delusional on occasion. When the last incident had included her throwing a heavy glass vase at his head—lucky for him she'd missed—he'd said enough was enough and left as fast as his feet could carry him. It was now clear Eva hadn't been able to see any fault with her actions, and instead lashed out at Wendy, who was a somewhat innocent bystander.

The fact everyone had been so clueless about Eva's instability was downright scary. Eva had most definitely deserved an Oscar for her performance. We each thanked our lucky stars, though. Based on what we'd learned, things could have ended much, much worse.

I dreaded the thought of having to get on the witness stand, look Eva in the eyes, and tell my story. However, JJ assured me it would all be worth it. The case should be a slam dunk and Eva would not be seeing the outside of a jail cell during her lifetime. I decided to take my mind off it with movie night. I had all the necessities, but one.

The doorbell rang, and I headed towards the door. I didn't need to look out the peephole to know who it was, so I just opened the door. Jack stood on the doorstep, his skin flushed and worry lines creased his forehead.

"Is everything okay? Your text said 911."

I moved out of the door and headed into the kitchen, Jack followed. At the counter, I picked up the bottle of chocolate syrup, put a drop on my finger, and turned back towards Jack. I leaned up against the counter.

"It is an emergency, Detective," I said, putting my finger in my mouth and sucking off the chocolate sauce. "The ice cream would've melted if you hadn't gotten here quickly enough."

Jack's eyes went as round as pool balls. He reached forward, grabbed me by the arms, and pulled me towards him.

"We wouldn't want that. Now, would we?"

He kissed me, putting every bit of his pent-up sexual energy into the kiss. His lips and tongue worked diligently to remove all traces of the chocolate.

For the briefest of moments, he pulled back and looked at me. "It's about damn time I got my chocolate sauce!"

I laughed, and he smothered it with another kiss worthy of letting the ice cream melt.

Epilogue

The jury came back unanimous, finding Eva guilty of three counts of first degree murder, and two counts of attempted murder. JJ was right, she would never see the outside of a jail cell again. During the six months since then, TAFT had finally gotten back to normal. Old clients had reinstated their accounts, and new clients were knocking down our door; all were making matches left and right. Jack and I were officially in a relationship and things were going great so far. He was scheduled to move into my apartment next week. Everything was finally smooth sailing.

Well, at least it was, before the two pink lines.

SOMETIMES YOU JUST STEP IN IT

Still haven't found your Prince Charming? Don't fret. Sometimes it's when you least expect it that you find love. More often than not, it ends up happening with a person that is already a part of your life in some small way. It could be the mailman, the guy next door, or even the hottie detective at the police station. Just ask our very own Callie Bloom.

If you do find yourself with one foot in the pile, stay calm and enjoy the sensation. Not everyone gets to step in something that actually does smell like roses.

This public service announcement is provided to you by TAFT

www.ingramcontent.com/pod-product-compliance
Lightning Source LLC
Chambersburg PA
CBHW030659120726
47905CB00001B/276